The Art of Moving On

A NaNoWriMo Novel by Mallory Lopez

Copyright © 2017 by Mallory Lopez

All rights reserved.

Cover artwork by Tiffany Lee

This is a work of fiction. Names, characters, businesses, places, events, and incidents are either the product of the author's imagination or used in a fictitious manner. Any resemblance to actual persons, living or dead, or actual events is purely coincidental.

For Farrin, thank you for being the person that understands me the most in this world.

To my parents, for being my parents. I'm not always an easy person to love.

Shout out to all the weird boys I've ever met. Don't ever change.

"God, it's so painful something that's so close is still so far out of reach."

-Tom Petty

RIP

The Art of Moving On

Chapter 1

"We need volunteers to make an announcement about Santa Spirit donations at the basketball game tonight, the football game tomorrow, and the pep rally at the end of next week. Would anyone like to volunteer?" I ask openly to the rest of the Student Council members.

Crickets.

"*Ummm...* okay..." I feel a warmth creeping up my face because nobody is responding. It's Friday and most students go to the football games so I'm not sure why nobody would volunteer...other than the sheer horror of speaking in front of billions of people, of course.

I'm not necessarily a bad public speaker, but I'm not great at it either. When I get blank stares and hear crickets I start to feel anxious. I take a breath and step up to the plate. "Ricky and I will take care of these three but next week we will need people to take turns making the announcement. Amelia, can you write up an announcement for us all to use?" I ask Amelia, our Student Council Secretary.

"Sure, that's no problem, Emmy. I'll write it now so you and Ricky can go over it before tonight."

"That would be awesome. Thanks, Amelia. That's all I have for Vice President." I sit back down in my seat next to my best friend, Ricky Rodriguez, at the maple wood rectangle table. Ricky and I serve as Student Council President and Vice President. Ricky is President and I'm Vice President, respectively. We have our meetings in the Student Council office, which is designed like a corporate meeting office. Well, a corporate conference room with a lot more junk stored in it like: massive rolls of butcher paper, boxes of cheap poster paint and markers, basic rolling chairs, a large white board, and an open space to make posters, etc. The office is mine and Ricky's second home.

"Great. Thanks, Emmy. Don't forget we are eradicating all lunchtime meetings. This is our last one, thank goodness. We'll be able to have our lunchtime back. Meetings will now be after school as we agreed upon last meeting. If nobody else has anything…" Ricky says, scanning the room.

"Oh! I forgot that Yearbook Committee needs to take our photos. They want one of each of us individually, one together, and then some action shots during a meeting. They've asked us what meetings they can attend to take photos," Amelia shares.

The Art of Moving On

"Cool. I'll sit down with Emmy and we can go over our meeting schedule and let them know what meetings would be good for them to come to. Is everyone okay with doing our individual shots and group shots next week after our meeting?"

"How about we sign up for times for individual shots before the meeting and take a group photo at one of the other meetings?" I offer.

"Perfect, I like that idea. Then we won't be here as late and it will be more organized. Amelia, can you set up a time slot schedule for next week's meeting and work with the yearbook photographer on times? Once we have set times we'll tape the schedule to the door and we can all sign up. Am, who is our photographer this year?" Ricky questions.

Please don't say it. Please don't say it. Please don't say it.

I wince and my insides tighten waiting to hear who the photographer will be.

Amelia looks at her notes. "Looks like it will be Dan Cosgrove. He's head photographer this year for the yearbook," she informs us. Amelia is a junior here at Mount St. Mary's. She's quiet but sweet as can be. She's an artist and is in almost all of my art classes despite being a year younger. She looks up at me and pushes her glasses up using the palm of her hand like a little kid.

Ricky takes a quick glance at me...actually, everyone in the room glances at me and my heart droops like a wilted sunflower. I do my best to act natural and hide my pathetically sad face. I know what they're all thinking. I've heard everyone's snide comments about how horrible it must have been when the Dan thing happened.

"Great. We all have our assignments for next meeting. Don't forget to sign up for a photo slot. This was a productive meeting everyone, thank you. Meeting adjourned."

The Art of Moving On

Everyone gets up, some people leave right away, and some people have a quick side chat. As soon as the first bell rings notifying us to get back into our classrooms everyone but Ricky and I scramble out of the room. Ricky rolls his chair closer to mine and leans in close to me.

"Is it okay that Dan is our photographer? I can ask for someone else if it will make you uncomfortable." I appreciate his sensitivity. Ricky has been really supportive (as any best friend would be) for the last month or so since the Dan thing.

"Yeah, sure. It's fine. I mean, he's head photographer so I guess it makes sense for him to do it," I reason, fidgeting. The thought of even *possibly* having to interact with Dan makes the acid stir in my stomach.

And makes me sad.

Really sad.

"Okay, as long as you're sure," Ricky says with a sigh. We start to gather our things as the second bell, the late bell, rings.

"Crap, we're late." I pick up my pace gathering my pens and notebooks.

"Well, no use in rushing now," he smiles angelically batting his eyelashes which makes me laugh.

"You know, for a guy who's probably going to be Valedictorian, you sure are a bad influence." I stand up, smoothing down my white button up Mt. Saint Mary's uniform shirt and green plaid skirt. He barks out an evil laugh as we leave the Student Council room.

Before we reach our classroom, I see a sight that makes my blood run ice cold.

The Art of Moving On

Chapter 2

"Emerald Evans-Green, step away from the poster," Ricky tells me sternly.

I can tell I'm shaking because I can hear the poster paper crinkle under my tight fingers. I feel a twitch in my left eye, and for some reason everything has a reddish tint.

I'm literally seeing red.

Given that Ricky used my full name, I know he is seriously afraid of what I might do right now. Nobody ever says my full name, Emerald Evans-Green.

Yes, that's right.

Emerald Evans-Green.

No middle name, either. My mom, Anastasia Green married my dad, Roger Evans. Mom decided to hyphenate our last name so that the Green lineage would be

9

carried on with her kids. She felt she was being progressive and thoughtful. And she was; so was Dad. He changed his last name to Evans-Green, too.

I don't hate my quirky name and I don't hate my parents for not giving me a middle name as a fall-back. I also don't hate my parents for insisting Green be included in my name. However, this did not stop kids from making the connection between Emerald and Green so I got plenty of teasing and some bullying growing up. As a young child I was resentful at times, but never hateful.

All throughout my childhood, teachers would give me a pitying look during roll call the first day of school. The worst was when some teachers (namely: 3rd, 4th, 6th, and 8th grade) were too lazy to say the Evans part and just said Green. This meant hearing every morning during roll call, "Emerald Green." I would slink down in my seat as children snickered as I meekly replied, "here."

Now that I'm older, I really don't mind as much. I occasionally get the chuckle from substitute teachers but by the time I got to middle school I was going by Emmy, so whether people use the full Evans-Green or just Green, there's no telling of the quirkiness of my full name. Everyone knew me by Emmy within the first two days of freshman year. I get a little testy when people leave out either the Evans or the Green. I'm proud of my parents and now that I've grown out of the embarrassment stage of having a silly name, I proudly own my name.

I'm surprised when Ricky, during my sheer moment of pain and anger, calls me by my full name, which I haven't heard out loud in probably three years since I started high school.

The Art of Moving On

"We can make another poster, Emmy," Ricky says with a softer tone than before. "It's not a big deal. We still have the extra poster we made last time–"

"It is a big deal!" I snap at him. "And exactly! We have an extra poster. We made an extra poster because we thought this might happen again." If I was a cartoon, red would fill my body from toe to head and steam would blow out of my nose and ears.

"Then why are you so mad?" he asks, approaching me carefully with his hands in front of him.

The anger seeps out of me and my eyes start to water against my better judgment. "Because we shouldn't have to make extras," I explain, defeated. "Because we work hard and the students think it's all a big joke. They don't care that we're trying to do something good for other people. Ricky, I made all these posters with my own two hands," I tell him, lifting my hands in the air. A selfish, lonely, solitary tear leaks out of the corner of my eye and runs down the side of my face.

He covers his mouth and coughs, "I helped," *cough*. I shrug my shoulders and hang my head low.

"I'm so sorry, Ricky. You're right. It's both of our work. It's just an epic bummer. A bummer of massive proportions." I sniff. I finally place the poster back on the ground and stand up to give him a bear hug.

"A total, major bummer, querida. It's weird that the last one was stolen and this one is only ripped." My loving (and very understanding) friend is Cuban and calls me querida, which he told me is like saying darling in Spanish. He kneels by me on the tile in the middle of the school's main hallway floor. "Hey, maybe we can tape it together. The rip is big but it's not a total disaster."

The Art of Moving On

Ricky Rodriguez is the sweetest boy alive and the best of the best of the best of friends. He hasn't exactly said the words, "I'm gay" to me yet but at this point it's sort of an understood fact between best friends. I don't want to push him into talking about anything he doesn't want to talk about but I've made it clear that he can tell me anything. I guess he's just not ready yet. Mount St. Mary's, I'm sure, isn't the easiest of schools to be openly gay in just as Cayden Springs isn't an easy town to be openly gay in. Though we do have a surprisingly progressive Catholic social teaching and even though Cayden Springs is a smaller city it's one of the more diverse towns in Oregon. Coming out under any circumstances in any area is, I'm sure, a difficult thing for someone our age, or any age for that matter. But like I said, other than hints here and there, we haven't really ever talked about it.

I inhale a massive breath in and clap my hands together.

Welp. Time for an attitude adjustment.

"You're right. It's not a total disaster and I'm thankful that it wasn't stolen completely," I admit smoothing down my white oxford uniform shirt. "Thanks, Ricky. Let's tape it."

A door opens in the hallway and Paxton Wright walks out of our Thursday AP English class. We make eye contact and then he eyes the poster laying in Ricky's and my hands like a dead corpse. He looks down as he walks by us on his way to the restroom and cheekily says, "That sucks, Green. Maybe you can put up another one." He smiles obnoxiously at us.

"Oh zip it, Paxton, I'm not in the mood." I'm not normally this short-tempered with Paxton but he hit two soft spots.

The Art of Moving On

A. The poster, and,

B. He called me Green. Not Emmy. Not Emerald. Not Evans-Green. Just Green.

He's patronizing me.

I've gone to school with Paxton for three years now and he knows that I don't like being called just Green. He is always trying to get under my skin. He's probably the one that ripped this poster to begin with, honestly. He looks down at his pants zipper and then at me with a smirk on his face.

"I am zipped but I'm about to be *un*zipped. Stop staring at my junk, Green," he loudly says as he walks into the restroom. I growl after him.

"I meant zip your *mouth*! I wasn't looking at…" I start to yell and then realize there's no way he can hear me anymore. "Perv." I turn to look at Ricky and he has a grin on his face.

"I'm pretty sure you guys are in love."

"*Ick*. No way, José."

"No, querida. Ricky. Me llamo es Ricky not José," he teases, patting my arm.

"Very cute," I commend him, smiling at his bad joke.

"I just think it's funny that he singles you out so much. It's like what little boys do in grade school when they like a girl. They go and push them around on the playground."

"You think he wants to push me on the playground?" I ask, chuckling.

"No, I think he wants to push your pu–" I dart to cover his mouth with my hand.

"*Oookay*. That's enough." I cut him off knowing his mind was about to land in the deepest of gutters. "Let's get some tape and get this fallen soldier back up." Rising to my feet, trying not to be embarrassed by his comment. Paxton and I don't hate each

The Art of Moving On

other, but we aren't exactly best buds either. And there's no way on God's sacred Earth that Paxton would ever want to touch me the way Ricky suggested. I've never thought about Paxton that way.

After running back to the Student Council office to grab our school approved big, blue tape, we delicately construct the ripped edges back together. Once we get it back on the wall, we step back to admire it.

Again.

On the poster, I painted an abstract Christmas tree a lá Picasso (which isn't easy despite what some may people think). Mrs. Timlin, my art teacher, allowed us to work for hours every day after school to make all the posters. That's on top of all the other homework and art projects and Student Council duties I also have. Next to it in colorful sharp edged letters it reads, "Donate to Santa Spirit." Underneath, in rounded block print it says, "See your homeroom teachers for a list of needed items."

Every year Student Council organizes a drive called Santa Spirit. Through a partnering non-profit organization, the school is assigned a certain number of families and the students bring items on the families' wish lists. Then, a week before Christmas, we go out and deliver the presents to the families. Since we were able to help so many families last year we were assigned enough to have a family for every homeroom this year.

It's mandatory at Mount St. Mary's Catholic High School for every student to complete a certain number of volunteer hours before graduation. This particular event is the most popular because volunteer hours are given for gift-wrapping all the items as well as the six-hour day delivering presents. In other words, it's a fast paced easy event. The

The Art of Moving On

gratification of giving back is also convincing to some students. It's one of the only events that all the students, faculty, and staff work on completely together.

Given that it's the beginning of November already, we've already assigned families to homerooms. Last week, Ricky and I put five posters throughout the school. I'm always dubbed "poster maker" in every club I'm in because I'm a visual artist. Specifically, I'm a painter and drawer. This year in Mrs. Timlin's class I'll be exploring sculpting as well as painting and drawing.

"It actually looks almost as good as new," I announce surprisingly. I grin and turn to Ricky. "Thanks for helping me. I'm sorry about freaking out. You know, it's not just about a poster for me."

"I know, Em, it's your art. You have every right to be passionate about it." He comforts me, slinging his arm over my shoulder. "It really does look good as new."

I feel a weight on my shoulder and before I know it there's another arm over me and another arm over Ricky. I don't even have to look to know who it is. After three years I can sense his energy. Okay, and the smell of his Irish Spring soap and the way it compliments whatever fabric softener he uses in some bizarre and entrancing way.

Wait, am I really thinking about Paxton Wright's smell?

"This one really is my favorite," Paxton gives his opinion as he stands between Ricky and I with his arms spread across our shoulders. My body tenses under his shoulder and my eyebrows lower.

"Nobody asked for your opinion and don't patronize me, Paxton. It's not nice," I respond to his sarcastic comment.

The Art of Moving On

"No, really, it is my favorite," he reaffirms in an annoying tone where I can't tell if he's being serious or not. Since he always singles me out, I've grown to assume that he doesn't know how to sincerely compliment me. I lean my elbow in his side just enough to push him away.

"Yeah, yeah, yeah," I mumble as I break away and head to our classroom for English class.

Just as I'm about to reach the door, Paxton leaps and twirls in front of Ricky and I, cutting us off. Before I can say anything, he opens the door for us and simply insists, "You first." I make squinty eyes at him not trusting his niceness. He smiles and his eyes twinkle. I have no idea how he does that. It's like his smile wipes away every annoying thing he says. It's unnerving how charming he can be when he's not being completely bothersome.

After class, Ricky and I walk out talking when we both look up and notice that my poster is no longer on the wall. Instead of being torn it's completely gone. It got stolen just like the other one. I heave a massive sigh and begrudgingly tell Ricky, "I can't believe we have a serial poster robber at school. What is the world coming to?"

"Maybe someone just liked it to so much that they took it." My shoulder seizes up by my ear from the heat of Paxton whispering in my ear.

I scoff and shake my head as he smoothly walks in front of me and greets some of his soccer buddies.

"I swear that boy wants you, Emmy," Ricky insists, watching Paxton walk off. He looks back and grins before quickly turning back around.

The Art of Moving On

"Yeah, wants me to go insane." We look at each other and laugh because we both know it's true. Paxton has acted this way towards me since freshman year.

As we walk down the hallway, I take a minute to shamelessly and objectively look at Paxton as he walks further down the hallway. I guess by normal high school standards Paxton could be seen as good looking. Okay, majorly good looking but I'll never admit it out loud. He's a few inches taller than me at about 5'11", has green eyes, short jet-black hair and he fills out his short-sleeve white Oxford shirt nicely. He has smooth naturally tan skin that's only a shade or two lighter than my own darker skin. I notice girls swooning over him pretty often. If he wasn't so weird he would probably be more popular than he already is, but he's mostly just seen as the class clown. He's usually so busy getting under my skin that I don't notice the details and particulars of what he looks like. That and up until a month ago, I was madly in love with Dan Cosgrove for three years.

***

After school I head straight for my old baby blue Volkswagen Beetle. My dad bought it salvaged and he fixed it all up for me. The engine is completely new including new leather interior and stereo. Modern retro. A little hipster but my dad loved buying it and now that it's been remodeled with his own two hands, he feels safe having me drive it. I love my powder blue car and I wouldn't change it for anything else. Not even an electric car or a hybrid and that's saying a lot coming from the founder and leader of the Environmental and Sustainability Club.

The Art of Moving On

As I open my car door (I call her Betsy) I hear a faint, "Fore!" and a hard slap against my neck and shoulder blades.

"*Ow!*" I turn around to try and figure out what hit me so hard that my neck is tingling. There's a soccer ball settled in between Betsy and the Honda next to me. I pick it up and look around. I immediately wish I didn't turn around because then I could avoid him or maybe run him over with my car. On accident, of course. I would never murder anybody. Not even Dan.

"Soccer doesn't start until the spring, Paxton. You might've missed that day in Kindergarten when we learned about calendars but spring isn't for another five months," I inform him as he jogs over to me.

"True but you don't get a body like mine by sitting around during the offseason." He flips up his shirt for a brief moment to show off his tightly muscled abs. I linger for a second too long and he notices. A cocky grin smears across his face. I curse myself for ogling so blatantly. He pauses for me to say something back but I'm still stuck on how his partially naked body looks to find a smart enough response. He juggles the soccer ball between his hands. "What's wrong, Green? Did you like what you saw? Because I can do it again," he offers, lifting his shirt again. I reach out and stop him.

"No. No, I didn't," I snap at him and look around to make sure nobody is looking at us. "Don't flatter yourself, Paxton. Don't you have a poster to go rip down?"

"*Woah.* Where are these accusations coming from?" He asks, smiling. He's enjoying this conversation a little too much. Every conversation with him makes me suspicious. He always has this secret grin on his face like he's hiding something. Paxton

The Art of Moving On

Wright is a wild card. I never know what he's going to say or do. It keeps me on edge and makes my stomach do funny things.

"Give it a rest. I know it was you. Who else would do something like that? I hardly doubt anyone at school would rip down a poster that was asking for Christmas donations." I cross my arms. "Implausible," I decide confidently.

"But not impossible," he counters. I let out a growl. He chuckles.

"I worked really hard for them to just be torn apart and thrown away. It's not cool, Paxton." The anger and sadness start bubbling back up inside of me.

"Did it ever occur to you, Green, that maybe someone thought they were so good that they wanted them for themselves to hang on their wall?" He holds the ball under his arm and stares at me. I scoff.

"No, it didn't because that's absurd. Who would want an original print of a non-objective Christmas tree, snowy mountains and wrapped gifts? That's weird."

"I wish you could hear yourself talk sometimes," he states seriously.

"Cut it out, Paxton." My exasperation shows and his eyebrows come together like he's confused. He looks up past my head then looks back down at me. His body becomes tense and his jaw firm. I turn to look at what he sees. It's Dan walking to his car. He sees us and waves.

Waves. Like we're his neighbors on a Sunday morning.

I swear it's like the last three years never even happened for him. Paxton gives him a curt head nod but his eyebrows are still pinched together. I ignore Dan, grunt and lean my head against Betsy in submission.

The Art of Moving On

"Look, Paxton, if you or someone you know is taking down my posters please tell them to stop. Ricky and I worked on those for a long time. They may just seem like posters to you but everything I make is art to me. I'm even using them in my portfolio for college. I value all of my art so please just let them be. I know we don't get along but if you could just do this one solid for me, I would appreciate it." I look up at him and he looks apathetic to everything I just said. This kid is so unreadable and so unbelievably frustrating. His expression borders between confusion and flat-out vacancy.

"Not everything is what you think, Green," he states monotone and turns to walk away.

"*Don't* call me Green."

"See ya later, *Emerald*," he yells back over his shoulder. My eyes instinctively narrow even though he can't see me.

"And keep your balls to yourself!" I shout and then immediately realize what I just yelled. I turn pink and look around to see if there are any witnesses. Only a few of his buddies across the parking lot on the field. Thankfully Dan already made it to his car and left, so he didn't hear.

"Next time my balls come near you, you won't be saying that," he touts and his buddies laugh.

"Gross, Paxton! That'll *never* happen!"

"It will, Emerald," he assures with a smile from across the parking lot.

My cheeks turn flaming red. *So* gross. I fluster to get my bag in the car and hearing him laugh at me doesn't help. I swallow my angst and slump into my car knowing I lost this battle with him.

The Art of Moving On

I try to let it go. I have to practice my announcement for the basketball game tonight. When you're working on boosting your confidence, speaking in front of a hundred people is probably not the best way to go about tackling your newly intensified self-esteem issues. Or I may be wrong.

I guess I'm about to find out.

Chapter 3

I'm in the middle of cooking risotto when Dad walks in the front door. He's in a pair of jeans and an old t-shirt. Grease stains line all of his clothes and tint his arms and hands. He looks tired but he smiles for two reasons:

A. He loves what he does, and

B. He's always happy to be home for dinner.

Dad was completely enamored with Mom and I'm not sure there was a day in the life they shared together that he wasn't madly in love. We always came first, even when he took a risk and quit his car mechanic job to open up his own auto-mechanic shop. He worked every single day to ensure that his shop was the most successful car shop in the

The Art of Moving On

city, but he never missed one single dinner. Family always comes first. This was especially true when he unexpectedly became a single parent.

After Mom passed away from an aneurism six years ago when I was twelve, we only had each other. When she passed we were lost, hurt, and confused but he never once retreated away from me, never missed a parent-teacher conference, never missed a bagged lunch, never missed anything. We've had our fair share of struggles (and fights), and still do, but at the end of the day we have a small, wounded, imperfect family that works perfectly for the both of us. I love our family of two. He still never misses dinner.

"Hey, sweet pea, that smells delicious," he greets me, closing the front door behind him. He comes to the kitchen and tries to give me a big hug.

"*Ack!* No grease hugs. I just changed clothes for the game tonight," I inform him, giggling and recoiling. "Shower first then dinner." He smiles. We go through this drill almost every night.

"Alrighty. I'll be out in a few and I want to hear about this game tonight. If there will be boys there, today is the day I teach you how to properly throw a punch," he jokes, making his way to his room in the back of the house.

I chuckle and shout after him. "There will be boys. It's a boys basketball game." He groans dramatically, then I hear his door shut. I shake my head and grin.

Since it is only us we have had to learn the hard, awkward way to be candid with each other. It is not easy going through puberty as a young lady with only a dad to talk you through things. It was horrifying then, but now we can joke about boys and I feel safe talking about things like what happened with Dan. Although, I did have to talk him

The Art of Moving On

down from going over to Dan's house with a shotgun. I left out the sordid details, of course. There are some things parents (and dads in particular) should never ever know.

Dinners have become important to Dad and me. We are both busy and we cross paths in the morning quickly. But no matter our schedules, we always try our hardest to be at home so we can eat dinner together. It's like our untouchable sacred time.

I finish setting the risotto and salad on the table just as he comes out and plops in the chair. He's clean, but his fingers have dark grease perma-stains. He matches them with his fashionable plain t-shirt and jeans look.

"This looks amazing, sweet pea. Thanks for cooking." He digs right into the risotto and makes a big plate for himself. "Now, what's this about a basketball game?"

"It's actually kind of a bummer. Well, that's not true. It's good for the President Vice President to support the sports teams by showing our faces at games. Ricky and I have to give an announcement at half-time about donations for Santa Spirit. None of the other Student Council members volunteered so Ricky and I are teaming up for it. I'm pretty nervous about it."

"Have you written a speech for it yet?" Some people shake my father off as just a talented grease monkey. Talented he is, but some people forget that he's a successful business owner. Not only did he go to trade school but he also has a degree in business. He knows his stuff. He's lived through a lot in his life and has managed to come out the other end a smarter man.

"Yeah, we went over it after the meeting today but it was just a quick writing and editing session." I attempt to stab my fork in a way that will pick up some of the spring mix in my salad.

The Art of Moving On

"And did you practice in front of the mirror a few times?" He knows me so well.

"Yes, I did. I'm not completely memorized but pretty close. It seems like I can always say my speeches fine but when I get in front of a lot of people all of my practice just flies out the window and I forget how to speak." I shove a forkful of creamy chicken risotto in my mouth.

"Well, let's try something less formal. How about you tell me your speech casually while we eat and do dishes? Don't perform or give the speech, just tell me like it's everyday conversation. Say it like the way you're talking now."

I contemplate for a moment. A new approach sounds like a great idea. "Yeah, okay. I can try that."

I spend the rest of dinner and washing dishes time telling Dad the speech and I manage to get through it a handful of times and he gives me helpful pointers after each time. By the time we're done, I'm actually feeling more confident than I have in weeks. The butterflies visit my stomach as I think about all the people that will be at the game, but I brush that off as normal jitters.

"Bye, Dad. I gotta motor. I want to get there early so Ricky and I have time to rehearse so we can watch the first half of the game."

"Motor? Kids are saying that again?" He looks at me with a grin. I chuckle.

"No. But I'm bringing it back," I announce confidently. He chuckles. "I'll be home by eleven, okay?" I smear some chapstick on my lips and straighten out my black and red Student Council baseball style shirt. It's a little bit tighter than it was when I wore it six weeks ago…I guess all that ice cream I ate after the Dan thing happened caught up with me.

The Art of Moving On

"Sounds good, sweet pea. Be careful."

"Always, Dad." I start to walk out the door but he stops me.

"And rock your announcement! Tomorrow's Saturday so I'll see you in the morning. Sleep in. I'll make breakfast when you wake up. Love you."

"Thanks, Dad. Love you too."

***

There are *way* more people at the basketball game than I thought there would be. It looks like half of the school is here. Not to mention the other team is from a town not far from here so all their students and parents are here on the opposite side of the bleachers. They're a sea of blue and gold, so it's easy to decipher them from our Mount St. Mary's black and red.

Ricky and I practiced our speech outside for about twenty minutes before the game started. We fight our way to the bleachers, finding a spot to sit. There are a lot of students I recognize that would probably let us sit with them if we asked. The problem is that there's practically no room. I scan the masses for an empty spot and I find a space just big enough to fit Ricky and I. I tug his shoulder and point to the spot. He nods, and we make our way to the open area. We manage to get to a spot, halfway up from the court. Ricky sits and scoots over. I slide in to do the same but only half of my butt fits on the bleacher. I nudge Ricky to squeeze further down, and he hesitantly does. Now we're sitting practically on top of each other like a couple of sardines.

The Art of Moving On

We settle in just as the whistle blows and the ball is flung in the air. Immediately, everyone is loud and yelling and stomping on the bleachers. There's an energetic sense of camaraderie, community, and just plain, flat-out fun. After a few minutes Ricky and I start joining in, even though neither one of us is well versed in basketball (or any sport for that matter), and have very little idea of what's going on. I focus on trying to match the player's names to their numbers. My shoulders start to ease and my cramped seat begins to become comfortable. There are a lot of people here but they all seem to be having a good time.

"I'm gone for five minutes, Eli, and you gave my seat away?" There's a body standing with the waistband of his jeans far too close to my face. I don't need to look up to know to whom the voice belongs. I can't ever seem to escape Paxton Wright. Eli, Paxton's soccer teammate and best friend, looks at Paxton and shrugs his shoulders like there was nothing he could do to stop us taking Paxton's seat. Eli eyes Ricky peculiarly for a few long seconds as if he's never seen him before and then focuses back on the game.

Paxton is standing over me holding a bag of popcorn in his hands. I finally look up and see that along with his dark blue jeans, he's wearing a brown leather bomber jacket with a white shirt underneath. His onyx hair is obnoxiously, perfectly imperfect, styled messy like an anime character. Paxton is the kind of guy that styles his hair like he didn't style his hair. Sort of in the same vain as girls wearing make-up for the "natural" look. He glowers down at me and his normally glowing green eyes are dim. I glance at Ricky to plead for help in dealing with Paxton. Ricky simply stares straight ahead ignoring me, trying unsuccessfully to hide his growing grin.

The Art of Moving On

Traitor.

I take a deep breath. "Aw, you brought us popcorn! You're so sweet." I smile innocently at him. He narrows his eyes, grins, and flicks a few pieces of popcorn in my face. "Oh, real mature, Paxton."

He squats down and suddenly uses his body to slide Ricky and I over towards Eli even more to make a spot for him on the bench. He only manages to get a tiny bit of room and is still practically squatting. I am now smashed between Paxton and Ricky, my shoulders scrunched together and the heat from the two of them is radiating enough to make me dizzy. Eli looks at Ricky again and gets a nervous look on his face. Ricky starts fidgeting. My eyebrows pinch together in confusion. There's some kind of energy floating between the two. I really can't focus on that right now. I'm already wound up tight about the announcement we're about give.

"Emerald," Paxton snaps me out of my assessment of whatever is silently going on between Ricky and Eli. I snap my head over and jump because there's a bag an inch away from my face. "Here, eat some popcorn. It'll help you poop."

"What?" I ask, thoroughly confused and grossed out.

"You have to poop. I can tell."

"You can tell no such thing."

"I can and I know you have to poop because you were just making a constipated face while you were checking out Eli."

"*What?*" There are so many things wrong with what he just said. "I'm not constipated, I don't have to poop, I don't have a constipated face and I was *not* giving eyes to Eli."

The Art of Moving On

He grins, knowing he got under my skin. "Giving eyes?"

"Yeah." My confidence falters. "You know, checking him out." Paxton's eyes slowly roam down my chest, down my legs and up to my mouth, lingering on my lips before reaching my face again. I grunt and shake my head knowing full well that he's patronizing me, like always. It still doesn't stop me from blushing.

"And did you like what you saw?" He asks cheekily. He smiles his sparkling, dentist-approved smile that makes my heart putter.

"I don't like Eli in that way, if that's what you're asking me. I barely know him."

He nods his head like he believes me. "That's good because you're not his type." He turns his head away from me and back to the basketball court.

"What's that supposed to mean?"

"It means you're not his type." He flings some popcorn in his mouth. I can't deny that his casual demeanor exudes a solid dose of confidence that makes me envious, slightly turned on, and angry all at the same time. My face is heating up again but I'm not sure if it's from my ferocity working its way up, or the embarrassment I'm feeling.

"Are you calling me ugly?" I ask with a frown. I'm not attracted to Eli but I can't help but feel like Paxton is insinuating that I'm unattractive.

He leans down close to my ear so I can hear him better. His breath on my ear tingles and it sends a shiver through my body. "Emerald, you are not ugly. I'm simply stating that you are not his type." His dark green eyes graze over me again. My body betrays me once again by flushing a heated pink like I'm going through menopause. The warmth radiating from our bodies being so close seems to amplify my blush. "When will you learn that not everything is what you think it is?" I shoot him a bewildered look.

The Art of Moving On

That's the second time he's said that to me and I have no idea what he means by it. I'm about to ask him but he leaps up from the bench.

"Aileen!" He calls out to a girl walking by in front of the bleachers. "Wait up!" The pretty red haired girl smiles and does as she's told. And just like that, Paxton disappears as quickly as he appeared.

***

Half-time comes faster than I expect. Ricky and I look at each other just as we are about to head onto the court as the cheerleaders finish their routine. I wipe my sweaty hands on my jeans. One of the volunteer parents offers me the microphone and I take it with my shaking hand. We walk out to the center of the court and I look out to the crowd. My stomach churns as the crowd is loud and moving about. I don't know why I was expecting a room full of quiet seated people. Talking over all these people won't be easy. I feel bile rising and I swallow it back down, praying that I won't puke from nerves in front of all these people. Sensing my hesitancy, Ricky takes the microphone from my hands and turns it on.

"Ladies and gentleman, I am Ricky Rodriguez, Mount St Mary's Student Council President." He passes the microphone to me and whispers in my ear. "Breathe, Emmy, you're going to be fine. Relax. You know what you're doing." I squeeze my eyes shut and attempt to zone everyone out. I take a deep breath.

"And I'm E-Emmy Evans-Green, S-Student Council Vice President. We want to thank you for coming out to support our awesome basketball team." A few people who

The Art of Moving On

are actually listening, clap and holler. I quickly pass the microphone back to Ricky as if it was on fire.

"Every year we plan an event called Santa Spirit. We collect donations for families that won't be able to put gifts under their Christmas trees this year." He passes it back. My eyes have no idea where or who or what to look at it. I tense up. The loud distractions throw me off and I start to get tunnel vision. The unruly crowd spikes my anxiety. My palms start to sweat again and my heart is about to explode like a firecracker in July. Ricky nudges me to keep going.

"Um–Every homeroom has a list of items needed," I pause awkwardly and swallow hard. Oddly, out of the myriad of black, red, blue and gold bobbing bodies I somehow manage to find Paxton staring right at me. His fingers are in his pockets, he's standing on one foot with the other crossed in front and leaning against the bleacher's railing. I can't explain it but having him to focus on relaxes me. I stare intently at Paxton and everyone else is instantly zoned out. The ruckus sounds like a mere white noise and the words begin to fall out automatically just like I practiced earlier at home.

"Every student was given a list to bring home and it is our hope that you will consider donating an item or two." I pass the mic back after only fumbling a little.

"Some of the families that we donate to are refugees from countries like Sudan. Some families are foster care families that don't always get to have a Christmas." He passes it back. I keep looking at Paxton and his eyes haven't left mine. He looks calm and thoughtful like he genuinely cares about what I'm saying. Never in my life have I been so happy to see his olive skin and gorgeous green-eyed face.

The Art of Moving On

"Once we have all the donated items, the students and teachers get together after school to wrap the donated gifts. Students are given volunteer hours to participate." Even though my heart is still pounding in my ears, I'm amazed how the words are flowing out of my mouth the same way they did when I was practicing with Dad during dinner.

"The best part about Santa Spirit is the day we all get to go out and deliver the gifts to families. There are no words that express the feeling of immense gratitude." He passes it back.

"Santa Spirit is the largest volunteer event at school and one that students, faculty, staff and parents are all involved in. Please consider donating items or your time to our most beloved charity event." I pass it back to Ricky to finish the speech. I want to take a breath of relief but every part of me is still fixated on Paxton and that part of me is tense, confused, and grateful. A spark ignites, hitting the block of ice surrounding the fragments of my broken heart.

"Emmy and I will be around if you would like to sign up to volunteer. Thank you and go Ravens!" Everyone cheers and Ricky nudges me to walk off the court with him, finally forcing me to break away from Paxton.

Once we are off to the side, Ricky is beaming. "See, querida? It wasn't that bad. There were a couple awkward pauses but you didn't puke or pass out! Let's go make some rounds and see if anyone wants to sign up." He hands me a clipboard. "Let's divide and conquer. I'll go this way; you tackle that side."

"Okay," I reply, still in a daze from coming out of what felt like an out-of-body experience.

The Art of Moving On

"Text me if you need me." He starts to walk away but adds, "Be proud, querida."
I smile warmly at him. We break off and go our designated ways.

Using my persuasive talking and general excitement about Santa Spirit, I'm able
to get four volunteers to sign up. It doesn't sound like much but for our first
announcement it's more than I was expecting.

"Can I sign up?" Paxton asks from behind me. My face blushes at the sound of his
voice. I feel like we shared some kind of inexplicable emotional connection earlier. He
was my anchor. I most likely would have choked in front of everyone if it weren't for
him. Of course, I don't dare tell him that. He has plenty of confidence as it is.

I turn and study his face. I can't believe I never realized just how beautiful his
green eyes are. I've never met anyone with green eyes quite like his. When they sparkle
they are panty dropping gorgeous. I blush at the silly thought and suck in my bottom lip.
He looks at me with an amused grin. I nod and manage to say, "Yes, you can sign up." I
lend him the clipboard and pen. I want to say something to him—something funny or
smart but my brain is unusually flustered by his close presence. Instead of saying
anything, I bite the inside of my cheek. When he hands me back the clipboard and pen, I
muster the courage to look up at him and lamely say, "Thank you."

"I volunteer every year. It's fun." His demeanor is light and casual as if we didn't
just have a strangely intense moment together. Considering I'm always the adult in
conversations with Paxton, I gain the courage to tell him what I really mean (despite my
better judgment telling me that he doesn't need a reason to be more cocky).

"No. I mean thank you for—you know…during my speech." I look at him
sincerely—a way I never have before...a way that I venture to say probably won't ever

The Art of Moving On

happen again. It's a soft, thoughtful, and grateful look and I hope he picks up on it because…I think…I think I want to hug him. My heart starts racing.

"It was nothing, Emerald." He keeps saying my full name and I'm not going to lie, I kind of like it. "I was just interested in what you had to say."

"Really?" I ask surprised, not knowing if he's being sincere or not. I'm enjoying this random, sweet exchange we're having and I hope for the sake of my sanity and his safety that he's not patronizing me.

"Yes, really." His eyes glimmer.

How does he do that??

"That's actually really sweet of you, Paxton." My smile reaches my eyes, which, I can factually say, hasn't happened in months. My heart swells at his surprising kindness.

I look to my left and see Ricky by the concession stand next to Eli. They look like they're having a conversation. It surprises me given the weird vibe they were giving off earlier. Paxton follows my eyes to see what I'm looking at.

"Come on, it's stuffy in here and it smells like sweat. Let's go outside." He leads the way before I can say anything. My feet automatically follow him.

The cool breeze whips across my face sending shivers down my spine as soon as we walk out of the gymnasium's back doors. I have no idea why we're out here or what we're doing. "What's up?" I ask once we've stopped in a grassy area by a streetlamp behind the gym and away from the parking lot.

"Tell me what happened between you and Dan Cosgrove."

Chapter 4

"Excuse me?" The sparkle in my eyes blows out abruptly like a candle leaving nothing but darkness and dancing smoke in its wake. I'm befuddled and quite honestly, offended that he would ask about such a personal matter. "Paxton…we don't do this." I shuffle my hands back and forth between us.

"Don't do what?" He studies my expression. He's challenging me on purpose. It's like he *wants* me to argue with him. It's like he likes to get under my skin just for kicks. I'm some sort of game he can play when he's bored. We were having such a sweet moment, too.

"Heart to hearts. We're not–" I struggle if I should say what I'm about to say next. "We're not…we're not really friends. And even if we were, I don't want to talk about

Dan. It still hurts, Paxton." I look up at him to gauge his reaction. He is majorly displeased. His square jaw is tight and his lips pressed together. His eyes have darkened like the forest at dusk. I let out a shaky breath and twist my fingers tightly together.

"Fine. We're not friends." He sounds harsh and defensive.

I don't mean to hurt his feelings. I think it's pretty obvious that we're not friends. He's just this random character in my life that just shows up and disappears as he pleases. One minute he's here, the next he's gone. One minute he's melting my heart, the next he's blowing a cool breeze over it. We don't hang out on weekends and we don't talk on the phone. I don't even have his phone number. We're not friends. We're acquaintances. Classmates, really.

"If we're not friends, then…" he says brazenly, walking closer to me. I take a small step back until my shoulders bump against the lamppost. Our shirts are flirting and his signature scent of soap and fresh laundry dances through my body and makes me salivate. My heart starts thumping erratically and I swallow so loud that I'm afraid it sounds like a car horn honking. His eyes move between my lips and my eyes.

Holy crap, I think he's going to kiss me.

I'm nervous, excited, and confused all at the same time. He lifts my chin with his finger and delicately presses his lips against mine causing a spark of warmth to radiate through my veins. It's a short, soft, simple kiss that makes me dizzy. I haven't kissed anyone other than Dan in three years. In fact, Dan is the only boy I've ever kissed. I feel like I just kissed again for the very first time, just like that silly Madonna song about virgins. I enjoy it more than I'd like to admit, but part of it feels wrong, like I still have to be loyal to Dan. He takes a step back and studies me. Even if I were able to speak

The Art of Moving On

through the softball in my throat, I wouldn't know what to say. I'm too shocked to even breathe, let alone say words that make sense.

"Tell me what happened with Dan Cosgrove," he demands again. My eyes start to water as an instinctual reaction to hearing Dan's name. My emotions are pinned somewhere between pleasure and guilt. I look up at him knowing that I must look like a lost puppy because he finally acknowledges my struggle. I see a quick hint of regret pass through his eyes. "You don't have to tell me now."

"Why do you want to know?" I meekly ask, desperately trying not to unleash the tears. I've cried so long and so hard over Dan. I'm surprised that there are tears left for him, but apparently there are because despite all my effort, they spill over and drizzle down my cheeks. Paxton doesn't answer but I can feel his energy change. "It hurts, Paxton. It just...*hurts*." He nods his head. I shock myself when I don't hesitate to lean into his thumb when it comes to intimately brush away a tear. I can't talk to him about Dan, but his touch feels so warm and comforting. He pulls back and reaches into his pocket. He takes my hand, and I let him. He places something firmly in my hand and closes my fingers around it tightly. He walks away without saying anything. I open my fingers and it's a grape Jolly Rancher.

It's official, Paxton Wright makes no sense.

Chapter 5

"Hey, what happened to you for the second half of the game last night?" I wonder as Ricky and I walk into the football stadium. There are more people here than at the basketball game last night but fewer fans from the other team. Butterflies emerge in my stomach the moment I step into the stadium.

"I should be asking you the same," he counters. I try to be cool even though I feel my face heat up. He notices and narrows his eyes at me.

"You know me so well," I sigh in defeat. "I had a weird moment with Paxton," I admit and anxiously await his reaction.

"I knew it!" He yells, jumping up and down. "I told you he wanted you."

"I haven't even told you what happened yet," I say, grinning at his tenacity.

The Art of Moving On

"Oh, querida, I can see it in your face. Something happened. And you liked it." He's in full gossip mode with his hand on his hip and one eyebrow cocked, waiting for me to spill the beans.

"*Guh*." I slump my shoulders down. "It was weird. He's just all over the place. I think he has ADD or something."

"Well, that's not news. Continue," he urges with a wave of his hand.

I'm hesitant to tell him Paxton kissed me because I almost believe it didn't happen. It was lightning fast but so delicate and sweet. He brought up Dan and then basically ran away. There's no easy way to explain what happened or how guilty yet exciting it felt. I decide to cut the kiss part of the story. "He asked me what happened between Dan and I."

"Say what? He asked you about your ex-boyfriend?" Ricky contemplates, no doubt internally thinking and asking the same questions I have. "What did you say?"

"I told him that I don't want to talk about because it hurts still."

"Okay…well, that was a good answer," he decides.

My conscience comes clean and I tell him, "I also might have told him that he and I aren't friends and therefore have no right to talk about what happened with Dan." I scrunch my face up waiting for Ricky's reaction.

He grimaces. "*Ay*, Emmy. Ouch."

"I know," I profess guiltily. "He just blurted it out and it took me off guard. I got defensive. I actually feel really bad about it now."

"Well, to be fair, it really isn't his business and you don't have to talk about it if you don't want to. And he is Paxton Wright. He probably won't even remember the

The Art of Moving On

conversation come Monday." I love Ricky's reassurance, but something tells me that in two days Paxton won't have forgotten that he kissed me. At least I hope he doesn't forget.

Wait...did I really just think that?

I shrug. "Yeah, you're probably right. How did your night end up?"

We walk across the bleachers to find a seat, bumping shoulders, fighting our way through the waves of bodies. I glance at Ricky who is nervously wringing his hands. Finally I'm not the only one nervous for this speech. The fact that he's never been nervous before but is now, is making me even more nervous. We should definitely practice this thing so I say it better than I did last night.

"Hey, we never got to talk about how the announcement went. Let's practice it once or twice before we go on at halftime. Were you able to get anyone to sign up to volunteer?" He asks, reading my mind.

"I did. I got about four volunteers, I think." I effectively turn from best friend mode to business mode. Ricky and I are good at that. We can get into a little tiff about Student Council stuff and then walk out of the meeting chatting about what movie we should see over the weekend. We rarely have disagreements but when we do, we are excellent professionals and even better friends.

"Good! That's better than I got. I got two, but there were a lot of parents there so maybe Monday and Tuesday the students will bring in some gifts from the families' lists."

The Art of Moving On

"We have less donations than we did at this time last year, but we still have a few weeks. It'll pick up. It would be nice though to get things sooner so we have more time to wrap."

Ricky bursts out a single laugh. "Do you remember last year? We had items sooner than we do now, and we were still in the office wrapping gifts like maniacs a week before delivery. The office looked like Santa's Little Workshop exploded all over the place." I laugh too remembering Ricky and I with a couple other students frantically wrapping gifts. There were ribbons and colorful paper flying everywhere. Thankfully there was no glitter involved, much to Ricky's disapproval. We were barred from using glitter due to the previous year. There are still traces of it in the carpet in the office.

"More like Santa's workshop on crack." We both blow out a laugh. "I think I prefer the basketball games," I say, bouncing a little to warm up. It's not freezing but there's a cool wind making it just uncomfortable enough to make me want to go inside.

We find seats on the first row near the bleacher stairs. "*Ay, ay, ay,*" Ricky complains as he sits down on the cold metal bench. "They're trying to freeze my cajones off." I laugh loud which makes him smile despite his chilly parts.

We are watching the game and it seems exciting given all the screaming, claps, hollering, and feet stomping. Ricky and I wouldn't actually know because neither of us know the first thing about football. It's too loud and chaotic for us to have a conversation so we fidget in our seats trying to keep warm until half-time.

Ricky elbows me and nods his head to the right. I look to the right and Eli, Paxton, Aileen, and some other pretty girl are walking up the bleacher steps. My heart skips a beat not knowing if Paxton will come talk to me or not. His group gets closer and

The Art of Moving On

we make eye contact. I momentarily stop breathing. I open my mouth to say something but nothing comes out. He looks away and keeps walking without any kind of head nod or hello.

Oookay.

"That was a cold breeze," Ricky comments about the walk-by. His eyes are dark and a scowl takes over his face. Though Ricky's broody reaction is unexpected, I do appreciate his loyalty to my side. "Some acknowledgement of existence would've been nice."

"Seriously. You'd never guess that we were just sitting with them twenty-four hours ago. I guess he is mad at me." *Or*, they didn't acknowledge us because they were with girls. Ricky and I let a long contemplative pause go before we speak again. "Maybe it was because Aileen and that other girl were with them." I stop for a second because I don't want to say what I'm about to say.

I don't want to believe what I'm about to say.

"Maybe they were on a date." Ricky still doesn't say anything but his eyes are remain dark. I shouldn't care whether or not Paxton is on a date. All he did was kiss me. It's not like it meant anything or like he asked me out. "You know, whatever. He and I aren't friends anyway, right? So whatever. He can give me the cold shoulder all he wants. It doesn't even matter." I realize a few minutes later that I sound like a petty little girl. Daddy didn't raise a petty little girl. He raised a hard working, smart, young woman. I take a deep breath and sit up straighter. The buzzer goes off signaling halftime.

***

The Art of Moving On

I can feel my hand tremble as I walk toward the center of the field, microphone in hand. I refuse to look at the bleachers. Instead, I focus on the blaring field lights and the dozens of moths and insects flittering around at a hundred miles an hour like bees around a hive. My breathing picks up as we hit our mark and I am visibly shaking. I don't know if it's from the cold air, the pending announcement, or a combination of both.

I scan the crowd once before Ricky and I get into it to see if I can spot him. To see if he'll be here for me tonight like he was last night. Ricky elbows me to hand him the microphone. Paxton is nowhere to be found. I shove my hands in my jacket and that's when I feel it. I wrap my hand around the grape Jolly Rancher that Paxton gave me last night. It fills me with a sense of calm and causes me to grin. I take another deep breath just as Ricky begins the announcement. I zone in. I zone in on the mission, what we're trying to accomplish and for whom we are accomplishing it for. I put my game face on.

I can do this.

I squeeze the candy in my pocket like it's my lifeline, grounding my mind before it floats away. I take the microphone from Ricky and introduce myself.

***

Once Ricky and I leave the field after giving a kick-ass announcement, we decide to walk around together this time and gather volunteers. He lets me lead the way. I decide we should target parents tonight. I see a woman standing alone holding a warm cup of coffee, and walk up to her.

The Art of Moving On

43

"Hi, I'm Emmy. I'm a senior here. Are you a parent of one of the players?" I ask her casually. She turns her attention to me and smiles. The way her smile brightens her soft-featured face makes my breath falter. I know that smile. She's tall, has dark brown, almost black, shoulder length hair that barely fits in the French braid it's in. The pieces of hair fall down in wisps, framing her face. She has olive skin like she could possibly be Greek or maybe Italian. Her smile deepens the small wrinkle lines around her eyes and mouth. Instead of the faint wrinkles aging her, they frame her features making her look naturally charismatic. After taking her in, my heart flops. I can't help but recognize that my mom would look eerily similar to her, if Mom were the same age.

Mom had dark brown hair that was always short. I remember her wearing only a little bit of light make-up too, just like the woman in front of me. She loved to garden. and was fairly tan as a result. On this woman the tan looks inherited, rather than from the sun like Mom's. The only other difference between this woman and Mom is that Mom had light brown eyes and this woman has vibrant green eyes that can only be described as…well…emerald. The way the stadium lights hit her eyes they look like wet moss sparkling on a tree. My shoulders ease and I immediately feel comfortable with her. Sure, it could just be my imagination but something about her makes me feel genuinely warm. My heart skips a beat the moment I hear her voice.

"Hi, Emmy. No, I don't have a player on the team. My son and niece are wandering around here somewhere though. Mount St. Mary's is my alma mater and I like to come to the games every now and then to show my support." Her voice is soft and smooth flowing just like Mom's. Their voices don't sound the same in pitch, but it's more like the melody of their voices are similar.

The Art of Moving On

Ricky usually lets me take the lead because what I lack in public speaking, I make up for in persuasive face-to-face conversation. I glance at him and he's not even paying attention. He's scanning the crowd like he's looking for something or someone...probably the younger Student Council members who have strategically dodged us the entire game.

"That's awesome of you to come. I take it you liked going to school here?" I ask her politely.

"Yes, I did. It's changed a lot." She quickly adds, "for the better. The facilities have all been updated inside and out. I can hardly believe it's the same school. Of course, one thing has remained and that's Nurse Ehsani and Mrs. Timlin." My ears perk up.

"I love them both. Was Mrs. Timlin as lofty and hippie-ish then as she is now?"

She chuckles. "She had just started working here when I was here. I think she must've been...maybe in her late twenties. And yes, she would tell us stories about how she traveled with The Grateful Dead and lived in San Francisco. Does she still tell her stories?"

"Yes! She's my favorite teacher. I'm actually an artist, so she's more like a mentor to me. I spend a lot of time in the art studio with her. She's incredible." I can't take my eyes off of this woman and it's probably freaking her out. I can't help it. It's like seeing a little piece of Mom in some strange way. It's confusing yet intoxicating all at the same time. I push aside the confusion for now and just try to enjoy our conversation.

"I'm glad she's still here and able to teach talented students like you." The more I listen to her talk the more my heart and my emotions become vulnerable. My heart keeps skipping beats, and then falling to my stomach all on repeat. I force myself to look away

The Art of Moving On

from her for a moment to recall the purpose of why I approached her. I take in the football players, the sound of the whistles, and helmets smashing against each other.

"Have you thought about volunteering for Santa Spirit? We would love having parents to come along when we go deliver gifts! I know it's a newer tradition here, but I think you'd enjoy it. I can't describe to you how rewarding it is to work hard to accomplish something for someone else. The families are filled with such love and gratitude. They welcome us into their homes and we get to spend a little time getting to know them and hearing their stories. Listening to their struggles really makes you reflect on how lucky you are. I truly believe that we are put on this Earth together to help each other. It's a beautiful and humbling experience. Santa Spirit is an excellent way to help some of the most kind hearted people in our community." I get a little passionate when I talk about things I really care about and believe in. I think that's why I'm good at getting people to sign petitions (last year I got enough signatures for the school to change Columbus Day to Indigenous People's Day) and sign-up to volunteer. I also selfishly want another chance to see her and talk to her, as bizarre and creepy as it sounds.

Her green eyes twinkle in a captivating way. "That was really beautiful, Emmy. I would love to volunteer. I usually buy a couple gifts on the lists but I would love to actually come in and help out this year, too." She grins, and I can tell she's flattered that I asked her.

All I can focus on are the features that remind me of Mom: the familiar brown, fine hair, her sparkling round eyes and wide mouth, the soft, melodic sound of her voice. I've never seen anyone that even remotely looks like Mom. My emotions and vulnerability are layering on top of each other, building up, and threatening to topple over

The Art of Moving On

at any moment. My throat starts to swell and my eyes begin to burn. I need to hurry and end the conversation before I freak her out by crying.

"Thank you. You can sign here and put down your name and email address and we'll let you know when we'll need help," I spew out quickly before I lose my ability to speak. She takes the clipboard, fills it out, and hands it back. I accept it with trembling hands.

"Thanks. It was good talking to you, Emmy. I'll see you in a couple weeks."

"Thanks, you too," I manage to force out. I turn away and take a shaky breath.

I cling to the clipboard with both hands across my chest as I walk out of the stadium without Ricky (who disappeared at some point in the conversation) and lean against the brick wall away from most of the crowd.

I'm trying to keep it together. The way she spoke was haunting at first then it soothed me in a way that I never thought could happen again. I wonder if she would still braid her hair while gardening like she used to. I wonder what flowers she would've chosen to plant this year. I wonder if I would still love the fresh flowers and dirt smell that came from her every time she came in the house after gardening or if I would've gotten sick of it by now. I wonder if she would still wear that ratty, old straw gardening hat she used to wear or if she would've gotten a new one.

I desperately want to know what Mom would look like if she were alive now. Would she look like that woman as much as I think she would, if she were only given the miracle to live? I just want to know Mom in the here and the now, but I'll never be able to, and it kills me. It shatters everything in me that I will never get to know what she

The Art of Moving On

would be like and how she would age. Twelve years on this planet with Mom was not long enough. I miss her

Mom died six years ago and I've cried for countless days, hours at a time, and sometimes so unbelievably hard that I actually thought I would pass out or die. I cry every now and then when I'm overwhelmed with longing but I've never felt anything like the way I'm feeling right now.

My heart bleeds, my muscles cramp and my breathing becomes quick and harsh. My chin is quivering and my eyes have filled up with so many tears that everything is blurry. I blink and the tears pour out unabashedly. I cup my shaking hand over my mouth to quiet my small sobs. My heart hurts, but it also feels open and welcome. I feel incredible sadness and loneliness, but also love and comfort in some inexplicable way. I finally start to regulate my breathing when Ricky walks out of the stadium and rushes to me.

"Querida, what's wrong? What happened?" I've stopped crying, but I'm right on the edge.

"That woman–" My voice catches trying to speak through the softball in my throat. "–reminded me of Mom. It was weird, Ricky, and confusing." He rubs my back in soothing circles.

"*Ay*, querida. Who was she?" I scrunch my eyebrows together, squeeze my eyes shut and think.

I'm such an idiot.

I curse myself. I never asked her what her name was. I don't even know with whom I was speaking. I let out a groan and a sob at the same time.

The Art of Moving On

"I-I don't know." I can't believe I never asked her for her name. Maybe it's because I felt like I already knew her.

"What's the paper say?" Ricky asks, gently pulling the clipboard down from my chest where I'm clinging on to it. We both look down, and I gasp loudly. I cover my mouth again, and am once again pushed forcefully over the edge. I start crying all over again. Ricky inhales deeply, and holds me to him. I look down once more to make sure my eyes were correct. No wonder why those captivating green eyes looked so familiar. The feminine loopy handwriting reads, Maria Wright.

Paxton's mother.

Chapter 6

Ricky calmed me down enough so I could drive home after the game. When I got home Dad instantly knew there was something wrong, due to my puffy red eyes. At first, I didn't want to tell him about Paxton's mom, Maria, and how much she reminded me of Mom. I didn't want to make him sad or feel lonely like I how I'm feeling. I never stood a chance at not telling him; he wouldn't allow it. He sat me down and I blubbered the whole thing out. He got choked up too but he didn't cry. He just hugged me and listened while I tried to explain my bizarre, confusing and conflicting feelings about my interaction. I feel sorrowful but also compassion. I constantly feel like I'm lost in this place between black and gray. I couldn't make sense of it, and I still can't.

He told me that it was a blessing to have met a woman that had a similar aura and presence. He said that maybe it was Mom giving me a gift in some small way. He also

The Art of Moving On

told me that he met a woman recently that had reminded him of Mom, too. It shocked him at first, but he saw it as a nice reminder that even though there might be people out there that look alike, nobody is the same. Nobody else is my mother and nobody can replace her, no matter how much they look or sound like her.

***

I smile from ear to ear when I sit down Wednesday morning and I see Dad cooking a french toast breakfast. "I thought I would make us something special for breakfast since I couldn't sleep." Dad sets down a plate with French toast and strawberries on it. "When's your pep rally?"

"It's on Friday, right before school ends. There's another football home game that night," I tell him, cutting into my syrupy toast. He hasn't taken a day off or gone in late to work in over a year. "When are you going in today?"

He sits down across from me. "I didn't sleep well last night so I might just hang out here for a bit," he states, noisily opening the newspaper. "I have Todd there to run things. Besides, Todd's got a decent head on his shoulders. He can handle things for a few hours." I'm not sure if he's trying to convince me of that, or himself. It makes me grin.

"Well, thank you for making French toast. I'm sure Todd can handle it. He loves the shop." Dad nods, engrossed in his paper. Todd Bartlett graduated last year, but he's going to the local trade school to become a car mechanic like Dad. Dad is trusting him more and more to take on responsibilities at the shop. He has this whole biker-tough-guy act, but he's actually a sweet guy no matter how much he tries to deny it. Todd is a year older than me and his reputation preceded him in high school, but just in the last six or seven months he's really stepped up, *grown up*, and I can tell Dad is proud of him.

When I shove the last piece of toast in my mouth I look at the clock and realize I need to get moving. I'm bummed I can't ditch and hang out with Dad for a little longer and lounge around. "Dad, I gotta motor." I hate being late, or even on time. I'm an early bird. I get it from Dad.

"All righty, sweet pea, put your dishes in the sink, and I'll take care of it. Have a good day at school. Be careful, huh?"

"Of course, I will." I walk to the kitchen, and put my dishes in the soapy water. I walk back, and get my things together. Before I walk out the door, I kiss Dad on the head. "Love you, Dad."

"Love you, too. See you tonight."

***

At school, I leave my Environmental Science class psyched about the project we were assigned. We have to pick a destructive way in which the environment is being impacted by humans and explain how, why, and what we can do about it. I already have something in mind. It doesn't have to be a paper either, so it allows me to use my art in a more academic way than usual—an opportunity I don't get too often. It's an ideal project for me.

The Art of Moving On

I meet Ricky by his locker before lunch. It's been an uneventful week, and I'm happy about it after all the weird things that happened last week.

"Hey, querida," he greets me as he spins his locker lock. "What is that look on your face? Why do you look excited?"

"I have a project for Environmental Science class that I'm really, really looking forward to. I already have so many ideas running through my brain."

"Your face looks like that for a class project? See, that's why we're best friends. You are the only other person I know that gets as excited for class projects as I do." He adjusts things in his locker so they look picture perfect and steals a glance at himself in his magnetic locker mirror. He flattens down the sides of his thick, neatly styled dark brown hair. I look up with a hesitant smile when I see Paxton and Eli walking toward us, most likely on their way to lunch from homeroom. Ricky looks up and sees them too. I can see Ricky physically tense as they come closer. He stands straighter; adjusting his shoulders back and lifts his chin a little higher in a way that defines his jaw.

"Emerald," Paxton says as his walk slows down. This is the first time all week he's talked to me. He's even been ignoring me in Environmental Science class. I have to be honest, I'm relieved that he is at least acknowledging my existence now. His cold shoulder was a little colder than I thought it would be.

"Hi, Paxton. Hey, Eli," I greet them as they stop in front of us.

"Hey," Eli says quietly to me then looks at Ricky. They have a second of eye contact before Eli looks down and fidgets like he's nervous. I don't know much about Eli, I don't have many classes with him. I'm not sure why he looks so nervous.

The Art of Moving On

"Are you okay, Eli? Do you have a big test coming up? You seem anxious and I always get that way before tests," I babble off at him because I genuinely don't know what else to say.

Paxton pats Eli on the shoulder and tells us, "Don't mind him." Paxton looks between Eli and Ricky before opening his mouth again. "It's just soccer stuff, you know, because tryouts are soon and we want to keep our titles of Captain and Co-Captain."

Eli gives us a small, quaint smile. "Yeah, it's just...soccer stuff."

I give the surprisingly shy Eli some reassurance. "You'll be great! You're a talented player, and I'm sure you have nothing to worry about."

His cheeks turn pink. "Thanks, Emmy."

I look back at Paxton who looks as normal as ever; thick messy pitch-black hair that makes his greener-than-green eyes pop. His smooth skin is olive, but still a shade lighter than his mother's. His frame stands tall and his modestly muscled arms are crossed in front of him. I would never admit it to anyone, but I kind of wish I was behind him right now because I've recently noticed that he has the nicest butt. It's his best physical attribute and I'm betting that it's due to soccer. He slides his hands in his pockets when he notices that I very non-discreetly checked him out.

I'm honestly so pumped for my project that I don't even care that he notices me looking at him. I think Stella might be getting her groove back. I give him a pleasant, casual smile. He looks at me suspiciously in return. There's an awkward silence where all four of us are just looking at each other.

"Can we talk for a second?"

The Art of Moving On

I nod and say, "Yeah, sure." The truth is I have been feeling guilty about what I said to him. He means more to me than just some random stranger. Maybe we are friends. I turn to Ricky. "I'll meet you in the office in a few, okay?" Ricky and I almost always eat in the Student Council office, even after we eradicated lunch meetings. There's not a good reason why we do it. It's just more peaceful than the cafeteria. Other SC members join us too, occasionally.

Ricky sends me a nod. Then he looks at Eli and they turn to walk to the cafeteria. I expect them to walk together but Eli quickly juts ahead of Ricky leaving him alone. I furrow my brow. I don't like that Eli just ditched Ricky. I know they're not friends, but they are acquaintances. I stifle a laugh because Eli looks awkward speed walking away from us. I shake my head and turn my attention back to Paxton. No wonder Paxton and Eli are best friends: they may be pretty opposite, but their weirdness matches.

"Paxton, I'm really sorry about what I said about us not being friends. I don't want you to think that I don't–"

"You met my mom," he states matter-of-factly, interrupting me. Oh, so this is what he wanted to talk about…his mom.

"I did. She's really sweet," I reply vaguely, purposely not elaborating.

"She likes you too."

I'm trying to figure out where this conversation is going. I look to the right, and my face falls. Paxton follows my gaze and sees Dan walking to lunch with his new girlfriend, Alexis, hand-in-hand. We say nothing as they pass us. I focus on my shiny black shoes until I know they've passed. I don't look up until he speaks.

"I'm sorry," he says. Before I can ask why he's sorry, and before I can ask for forgiveness, he walks away and once again leaves me bewildered. He does it so often that you'd think I am used to it, but I'm not. One day he kisses me, the next he ignores me. One day he mocks me, the next he does something nice. I wish he would just pick a direction, and stick to it. I don't like not knowing what to expect. It makes my heart and stomach do funny things.

He turns abruptly and marches back to me. "You have something right here," he informs me, pressing his finger against my uniform shirt's neck button.

"What?" I look down, embarrassed. Once I see there's nothing there, his finger slides up and knocks my nose.

"Got you," he says, turning away grinning.

"Seriously, Paxton?" I yell after him. He just keeps walking. He's infuriating.

"Hey," I greet Ricky as I sit down next to him with my lunch. "What's up? Things got weird in the hallway, huh? Paxton can be so completely frustrating." I look up from my PB&J and his look has me surprised. He looks sad. In fact, he's been acting kind of strange this week. I shake his arm gently. "Hey, what's going on?"

"I don't really want to talk about it right now, querida. I'm okay but…we can talk about it later. Sorry I'm being a downer."

"Don't worry about that. We can talk whenever you want. You know I'm always here for you." Before I take another bite of my PB&J, I stop myself to say, "You know what, let's do something fun this weekend." That makes him smile. "I hear that there's party after the football game on Friday. You want to go? I haven't gone to a party since the Dan thing happened." Ricky would come with us every now and then, but he

The Art of Moving On

complained that he felt like a third wheel and would mostly stay at home working on whatever school project or paper he had at the time.

He releases a massive sigh, and his somber look turns darker as he stares at the ground. "Querida, I hate that I have to tell you this, but you keep saying 'The Dan Thing' and I don't think you've actually said the words out loud. You can't keep calling your breakup with Dan 'The Dan Thing.' I think it's holding you back. I'm sorry, I know it's hard but, querida, you need to start moving on."

Stunned by his confession, my eyes start to fill and my throat tightens. My breakup with Dan was not mutual. One day, when we went to The Café to get pie and study, he told me that he had feelings for someone else and that he hadn't really been feeling anything for me for awhile and thought it would be best if we broke up. This was all after we had sex the day before. It wasn't our first time but still, we had been sleeping together for a while and I loved him. I was completely enamored and had been for three years. Hearing him say that he hadn't had real feelings for me for a long time after having had sex with him less than twenty-four hours beforehand hurt. Like, *BAD*. I couldn't even finish eating my pie. And I love pie.

So when Dan broke it off, I was turned upside down. And as Ricky just pointed out, I'm still not up right. We spent *three years* together. In high school years that's practically a decade. I gave myself to him mentally, emotionally, and physically. Hearing he had feelings for someone else was like having my insides knifed up. It felt like all of my guts were tumbling out of me. I thought for sure all hopes of happiness and love and family were tossed out the window without a single glance. He was my *everything*, and I thought I was his.

The Art of Moving On

Naïve.

A week later, he started dating Alexis Fischer and I was done for. If that wasn't enough…the next week I heard girls gossiping about how she had been fooling around with him since the start of the school year *before* we broke-up. Because we had dated for so long, our breakup quickly became public knowledge and the whole school knew by the next day. Two days after he shattered my heart, they officially came out as a couple and the news that he cheated on me spread like wildfire. Everywhere I went, students gave me pitied looks and gossiped about how much it sucks to be me. Teachers looked at me sympathetically. Even Paxton Wright didn't bug me for a few days. That was the last nail in the coffin for me. I felt used, dejected, and broken as if there was something wrong with me, like I wasn't good enough, like I was too boring to be around, to ugly to be seen with.

After spending a couple weekends in my pajamas, not showering, listening to Beyoncé's *Lemonade*, Adele, and eating nothing but pints of Americone Dream, Ricky swooped in and gave me some tough love. He literally dragged me across my carpeted bedroom floor, into my bathroom, dumped me in the shower and turned the water on. It was like an episode of *Intervention*.

I loved Dan. Or at least, I always thought I did. Dan and I dated for years, and it was so easy. We hardly ever fought, we had the same dedication to our art (photography for him and drawing and painting for me) and to our studies, and we were physically attracted to each other. It seemed perfect. But, our relationship was merely convenient. There was never any passion, no heated arguments, we agreed on everything. It was like being in a relationship with myself which leads me to believe that maybe I really am

The Art of Moving On

boring. I'm still licking my wounds, and it's leaving me vulnerable and constantly anxiety ridden. My self-confidence is now slowly starting to rebuild itself from the ground up.

I don't want to talk to Dan (I still haven't spoken a single word to him). I don't want to be in the same room as Dan. I don't want to see Dan. I don't even want to breathe the same air as him. I don't hate him like I did a month ago, but still…I'm *hurt*. I felt physically debilitated after it happened. It was a knockout blow, and I'm trying to get back up as best as I can. I know I have to face Dan and interact with him eventually. I just want to be in the right mindset when I do. Luckily for him, I don't feel the impulsive urge to hit him anymore.

But, Ricky is right. His tough love hits me like a ton of bricks. I tilt my head up toward the ceiling. I do my best to speak through the softball in my throat. "I guess I'm not doing as well as I thought I was."

"You're not doing *bad*, querida. Sometimes other people see things that we don't. You deserve so much better than that dick. I know you don't want to hear this either—"

"Oh god, there's more?" I groan.

"I really think there's something between you and Paxton. Well, there could be something, and I hate to see Dan holding you back. I don't want you to hurt anymore. I'm sorry, Em, I had to say it. You can call me a jerk but he's still holding you back, and you're so much better than that."

"You're not a jerk. I didn't want to hear that but I know I needed to, I guess." I sniff and lean on Ricky's shoulder. He puts his arm around me and hugs me.

"So, about that party..."

The Art of Moving On

I chuckle in his arms in spite of myself. "If you mean the *pity* party, it's happening here, right now."

"I mean it," he announces getting this burst of energy. "Come on!" He shakes my shoulders in attempt to literally shake my sadness away. His face lights up and his mood is a complete 180 than it was ten minutes ago. "You brought it up! We're going. This is happening."

"We're going?" I ask incredulously, but he hears what he wants instead.

"Damn right we're going! That's the attitude!" He slaps the desk in excitement causing me to laugh.

"You're acting like a crazy person, Ricky. Ten minutes ago we were–"

"Sh!" He swiftly covers my entire mouth with his hand. "We deserve this. We deserve to cut loose! You have to admit we deserve this."

As soon as he feels me smiling under his palm he removes his hand carefully as if he's still expecting a fight from me. He has the widest grin on his face. If this will make him happy then I will for sure go with him.

"Say it, Emmy. Say, 'we deserve this.'"

"Yeah, okay, I guess we do," I say noncommittally. Ricky rises to his feet and turns my chair so it's facing him.

"No. Say it, Emmy. Say it like you mean it. We deserve this!" He practically shouts. I can't contain my grin anymore, and I give in to his charade.

"We deserve it, Ricky."

"Say it louder!"

Through a fit of laughter I shout, "We deserve it!"

The Art of Moving On

"Show me the money!" Ricky yells.

I bend over in my chair busting out laughing at his sudden burst of hyperactivity. He's gone mad. I try to compose myself and tug on his shirt, telling him to sit back down. We both take a deep breath and chuckle again. I sigh in contentment.

"So, I guess we're going to this party, huh?" I joke. "Time to get back on that horse."

"What kind of horse are we talking about? Paxton? You should definitely ride that horse. It's about time Stella got her groove back." He cackles a laugh, which makes me laugh until we're in a fit of giggles again. I playfully shove his arm.

"You know what? I was thinking the exact same thing." His mouth drops.

"You want Paxton?!" His eyebrows shoot up.

"No! I meant it's time I got my groove back. I don't think I'm ready for boys. Parties—sure. Boys—not yet. And I'm certainly not ready for Paxton, nor will I ever be. He's too unpredictable."

"Never say never, chica," he taunts raising his eyebrows.

"He's so random. He asked if we could talk and all he said was that his mom liked me. That's it. Oh, and then he said sorry and walked away, but not before bonking me on the nose. I have no idea what he's sorry for, and I couldn't even ask him because he literally ran away. Ricky, boys literally run away from me." I'm joking but my face starts to frown because it is actually true. Dan couldn't have ran faster.

"*Nooooo.* No. Stop it. Don't get sad again. That is not true. Paxton is just a little bit weird. I don't get him. *But* I still think he wants you, and weird or not—that boy has got some killer looks." He cocks his head to the right and looks up like he's remembering

The Art of Moving On

something. He turns hesitant. "Although, before I could find you at the football game, I saw him with Aileen again. I'm not sure what the deal with that is."

"Well, it doesn't matter. I don't need to know about his love life and he doesn't need to know about mine. It's not my business," I firmly tell Ricky. It isn't my business…but I have to admit, I am curious.

"You're right. Enough about Paxton and Eli. Let's get our party on and forget about them," he says smiling. He holds his soda cup up and I cheers him with my reusable water container. I smile back at him but something strikes me as I swallow my drink…

We never said anything about Eli.

Chapter 7

I've given the Santa Spirit announcement twice now in front of over a hundred people.
Ricky and I have special seats on the gym floor along with the cheerleaders, football
team, coaches and Principal. The cheerleaders take their fifteen minutes to perform two
routines and hold up a giant poster for the football team to run through. Once everyone
settles down the Principal gets up and riles up the students. I know our time is about to
come and I'm starting to get nauseas from anxiety. As Ricky and I get up, the everlasting
smell of sweat along with that stench that floats between floor cleaner and damp mops
permeates makes me groan and put a hand over my stomach.

Once everyone is settled Ricky takes the microphone from Principal Jones. I scan
the crowd to see if Paxton is looking at me so he can be my anchor but I can't find him.
It's so dumb of me to expect to find him out of the hundreds of students staring at us. I

The Art of Moving On

reach into my pocket hoping to find the comfort of the Jolly Rancher even though I know it isn't there. Every rehearsal and every word of the announcement vacate my head, and sheer panic sets in. I get hot and I can feel my face turning pink. My heart is beating so hard against my chest that I think it might actually escape. My breathing picks up as I'm looking at the crowd of students closing in on me and my eyes somehow find Dan.

Dan used to be my anchor. I remember how we would cup each other's faces as we kissed. His flawless black skin and dark features I found so beautiful. I could never get enough of him. His lips are thick and soft as feathers. His eyes as deep, dark and mysterious as black holes. I used to get lost in them. I loved them. I loved *him*.

He used to be my anchor.

Right now, he's sneaking kisses with Alexis, holding her close, and every other person in the gym just vanishes. I can't stop staring. I can't stop thinking about every touch, every moment our skin and souls came together and created magic, every intimate moment we had. A few seconds ago my heart was about to explode and now I suddenly can't feel it beating at all.

I think Ricky is nudging me but I'm frozen. All that exists is Dan and Alexis kissing, leaving me on the outside looking in like an orphan peering through a happy family's home window. I sway from a dizziness taking over my entire body like I'm drunk. The nudging against my arm stops. Dan tucks a lock of her hair behind her head the way he used to do with mine. He uses the opportunity to lift her head and kiss her sweetly with his plump heart-shaped lips. They continue to kiss. Seeing them embrace each other intimately hollows out a new a cavity in what I thought was my already shredded heart. Yet, I can't stop staring.

The Art of Moving On

Ricky stops talking and is pulling me back to our seats. My eyes still haven't left them. They don't even notice what's going on around them. They look at each other like they're the only people that exist. Everything Dan and I had, he now has with her. I shake my head to clear my tunnel vision. I yank my arm away from Ricky. I tear my eyes away and run straight across the gym floor, leaving scuff marks in my wake. I slam the bar down on the gym door and I don't stop running until I'm outside the school doors and in the cool autumn air.

I take a huge gasp of air. The chilly air serves as a splash of cold water in the face that I so desperately need. I lift my arms so my hands are resting on my head. I pace back and forth trying to get ahold of myself. I can't believe I let Dan have that much control over me. I was trying to do better. I was going to get my groove back this weekend. I thought I was getting over it. I thought I was moving on. I take in deep breaths and close my eyes. I hear the door burst open behind me. It scares the living daylights out of me and I throw my arms down to attempt to look like nothing is wrong with me. Once I recognize the face in front of me I fling myself forward and wrap my arms around him.

"Dad! What are you doing here?" I cling to him as if my life depended on it.

"I wanted to come see you be Student Council Vice President in action. I knew how nervous you were so I left the shop to come and be here when you gave your announcement. Sweet pea, are you okay? Tell me what happened." He doesn't let go of me until he kisses my forehead. He guides me by my shoulders and sits me down on the cement step.

The door bursts open loudly once again and my dad and I both jump and turn around. Paxton is standing halfway out the door and halts as soon as he sees us. My

The Art of Moving On

eyebrows rise in curiosity. I so badly want to know what he has to say to me but all he does is stand there and stare. After a moment he stammers a few unintelligible words, scratches the back of his head and then goes back inside. I'm stunned that he came out to find me. Part of me wants to run after him. Instead, I wince and lean my head against Dad's shoulder.

"Do you want to go…" Dad points back to the door. I shake my head "no." I can talk to Paxton later. He puts his arm across me and I lean into him. "What happened?" He asks me again.

"I just…panicked and then I saw Dan. And it was awful, Dad. He was kissing his new girlfriend and..." my chin starts quivering as I'm getting the words out. "It just hurt so bad. I thought I was doing well getting over it but I don't know. It just *hurt*. And I know I shouldn't be crying over a stupid boy, and I shouldn't be letting him have this much control over me. Half of me is sad and half of me is so mad that I'm still letting him hurt me. I'm mad. I'm angry with myself. I don't want to feel like this anymore." Dad shakes his head.

"Emerald Evans-Green," He starts. "You were in love and everything you are feeling right now is completely valid. Look at me." He sits me up so I can look at him. I swoop my knuckle under my eyes to clear any runny make-up. "None of this 'should or shouldn't' business. You're allowed to feel hurt and sad and everything else that you are feeling. Don't be angry with yourself for having emotions. You're human. You love so deeply and so passionately just like your mother. You can't just will that away. I can promise you that it will get easier. And there's no timeline for these kinds of things. So don't be concerned with 'should and shouldn't.' They don't exist."

The Art of Moving On

"Dad, thank you for being here," I sigh into his shoulder.

"I will always be here when you need me, Emerald. I promise." He kisses my head. "Now, school is going to let out in a few minutes. You still have Student Council and the game tonight, right?"

"Yes." I groan. "And I promised Ricky we would go to the after party but I don't know..."

He nods his head. "Good. I think you should go out. It's been awhile since you had fun. The bell's about to ring, and I should get back to the shop. I'll see you at home for dinner, okay?"

"Okay." We stand and hug. "Love you."

"Love you, too. Now go be a kick ass Vice President." I smile and he walks to his car. I turn around and walk back inside to my locker with a heavy heart.

***

Ricky drops everything (literally, his books and papers go flying everywhere and float down to the carpeted floor) and rushes to hug me as soon as he walks into the office and sees me. "Querida, thank God you're okay. Do you want to talk about it?"

"I'm okay...I think I'm fine. It was just...Dan. I panicked and then I saw him kissing Alexis and..."

"*Ssshhh*. It's okay. I understand. I'll have Yearbook give us another photographer, too."

"No. No, it's okay. I need to be able to be normal around him. This will be good for me. It'll help me move forward like you said," I assure him. "I'm fine, really. Just super embarrassed."

"We don't have to go out tonight–"

"Yes, we do. And we are. And we are going to have fun. I don't want him to have this power over me anymore." He tilts his head and smiles.

"I love your new found determination about this party. We *are* going to have fun. Now let's get this meeting over with. Also, I'm using my executive powers and neither of us will ever do another announcement ever again. We'll make the minions do it." I smile and hug him.

CHAPTER 8

Traci Dougan lives in a ten-bedroom mansion on the west side of Cayden Springs. Her driveway has a loop, and the entire front of the house, including all of the trees and bushes, are all lit up for display. She has an extended front porch lined with four antique, white, ionic columns and ornate, over-sized, double front doors.

I've been to her house for parties with Dan a number of times, and her parties never fail to disappoint. Something dramatic always happens. One time Todd got in a fight with some guy from another school because (supposedly) Todd slept with his girlfriend. His best friend, Brett Dixon, had to break it up. Todd really is a good a guy, despite his drunken escapades…in and out of the sheets.

The Art of Moving On

"You nervous, querida?" Ricky asks as we pull up in his old, dark green, two-door Honda Civic behind another car in Traci's loop driveway. "Because you shouldn't be. You look incredible tonight. I'm glad you decided to wear that red lipstick." I'm wearing my tightest dark blue skinny jeans with black shiny pumps, a fitted black hooded long-sleeve Henley, and red matte lipstick. "Paxton isn't even going to know what hit him and Dan will be groveling for you to take him back."

"Paxton? Who said anything about Paxton? And Dan and I are *never* getting back together–"

Ricky interrupts me to sing, "We are never, ever, ever, getting back toge-"

"*Wow*, okay, save it for the Taylor Swift concert," I respond loudly. I laugh and cover my ears in jest.

"Oh, please," he says. "My T-Swift game is on. point." He pulls down the vanity mirror to check himself out. Ricky is an excellent dresser. He's wearing perfectly fitted black jeans, with dark mustard yellow hipster shoes and a dark blue button up with the sleeves rolled up.

I pull my mirror down to do the same. My brown hair is tightly curled so it looks shorter than it really is. Curled, it sits right on top of my shoulders. When it's straight, it hits my collarbone. I smooth down a few flyaway hairs and make sure that I don't have lipstick on my teeth. I flip the mirror back up with a snap and look over at Ricky who is making "sexy" faces at himself in the mirror. I bust out laughing, happy that he's in a silly mood. He stops making faces and goes back to his hair check.

"I'm going to leave my purse in here and just take my gum, lipstick and phone, okay?" I think the few valuables I have are actually safer here in Ricky's old car parked

The Art of Moving On

outside a big party than my posters are on the school wall. I swallow the frustration bubbling up and push the thoughts out of my head.

"Sounds good to me." He snaps the mirror back up. "Because you are getting duh-runk tonight, chica!" I giggle with him and then pull back his reins.

"No, no, I am not getting plastered tonight, Ricky. I'm going to have *a* drink, but seriously, I have to end up back in my bedroom by one in the morning. I have curfew and I've never missed it," I tell him seriously.

"Ok, ok, whatever you say. We look hot. Let's do this."

We get out of the car and make our way to the elephant size front doors. There are few other people standing around outside loitering and smoking cigarettes. As we get closer we can hear Drake playing. I get nervous as we open the door. The party looks like a scene from a high school movie...minus the girls making out. There are people everywhere with red cups. Girls and boys are flirting, dancing, or kissing. The entryway already smells like sweat and stale beer. We walk in a few steps when Paxton appears. He throws his hands up and yells, "The President and Vice President have arrived!" People nearby scream and clap. I'm sure most of it is because Paxton yelled, and not actually because they care about Ricky and I arriving, but it's the loudest welcome I've ever had. My eyes grow wide and my face turns pink. I instantly get embarrassed and anxious while Ricky takes a few bows. Paxton's short attention span takes over, because he walks away without saying anything to us.

"That was awesome," Ricky says excitedly loudly over the music. "We're going to have to start coming to more of these." *Oh no.* We've been here five minutes and he's already turning into a party monster.

The Art of Moving On

"Let's go to the kitchen so I can get a drink."

"To the kitchen!" He exclaims animatedly with a fist in the air. I can't help but chuckle and follow him.

One dining room and two living rooms later, we get to the kitchen. People kept saying hi to us along the way, and I felt bad because I only knew about half of them. A lot of people know us because of Student Council, but Ricky is better with names than I am.

The kitchen is about five times the size of mine. Everything is oversized and dark granite. Next to one of the granite islands is a keg of beer in a blue plastic tub with ice around it. I pull a red cup out of the plastic package on the counter. I go to grab the spout of the keg when someone beats me to it.

"Hey, Emmy. You look really nice tonight," some beefy guy with blonde hair compliments me. I can't remember his name, but I think he's a junior and plays varsity baseball. He's cute enough, but I'm not interested.

"Thanks," I reply politely as he pours the beer in my cup.

"What do you say…want to take a shot with me?" The cute blonde asks, smiling at me.

"Um…" I'm not used to being hit on. I'm not used to being *single*.

"Yes!" Ricky answers from behind me. "Yes, she would love to." I turn into him.

"What? No, I don't even know him," I mutter to him.

"Who cares, chica? He's cute; now do the shot. It'll put hair on your chest." He flips me around and pushes me to the counter so I'm standing next to blondie. It's been awhile since I've taken a shot, and I'm not entirely positive that I won't chuck it back up.

The Art of Moving On

Blondie puts his hand on the small of my back. Dangerously close to my butt. I do not approve. I shimmy towards the left so his hand drops. "Here." He passes me a shot glass with clear liquid. "Vodka. Cheers to you, Emmy, looking sexy as hell."

"Umm," I mumble but Ricky lifts my elbow informing me to down my shot like blondie just did. I down it all at once and then chug some of my beer. The burning in my throat is horrific. I instantaneously feel my insides starting to get warm and my cheeks redden. The burning is still there so I chug more of my beer. It must not have been filled all the way because I clear the cup easily and blondie pours me another one.

"Thatta girl. I had no idea you could put it away like that, Emmy." He pumps the keg a few times without taking his eyes off me. My face burns brighter until the warmness matches the warmth in my insides. "Damn, you're fine as hell." I have no idea what to say to his forward comments, so I just say nothing and try to avoid eye contact. He finishes filling my beer.

"Um, thanks. Ricky and I are going to go walk around," I mumble awkwardly trying to tell him "good-bye" and "thanks but no thanks" all at the same time.

"Sure thing, sexy. I'll come find you later." He looks me up and down like he's visualizing me naked. I'm supremely grossed out, so instead of saying words I just turn and start walking in the opposite direction trying not to gag.

"Gavin wants you so bad!" Ricky states as he locks our elbows together as we start to graze around the rest of the house.

"Gavin! *That's* his name. I couldn't remember. I'm not interested." I tell him honestly, taking a gulp of my beer. It tastes flat and stale but it's making my tummy warmer so I keep drinking it. We walk into another dining room with hardwood floors and a fancy cabinet with fine china, crystal bowls, and glasses. We stop and talk to a couple people from Student Council. We start to make a move to continue doing our rounds of the house but a girl gets in our way.

"Shots! Shots! Shots!" A girl I've never seen before in my life is on roller skates pouring out shots. I fear for the damage she's doing to the hardwood floor but, hey, not my house.

"You're such a talented skate–" I try yelling to her through the music.

"Shots! Shot?" She says at me. Or asks at me. I can't really tell.

"Oh, no, I was telling you–"

"Shooooots! Shots," she hollers, shoving a mini plastic cup of clear liquid in my face. I grab it so it doesn't fall on the already sticky floor. Everyone is having fun chanting "shots" with her. I have nowhere to walk and nothing to set the shot down on, so I decide I might as well swig it back. I follow it instantly with chugs of my stale tasting beer. "Shots!" She keeps saying, and people keep yelling. I'm starting to think that the only word she knows is, "shots," and I think I'm getting drunk enough to actually believe it. I turn around and I can't find Ricky in the bodies that suddenly have surrounded me.

I have to pee.

I push through the bodies and head for the bathroom. I'm magically the only person in line—wait, if I'm the only one in line that means there is no line, right? Right. I think. I shake my head and as soon as a boy walks out, I walk in. I close the door behind me, but someone stops the door and walks in, shoving me further into the bathroom, and closes the door.

The Art of Moving On

"Paxton! What are you doing? I have to pee," I whine to him, floored that he just followed me into the bathroom. I hope nobody saw. The last thing I need are rumors about how Paxton and I hooked up in a bathroom. *Gross.*

A light bulb goes off in my head and I remember to ask, "Hey, have you seen Ricky?"

Crickets.

He just stares at me with his scintillating green eyes. I take his silence as an invitation to peruse the rest of his body. He's wearing a plain white t-shirt that looks as though it's been worn a hundred times. The fabric is worn and has a tiny hole in the seam of the collar. A black hoodie covers the shirt and his dark purple beanie covers his hair. I love it when guys wear purple. It's a statement against society segregating and assigning colors to gender...or something...

I think I'm officially drunk.

I look further down and his dark jeans hug him terrifically in all the right places. I look back up at his face and he's grinning. I blush and suddenly feel very self-conscious. I hope that I look as good as he does. "Why are you grinning?" I ask suspiciously but can't help curve my lips up. He's too damn cute.

"I like it when you do that," he admits, taking a step closer to me. He smells musky and clean like soap and I'm finding it distracting...and addicting.

I want him closer.

I succumb to his bait and ask, "Do what?"

"Look at me like a piece of meat."

I bust out laughing, thankful that he broke the ice. He chuckles with me. "I do," he attests. "Or maybe I just like that you like what you see when you look at me." I stop laughing and take in the complexity of what he said. It takes me a second to absorb his confession through my foggy drunk mind. I look him in his eyes trying to read him.

But he's Paxton Wright and Paxton Wright is unreadable.

The liquid courage comes over me, and I step right up to him, grab his head gently, and lean forward to kiss him. I don't kiss him softly but playfully. I push my lips harder against his and the second I feel his mouth start to open I pull away. The whole kiss lasts about five seconds. My assertiveness surprises him and leaves him paralyzed. I grab his arm and whisper in his ear, attempting to sound sexy. "I have to pee. Get out, please." I think I accidentally slur, but I grin anyway as he walks out with a "What in the hell just happened?" look.

I successfully Paxton-Wrighted Paxton Wright.

Now he knows how it feels.

***

My cup is empty again so I push my way back to the kitchen.

"Emmy Evans-Green! Back for more!"

Oh shoot.

I forgot about blondie. Gavin jumps off the counter with his arms open. His words are coming out sloppy, and his face is pinker than the last time I saw him. Someone has had one too many shots.

The Art of Moving On

"Hi, Gavin." I avoid his hug and go straight to the keg. He drops his arms and grazes my hand.

"Here, I'll get this for you," he takes the spout from me and pours my cup as if holding down a tab is an arduous task.

"Um…thanks." I try not to roll my eyes. Instead, I look up and around the house. My eyes get caught on Paxton and Aileen talking by a giant fireplace. I'm wondering what they're talking about then my breath hitches. I see Dan and Alexis. She's sitting on his lap and they're canoodling for all the world to see. My heart beats and then flops upside down uncomfortably.

"So?" Gavin looks at me expectantly with a grin on his face.

"So…" Apparently he was talking to me while he was pouring my drink and I missed every word.

"Want to do another shot with me?" He asks, smiling. Gavin has a snaggletooth, far different from Dan's flawless smile, but it's actually kind of cute. However, he has a baby face that's more suitable for the word "adorable" than it is for the word "sexy." He seems overtly cocky for someone with a pink baby face.

Hm, drunk Emmy is really judgmental. Or maybe I'm always this judgmental?

"*Uuhh,*" I look back up and Dan and Alexis are still kissing. I scan to the left and Paxton and Aileen have gotten closer to each other and look as if they are in a heated discussion. Ricky is still missing in action. Aileen laughs at something Paxton says and he smiles brightly. I frown and somewhat reluctantly mumble, "Sure. Why not."

"Yeah! That's the spirit, babe." Those words coming from his mouth make me want to hurl. He pours us two shots.

"Cheers to this fine ass woman standing in front of me. May she make me a lucky guy sometime." He winks. My eyes bulge and I'm disgusted by what he is suggesting. I will *never* hook up with him. "Bottoms up." He clanks our mini glasses together and I swallow it down despite his rude keg-side manors. I chug some more beer to clear out the burning of my throat.

"Um…I gotta go," I say, turning around to walk out of the kitchen and away from Gavin before I get rude. I'm almost drunk enough to lose my filter.

"If you say so. You know where to find me, sexy girl." As I walk away he takes a handful of my butt and squeezes. I nearly jump out of my heels. A fire burns inside of me and it's not from the shot. Well, not entirely.

"Hey! You better watch–" I'm interrupted when a body jumps in front of me facing Gavin.

"Dude, not cool. Don't touch her like that. She's not your property that you can touch and grab whenever you want. She's not a piece of meat and she's certainly not yours," says the body in front of me. I lean forward and smell the delicious scent of woods and citrusy cologne. It's so yummy I go dizzy. Or maybe that's the alcohol. He has such a nice frame and such a soft sweatshirt on. I chug the cup until it's empty again. I sway on my feet a little so I lean my head against the boy in front of me and grab a handful of his delectable smelling hoodie.

"So, what? She's yours now?" Gavin asks incredulously.

Crickets.

"Just stand down, Gavin. She's a person not a possession," the body says firmly.

Crickets.

The Art of Moving On

Majorly uncomfortable crickets.

"Fine. Go ahead. I get it. She's all yours, asshole." The body shakes his head at Gavin who I can see saunter away.

"Jerk!" I shout at Gavin's back. The body turns around and I end up against his chest taking in the smell of him from the front. It's intoxicating. "My beer is gone," I slur.

"I think you've had enough, Emerald." I finally look up at his eyes. His eyes that are the same color as my name. His eyes that compliment his face so deliciously it makes my mouth water. I sigh into him.

"Paxton…" I start.

"Yes, Emmy?" He asks absentmindedly as he takes my cup from me and puts it on the counter.

"I forgot what I was going to say." I slump my shoulders and mumble into his chest. His hands are on my side and I want to tell him to put them on my bottom. I wish it were his hands that grabbed me and not blondie's.

"I'm flattered that you want me to touch your butt but I'm not going to."

Oops. I said that out loud.

"Yup, you just said that out loud too."

"Crap." The room slowly starts to spin. "Paxton…I don't think I want to stand any more. Can you hold me?" His hands are still on my hips trying to keep me from swaying.

"I already am holding you."

"Oh." I decide his hands on my hips aren't enough to keep me from falling. I ignore his comment and jump up on him with my legs wrapped around the front of him. He stumbles backward and his body stiffens. "Uh, ok. I didn't know that's what you meant."

"You feel so warm and cozy, Paxton." I snuggle my head into his neck. My eyes suddenly feel heavy and are having trouble staying open. "Can I just go home with you? That way we can wake up and your mom will be there in the morning, and we can eat breakfast with her, and talk to her all morning." He chuckles and starts to walk without touching me at all. I'm clinging onto him completely by myself.

"That's officially the weirdest thing a girl has ever said to me." I start slipping down, and he finally acquiesces to touching me and grabs my thighs to pull me back up.

"Jeez, you don't have to act repulsed to touch me." He chuckles. I'm not sure why he's laughing. I grunt. "Where are we going?"

"To Ricky's car so we can get you home." I start to slip down with each step, so I grab my legs tighter around him and push myself up. "Jesus, Emerald, you have to stop doing that."

"Doing what?" He looks at me like I should know. He gestures down below and I feel what he's talking about. "Oops. Okay, you can put me down now. I can walk."

"You sure?" I nod. He slowly puts me on the ground, and I stumble a little.

"Okay, maybe not. Piggy back-ride?" Even though I would like to be wrapped around the front of him again. He laughs out of nowhere.

"What's so funny?" I pout.

"You said that out loud, too," he says, smiling brightly. I groan.

The Art of Moving On

"Well, I didn't mean it. I'm drunk. Nothing I say counts," I rationalize.

"Debatable. Hop on," he says, offering me his back. I jump on and it's much more comfortable than being attached to his front, even though I liked it better.

"Stella is definitely getting her groove back," I giggle at my scandalous thoughts as I snuggle into his neck and give him tiny kisses below his ear.

"Jesus, Emerald, you are not making this easy. And who's Stella?" He grunts, and I can tell that he's getting irritated with me. I don't want him to get mad and make me walk, so I stop kissing him.

"Are we there yet?" I ask, suddenly noticing that we're outside.

"Almost. Ricky should be out here waiting for us. I texted Eli."

"Oh, thank God. Wait, why Eli?"

"Ricky and Eli were hanging out together."

"Oh," I simply say, not even caring to process what those two could possibly have in common.

"*Aaand* we're here." He carefully puts me down. I grab his arm for balance as I take off my heels. He sighs. "*Aaand* Ricky is not." He pulls his phone out again and sends a text.

"Do you hate me?" I ask, leaning against Ricky's car. It's dirty but I'm too tired and drunk to care. Paxton looks at me with a smirk.

"No. I don't hate you. I actually think I like you a little bit more after tonight." Before I can spit a rebuttal, Ricky shows up.

"Hey, guys," Ricky greets us as he and Eli speed walk up to us. "Sorry for the minor delay. Gavin caught up with me, and I had to convince him that you and I aren't dating, and that you and Paxton aren't dating, and that you and Dan aren't dating, and that basically nobody is dating anybody." He fidgets around looking uncomfortable. He adds, "That guy seriously wants you."

"Well, I want none of him. He's a pig," I announce, swooshing my hand through the air.

"Right. Well, let's get you in the car. Are you going to puke once we start driving?"

"No, of course not. I'm a lady. I only puke in toilets," I announce as if I'm royalty. Paxton laughs. "Don't laugh at me, Prince Wright," I continue saying in my hoity-toity voice. They all laugh, and I'm not sure why. Paxton opens the door and helps me get in. He takes a hold of my hand, and I feel the heat from it seeping into my bloodstream making my entire body warm up. "Until we meet again. Don't forget to go find your Princess Aileen. She's probably awaiting your return." He grins and shakes his head like I'm loony when I start to sing the '80s song, *"Come on Eileen."*

He leans into the car and against my ear he whispers, "Not everything is what you think it is, Emerald." I look into the forest of his eyes.

He really is beautiful.

He kisses my hand and places it on my lap.

"Not as beautiful as you are, Emmy," he confesses, still looking at me.

"All right, not to ruin this Kodak moment but we should really get going," Ricky orders us, causing Paxton and I to snap out of it.

It's probably for the best. It's time to leave before I say even more things that will embarrass me tomorrow. I have a serious case of word vomit tonight. Speaking of vomit…

I make it five minutes before I puke half inside and half outside of Ricky's car.

***

"*Uuuggghhh*, why are you calling me so early?" I groan and ask the voice in my ear.

"Emmy, it's noon. I deposited you to your bed before one in the morning. You've slept almost twelve hours. Up and at 'em, chica," Ricky tells me in a chipper voice.

"I wonder why my dad didn't wake me. We were supposed to have breakfast. Anyways, what's up?"

"Nothing. I just wanted to check on you to make sure you were okay. There's water by your bed and some Aspirin." I look on my nightstand and sure enough there's a cup of water and two white pills.

"Did I ever tell you that you're the bestest friend in the whole wide world?" I roll over to pick up the pills and water. I pop the pills in my mouth and attempt to hold the phone up to my ear with my shoulder and drink some water. I end up spilling water all down the front of me. The spillage makes me realize that I'm still in the same clothes from last night.

"You just spilled a bunch of water, didn't you?"

"Yeah," I admit reluctantly. "Should I be afraid to look in a mirror?" I ask but I already know the answer.

The Art of Moving On

"Depends. Are you done tossing your cookies?"

I groan loudly as my memory comes back to me in full force…as does the smell.

"Ricky, I'm so sorry. Let's go get your car washed and detailed later."

"I'll take you up on that. Pick you up around four? Car wash and dinner?"

"It's a date," I confirm.

"Oh, querida, if that's your idea of a date, Dan did more damage than I originally thought."

Crickets.

I know his jab is harmless and if I didn't feel like poop I would probably laugh. Right now, it just makes my heart *womp.* "I'm sorry," Ricky says.

"No, it's okay, I just have a bad headache. I have to go find my dad and apologize for missing breakfast."

"Okay, see you in a bit. Te amo," he says purposely in a high-pitched voice that only dogs can hear. I move my phone away from my face.

"Yeah, te amo too," I mumble, still groggy. He laughs and I hang up.

I somehow will myself out of bed and into the living room where there's no sign of Dad. I look in the kitchen and he's not there either. I push the screen door out and am smacked in the face by a cloudless sky and chilled air. It's way too bright for my eyes and brain, but it feels unbelievable on the rest of my body. I use my hand as a visor as I walk down to the driveway where Dad is working on an old 1985 dusty, mint green El Camino. Not exactly the car I would've picked up to restore, but Dad can be random like that.

The Art of Moving On

"Hey! Look who's finally awake. How you feeling, sweet pea?" He asks, standing up straight from bending over the engine.

"A little bit like death but I'll make it." There's no pretending that I didn't drink or that I'm not hungover. I would never sleep until noon unless I was sick, but since I went out the night before… well, Dad's a smart guy. He can put two and two together.

"Rough night last night?" He questions, squinting his eyes from the sun.

"Yeah…rough day." I'm not proud that I got drunk, and I'm embarrassed that Dad knows.

"I figured as much. Don't make that a habit, okay? Let this hangover be punishment enough," he says sternly, waving his wrench at me.

"More than fair. Sorry, Dad."

"It's okay but you can't go and drink away your problems every time you have one. You broke curfew, but luckily Ricky was looking out for you. I'm not happy about it, let that be clear, but I know that's not like you. Last night was an anomaly, *I hope*, but I need you to understand that, okay? Next time anything like this happens you're grounded."

"Of course, Dad. I understand. Sorry about breakfast. How about lunch? I bought some chicken the other day that I was going to fry up. How about some fried chicken, and I can re-heat some black eyed peas and cook some collard greens?" I suggest, hoping that food can redeem me even if it's only a little. The guilt is the punishment, not the hangover.

"Grandma's recipe?" He asks, even though he knows the answer.

The Art of Moving On

My grandparents on Dad's side live down south near Savannah. We don't get to see them that often but Grandma came up for an extended visit when Mom passed away. She wrote down all of her old soul food recipes that she got from her grandma and now I have them. The recipe cards are merely frail bits of paper but I know all the recipes by heart now and I don't even need to look at them any more.

"Of course."

"Sounds great. I'll come in and take a shower in a few then come help."

"Cool. Actually, I need to shower too." I don't even have to lift my arms up to smell my stench. The sweat and vomit aroma floating from me is putrid. Everything in my room is going to need to be sanitized and washed. My head throbs and my stomach churns just thinking about it.

"Oh, good. I wasn't going to say anything but you look and smell worse than I do," he jokes.

"Oh, *HA HA*. I'll see you inside." I walk away to hop in my desperately needed shower.

Much to my chagrin, all the other memories from last night come cascading back to me just like the water trickling down my body. Too bad no soap in the world can wash the embarrassing memories away no matter how hard I scrub. Seeing Paxton is going to be completely cringe-worthy. There's no way he's going to let me live any of that down.

The Art of Moving On

Chapter 9

Monday is going so smooth that I should've known something was up. Ricky and I had a

calm but productive lunch in the SC office. Paxton hasn't even looked my way at all

today, and I am honestly grateful for it. It's no surprise that I'm full of relief on my way

to one of my favorite classes, Environmental Science. I can't wait to get started on my

project that we were assigned last week. I already know what I want to report on and

have thoughts on how I can integrate my art in.

      Mr. Kirkland is writing on the whiteboard when I enter the room. I sit in my seat

and begin to take out my notebook. We don't have assigned seats in this class, but

everyone always sits in the same seat they sat in on the first day of class. If one person

sits elsewhere the whole seating shifts and it becomes chaos. Okay, it doesn't really become chaos but it makes way for a few grunts and eye rolls. I'm surprised when Dan

sits down in front of me (his pre-break-up seat) and not in his new normal seat, which is

two seats behind me. I could go further into the seat dynamics in every one of the classes

he and I share, but it's petty and confusing. Let's just say, when he broke up with me six

weeks ago the entire seat chain of every class was thrown off and Dan and I were to

blame. Turns out, people can get really attached to their non-assigned seats.

There are many eye rolls as more students trickle in. My heart flutters wondering

why Dan is sitting in front of me again. Paxton strolls in and takes note that the classroom

is off balance. He takes advantage of this and sits right behind me, which further

complicates the seating dynamic. I hear a resounding, "ugh," as the next few kids enter

the room. My nerves are becoming a wreck, and I wish Dan would explain his action. I

have no doubt that Paxton is sitting behind me to get on my nerves somehow. I'm sure

I'll find out during class when I'm taking notes and trying to pay attention. Paxton is

really good at disrupting and distracting me. I'm certain it's what he does best. Being

sandwiched between them makes me want to crawl under my covers and never leave my

bedroom again.

Staring at the back of Dan's head reminds me of playing with the little black

dense curls and how much I loved it. I remember last year for our 80s themed dance he

grew his hair out specifically for it and then cut it in a flat top. I thought it was the cutest

thing in the entire world. I remember how we made love in his Land Rover after the

dance, and he held me until we had to go home.

Another memory comes flashing back. I remember him being upset that I had run

my fingers through his hair so much that it left his hair a little lumpy and poofy in some

The Art of Moving On

spots. He scoffed at me and told me that his parents and older brother would know that he had been fooling around. The memory turns bitter in my mind. It's funny how we only remember the good memories until our subconscious has a reason to find a sour one. I don't get a chance to shake my memories before Dan turns around.

Our eyes meet immediately and I am thrust into pain once more. Looking into the eyes of a person you once loved is indescribable. But if I had to try to describe it, it would be akin to looking into someone's eyes whose memory of you has vanished completely. His eyes are mostly vacant. Vacant and casual, as if I was just someone he happened to pass in the grocery store aisle. It's jarring and a new form of pain that he's evoked in me. I can sit here now and confidently say that the opposite of love isn't hate. The opposite of love is apathy. His entire demeanor is indifferent. He looks at me and sees nothing but a classmate.

It freaking hurts.

I can't decide if I'm going to cry, vomit from anxiety, or punch him in the face. Or all of the above.

"Hey, Emmy…are you okay?" He deigns to ask me.

"No. What do you want?" I ask monotone as to not give away any emotion.

"Look…"

Life lesson: be wary of any sentence that starts with, "look" or any conversation that starts with, "We need to talk."

"We need to talk," he says casually.

He's two for two. This conversation is headed straight to the crapper. Then again, I should have predicted that as soon as he looked at me.

The Art of Moving On

"I'm taking photos for the yearbook and we're scheduled to shoot the Student Council members on Friday." I stop him there because I know what he's going to say.

"Yeah, I know, Dan. I'm Vice President. I know what you're thinking, and I'm fine with it, okay?" I snap at him. "There won't be any problems. You don't need to find us a new photographer," I tell him upfront to save us both time. I roll my eyes and cross my arms.

"Uh, well, that's cool, but I was actually just going to ask if you could switch your time to fifteen minutes later. You're the first one signed up at 3:15, and I was wondering if you could come in for your photo at 3:30 instead. I need the time to set up the equipment and make sure the lighting is right."

Lighting.

Lighting.

He has to make sure the *lighting* is right.

He didn't want to clear the air about us being alone in the same room for the first time since he broke up with me. Technically, the last time we were alone in a room together was when had sex the night before he broke up with me. You know, since he broke up with me in public at The Café while I was eating pie. I thought I had gotten incredibly better on my anger/hatred. But I feel a fresh douse of anger seeping over me like honey over my head, slowly covering every crevice.

I snap out of my anger when a heavy hand squeezes then rubs my right shoulder. I turn to the right to see who it is, and there's nobody there. Of course there's not. "That works perfectly since we need some time to discuss our project." I whip my head to the left, and Paxton's head is mere inches away from mine. He's leaning over and looking

The Art of Moving On

just as casual as Dan. I'm befuddled as to how this is simply casual for either of them. I seem to be the only one thinking logically. And having feelings for that matter. Perhaps boys don't have real feelings?

That's absurd.

I shake my head to refocus. I appreciate Paxton trying to save me by making up some school project so I go along with it.

"Oh, yeah, I almost forgot. Thanks, Pax. Yeah, 3:30 works better for us too," I attempt to match their casual demeanor.

"Awesome, you guys. Thanks." Dan starts to turn around then turns back and says to me, "Glad to see you're doing okay." Then turns back around. His last comment leaves me with a sour face and grinding teeth. I glance at the classroom clock and class should've started by now, but Mr. Kirkland is still jotting on the whiteboard.

"So, partner," Paxton says.

"Uh, yeah, thanks. You really didn't have to do that—fake a project to bail me out. Also, thank you for the whole Friday night thing. I'm really embarrassed, and it was cool of you to help me out," I thank him shyly, looking between the pencil I'm twirling in my hand and toward his eyes but never actually meeting them. He grins.

"Don't mention it, Green." I look at him and clear my throat obnoxiously so he takes note of what he said. "Sorry, *Emerald.* And I didn't fake a project." A grin shines across his face. My eyebrows inch together.

"What do you mean?"

"Our new project," he states. He stops twirling his red pen. Of course, the only pen he would have on him is red. He probably swiped it off a teacher's desk because he

The Art of Moving On

came to school with no pens or pencils. It irks me when students come to school ill prepared. How hard is it to bring a pen or pencil and a notebook? That's literally all you really need to survive. I massage my temples and try to cool out. This is not how I thought my afternoon would go.

"What are you talking about? What new project?"

"Our new partner project," he informs me pointing to the whiteboard just as Mr. Kirkland speaks.

"Okay, everyone, I've assigned you partners for your project that I assigned last class." I look at the board.

Hell on a graham cracker.

Paxton's name is beside mine.

I raise my hand before I even know what I'm going to ask. "Mr. Kirkland?"

"Yes, Emmy?" His pointed nose and round glasses face me. He looks reminiscent of Steve Jobs. Or a grown up Harry Potter. I give a silent *rest in peace* for Mr. Jobs before I answer.

"Um, last week when you assigned us the project you never mentioned anything about partners so I'm just wondering why we have partners now?" I get hisses from students telling me to "shut up" and "it's a good thing."

"Settle down, class. It's a good question." Audible scoffs abound. "A student came up to me and made their case as to why the project should be a partner project and I agreed. So, it's settled. You have partners. *There is no switching partners.* I expect double the effort and double the creativity. The bar is set high."

The Art of Moving On

I turn around to look at Paxton and his balsam eyes greet mine with a twinkle to match his grin. I turn back unsteady and a little frightened that Paxton and I are about to share some forced time together. I look back down at my notebook and tap it a few times with my pen. I reach into the small front pouch of my bag and twist to Paxton's desk to set down a blue ink pen so he'll have one for his next class. He looks confused then looks at his red pen and huffs a laugh through the back of his hand, shaking his head.

The bell rings at the end of class and we all stand to collect our things. "So, about this project…"

"Yeah. I already have an idea and I think it's going to be great and a lot of fun," I inform him excitedly. Maybe partnering with Paxton isn't the worst thing. At least now I have someone to be excited with.

I think.

"Well, I also have an idea that I think is really great."

"Oh. Okay. Um. When do you want to get together?" I'm biased, but I'm pretty sure my idea is better. Not that Paxton isn't smart; it's just that this type of project is right up my alley.

"*Ooo*," he coos in a high-pitched voice. "Are you asking me out, Miss Emerald?" I shoot him a heavy eye roll. He gets the hint and goes back to normal as we make our way down the hall together. "Wednesday. We get out early. Your house or mine?" He asks, moving his eyebrows up and down suggestively. "I know how beautiful you think I am, and how badly you want me to grab your ass."

"*Ssshhh*, Paxton!" I whack his arm. My face turns as red as a cherry. "I never said that. And the library, right after school."

The Art of Moving On

"Yes, you did. In the library, right after we eat lunch together," he counter-offers. "I don't do projects before lunch." I contemplate his lunch offer.

"No, I never said that, Paxton. Library, right after we eat lunch with Ricky in the SC office."

"You definitely did, Emerald. Library, right after we eat lunch outside alone. I'll make us a picnic. Later, Emmy." He breaks off down another hallway. He walks backwards and hollers, "Oh, and that shirt brings out your face skin nicely." He turns back around and enters his next class before I can say anything.

My white oxford shirt brings out my face skin nicely?

That's by far the weirdest thing anybody has ever said to me.

I make my way to my TA period. My Prayer and Spirituality teacher, Mrs. Novoa gives me a stack of quizzes from her junior class and a red pen to grade them. I take my stack and head to the library. Ricky greets me shortly after with his stack of papers to grade from a Sophomore English class. A few minutes later Paxton shows up at our table with his own stack of papers to grade. He whips out the red pen he had earlier, and starts grading without saying a word. Ricky and I look up and make confused looks at each other, but end up shrugging our shoulders. He's never graded papers in the library before. I look back up and take notice of the red pen. So *that's* why he had it. Not because it's all he had but because he was going to use it for grading during his TA period. I curse myself for being judgmental and for allowing Dan to put me in a bad mood.

Paxton's right.

Things aren't always what I think. I let out a "*hm*" and Paxton looks up at me, down to his pen and the back at me. I grin at him and slowly shake my head a little. He

The Art of Moving On

grins back as if we just had a silent conversation. He knows he's right. We go back to grading.

Chapter 10

Wednesday morning I eat with Dad again. Bacon, eggs, and orange juice. It's our Wednesday thing. I'm not sure when or why it started, but for the last few years we always get up, and he makes bacon and eggs for us. Normally we eat cereal, yogurt, or toast before we rush out to conquer and destroy our daily tasks.

"Thanks, Dad." I sit down to my plate. "Hey, I've been meaning to ask you, what's with the 1985 El Camino in the driveway? Seems like an odd project to pick up."

"Look at you smarty pants! Knowing it's an '85! That's my girl! It is a little quirky, but a woman bought it off Craigslist for real cheap and asked me to restore it for her and redo it with all the bells and whistles. I can't say no to an intimidating project. It

96

needs a lot of work so I figure I'll work on it here every weekend, and Todd will probably come by and help with it, too."

"That's actually pretty cool. Are you going re-paint it green?"

"Yeah, but not a mint green. I'll do a dark metallic type green so it shines in sunlight. I'm going to put in a brand new black leather bench. Those cars don't have bucket seats, you know. Then I'll take it to my tech guy to put in a nice new stereo. This lady was pretty adamant on wanting all the new stuff with a vintage feel. Kind of like Betsy."

"In that case, I can't say I blame her. She picked the perfect guy to do it."

"Sure did. We'll just have to live with a funky car in the driveway for a while. I think I'll get Todd over here this weekend to help out."

"Sounds pretty cool. I can't wait to see it when it's done. Oh, hey, I won't be home until later today. I have a project I'm working on with Paxton, that kid I told you about."

"Paxton. The one you think is weird and annoying?"

"Yes. Well, he's not so bad. It will be interesting to work on a project with him though. I'm not sure how serious he'll take it. He's kind of a goofball." He chuckles.

"Well, that sounds like fun. Are you guys coming here or going to his house?" He takes a bite of toast and some crumbs stick to his stubble.

"Library. Neutral territory." He chuckles again.

"It's a project, sweet pea, not a battle. I'm sure Paxton will have many ideas that will contribute to the project. Don't be so quick to judge. I know I didn't raise my daughter to be judgmental." I groan because he's right. I've been really judgmental when

The Art of Moving On

it comes to Paxton. Even though he can be childish at times, he can be full of pleasant surprises.

"You're right, Dad."

"I'm the Dad. I'm always right," he says smiling brightly.

"Oh, hardee-har-har. I'll be back around 2:30."

"Put your dishes in the dishwasher. I'll wash the rest when I get home." I clear my plate easily and quickly, crinkling the rest of the bacon in my mouth.

I freaking love bacon.

I tried being vegetarian for a while, but it didn't work. I just love meat too much. Part of me does feel bad about still eating meat. The conditions that cows, chickens, and pigs live in are horrific. The chemicals they pump into them are horrendous and completely unethical; not to mention unhealthy. It makes me sick just thinking about it. But when you're only cooking for two and one doesn't eat meat and one does, it's difficult to make a balanced meal to fit both our needs easily. I quit and now only buy organic, free-range meat. I also tell myself that millions of years of evolution have ensured that I was built to eat meat. I feel it's a natural part of my body and my body's desire to eat meat. I remind myself of that to try and make myself feel better about it. Maybe when I go off to college I'll give it another try.

When I leave the kitchen, Dad is just finishing his food. He's taking his time, which tells me he's working on the El Camino this morning before heading to the shop. I kiss the top of his head after I grab all my school stuff. "Are you *motoring* out of here?" He asks. I laugh.

"Yes, I'm motoring on out. Love you."

The Art of Moving On

"Love you too, sweet pea."

***

I'm sharing a moment with Paxton that I never thought I would share with him or, frankly, with anyone. After school we met up; he pulled a bag and a blanket out of his locker and I followed him to the soccer field. Paxton tells me the girls soccer team is having a cross-training day and that they wouldn't come to the field to practice. I have no idea what a cross-training day is, so I decide to believe him.

He spreads out a large old pale flower patterned blanket that looks like it has rested on the back of a grandma's sofa for about twenty years. Maybe thirty. He pulls out a reusable cooler bag out of his trunk and then sits on the blanket. He taps next to him, motioning for me to sit down. I join him noticing some butterflies in my tummy starting to flitter around unexpectedly. Or maybe they're just hunger pangs. He pulls out two Capri Suns, two small bags of barbecue chips, two peanut butter and jelly sandwiches, an apple, and a banana. I am insanely impressed. "Your meal, madam," he declares in his own version of a hoity-toity voice.

"Why, thank you." He places one of each item in front of me but studies the sandwiches through the clear baggies. "Are you trying to figure out which one is poisoned?"

"Actually, yes. One is P.B. and J and one is just jelly and bananas. I'm allergic to peanuts." He finally hands me mine.

The Art of Moving On

"I didn't know that. That's good to know. Like…how allergic?" I ask, biting into my sandwich. He even cut the crust off and cut it diagonally. It doesn't seem like much but coming from Paxton…I can't explain it but it mends a little piece of the crack in my heart. He's so thoughtful.

"Like throat closing, everything swelling, emergency room, shot in the ass allergic. But only when I ingest them. I can be around them and be fine. Some people can't even be around peanuts." He opens his chips. He's now shoving his barbecue chips in his mouth along with his jelly and banana sandwich.

"You're creating a very strange mix of flavors in your mouth right now," I comment.

He shrugs his shoulders nonchalantly and says, "Meh. I like it the way I like it." He winks, and I can't help but smile and feel a movement of the butterflies in my stomach.

"That's a great attitude." I adore his ability to be genuinely himself all the time, quirks and all. I look down at the grass. This whole lunch is really great. I can't believe he went to all this trouble for me. I know it doesn't mean anything. It's just us being partners and having fun while doing school work, but it's still really sweet of him.

"Pax, it's really thoughtful of you to go to this much trouble to feed me. It's really nice outside and the P.B. and J…it's all…really nice. Thank you." He's been doing such sweet things for me lately; I don't know why I keep getting so surprised every time.

"You have jelly on your chin and peanut butter on your cheek. I never would've thought that you ate like a little kid," he blatantly tells me. Well, maybe that's why I get surprised. I turn pink and look away to use the back of my hand to wipe my face off since

The Art of Moving On

I don't have a napkin. I turn to face him again, and he is holding a napkin an inch from my face. I didn't know it was possible, but I get even more embarrassed.

"Um, Thanks. You know, your shirt really brings out your face skin," I tell him to take the focus off my Neanderthal eating habits. I study his reaction. He tries to hide his grin but fails.

"I think the blue one does it for me, honestly," he says.

"No way." I smile and wave my hand in front of him. "White oxford is your shirt. Definitely. It takes your natural olive complexion and makes it pop. All of that combined with your black hair makes your eyes really pop. And your hair pops too, for that matter. There's basically a lot of popping happening." I wave my hand in front of his body.

"Good popping or bad popping?"

"I think that depends on the person," I state self-assuredly. He narrows his eyes at me, but a confident grin remains on his face.

"Is it good popping *to you* or bad popping?"

I'm hesitant to inflate his ego and let him know how good his "popping" makes me feel sometimes. I tilt my head and contemplate. Finally, I nod. "Good Popping." I've finished my sandwich and chips. I grab the apple and the banana. "Okay, who gets the banana and who gets the apple?"

"Well…" he starts, eyeing the banana.

"You had banana on your sandwich," I reason in favor of me getting the banana.

"I love bananas though. Enough to eat two in one meal," he claims convincingly.

"Really?"

"Yeah, I love bananas. Bananas are, like, my thing."

The Art of Moving On

"Wow. Okay, so you want the banana?" I ask, holding the banana in front of him with one hand as I hold the apple to my lips with my other hand.

He grabs the banana but then rapidly changes his mind. "Just kidding. I'll take the apple." He throws the banana back on me so it lands on my lap while I'm midway into a bite of the apple. I pull out my teeth from the apple and offer it to him knowing he'll hand it back since my teeth prints are indented in it.

Except it's Paxton Wright and he takes the apple back and immediately takes a bite out of it. Using my teeth marks, too. I shake my head and grin.

When we're done, we clean everything up and open the trunk to put everything away. Paxton pulls out his soccer ball. The same ball that smacked me in the back a couple weeks ago. "You know we have to go work on our project," I harp on him while he plays with the ball on the grass.

"Yeah let's work on it," he agrees, looking down at the ball as he taps his feet against it in a bunch of fancy ways and then flips it up and starts using his feet and knees and even his head to bounce it around. No wonder he's the co-captain of the soccer team.

"We should to go to the library or something."

"No, let's do it here. Come out here on the field." I grunt and tilt my head back, but my feet still move forward.

"We need supplies—like a table and chairs, papers, books, and...come on, Paxton. We said we would work in the library." We've had such a nice time that I hate being Debbie Downer.

"Grab a paper and pen." I do what he tells me and pull out my notebook from my backpack in his car. I walk back out to him on the field.

The Art of Moving On

"My idea is to focus on the destruction of the rainforests. We take it back to basics, you know? Keep it O.G. We can talk statistics of the destruction of rainforests, and how we can help." I'm jotting down his notes as he plays with the ball. "Okay, your turn." He walks up to me with the ball below in front of us. He takes the pen and notebook. "Here, use the ball."

I don't know anything about soccer and I really don't want to embarrass myself again today so I just lightly toe it around. "Um, okay. I actually think our ideas are sort of the same. They go along perfectly together. The rainforests are being destroyed. The rainforests were home to a lot of species. One of those species is gibbon, a type of ape. I want to focus on the different types primates going extinct, specifically gibbons, and how and why their habitat is being destroyed. We can talk statistics, but also raise awareness about ways we can help. I think it would be really cool to find a way to show our project not just to the kids in our class but the whole student body." He's jotting down notes, and I'm getting more and more comfortable with the ball. I'm actually getting excited. With Paxton's help this project can be a lot bigger than I had originally planned.

"Okay, so: showing the facts, finding out a way we can help, and then give the information to the masses so they can learn how to help."

"Yes. We need to do some research. How about Friday?" I ask, looking up at him. He grins with one hand in his pocket and one hand holding the notebook by his side. He looks at me for a moment and it causes me to fidget.

"You want to do research on Friday night? Are you asking me on a date Miss Evans-Green?" His use of my whole last name makes me smile.

"It's not a date, Mr. Wright. It's research," I tell him directly. "In the library."

The Art of Moving On

"My house. Libraries close early on Friday."

"Uh–um." Being in Paxton's house evokes an intrigue in my mind but also makes me nervous. "Okay. Will your parents be okay with it?" Being alone in his house sounds a little…tempting. I shyly lead my eyes to find his. The butterflies in my stomach go berserk. His eyes nearly take my breath away. I've never seen eyes quite this green. He oddly looks the same way at me—like there's some sort of desire in my eyes. We're having some kind of moment, but I've been out of dating and flirting for so long I'm not entirely sure what our bodies are saying to each other...if anything. I could be reading into it too much. I break our eye contact and look around the field waiting for him to say something.

"Yeah, it'll be fine. Come over at seven. Is that cool?" He picks up his soccer ball and walks back toward his car. I'm assuming I'm supposed to follow, so I do.

"Yeah that works for me. Text me your address." I hand him my cell.

"Do you need a ride home?" He taps in his name and number. "I'll call you later so you have my number."

"Okay, and no, I have Betsy here in the next parking lot."

"Betsy," he repeats, monotone. I wait for him to say something about Betsy, but all he says is, "I'll see you Friday night." He slams his trunk closed.

"Well, I mean, technically, I'll see you tomorrow–"

He gets in his car and shuts the door, ignoring everything I just said. I let out a small exasperated sigh.

He puts his shades on and rolls down the window. "I'm going to call you later."

"Right," I respond sarcastically and roll my eyes. "Later, Paxton."

The Art of Moving On

I stroll onward to my car as he zips out of the parking lot in his old as dirt, gray Subaru Outback.

***

Ricky comes over for dinner and "Must See Thursday." It's when all of our favorite drama shows are on. Dad lets us have the TV for the night. Tonight I made red beans and rice, chicken, and green beans.

"Ricky, how are things going? I haven't seen you since you were stumbling in at one a.m. with my drunk daughter in tow," Dad reflects cheekily. Ricky grins awkwardly. I groan.

"Yeah, sorry about that." Dad smiles, showing Ricky he was just giving him a hard time. "Things are going okay. Being a middle child and the only son in the house can get a little…hectic. Lately it seems like everyone's in my business. It's everything I can do just to get in and out of the house without an interrogation." This is the first I'm hearing about this. I guess we never really talk about his family. He hasn't said anything, and I instantly regret not having asked. I've been so mopey over Dan to even ask how things are with his family. I know his dad has a bad temper, and his house is chaotic, but he hasn't mentioned anything to me lately.

"Well, you know you're welcome here anytime you want," Dad offers.

"Thanks, I appreciate that. Your southern food is pretty delicious, Emmy. I'm going to have to teach you how to cook Cuban food. Real Cuban food."

The Art of Moving On

"Now that sounds good. And, yes, dinner was excellent. Thanks, sweet pea. Load the dishwasher, then I'll do the other dishes. I bought you guys ice cream, too."

"*Ay!* Gracias, E.G.!" Ricky squeals. E.G. is what Ricky calls Dad for short. Dad leaves to go to his room for the evening.

"So…yearbook photos are tomorrow…" Ricky says cautiously. I throw my head back and groan.

"I'm sure it will be fine. We'll be together for like three minutes, and that's it. I don't plan on having any kind of conversation. I'll just keep it…purely business. I'll just stick to business, and it will be fine." I do my best to convince myself that everything will go smoothly with Dan tomorrow.

"Then you have your project tomorrow night with Paxton, too," he reminds me, and I groan louder.

"Why must you remind me of all these things?"

"I can't believe you're going to Paxton's house," he nearly squeals. I have to admit, I am excited to work on this project.

"I know. It's going to be weird to be in his house." I wonder if I'll see his room. The thought of being alone in his room actually causes my heart to skip a beat. I shake it off. "Did I tell you he called me last night?" I ask, smiling.

"No! Details, now!"

"It's funny after the fact, but it was annoying last night. I just turned my lights off to go to sleep, and he called me; it was like, midnight. I picked it up, and he said, 'It's Paxton.' I said, 'hi.' He said, 'Okay, bye.' He hung up before I could even say goodbye.

The Art of Moving On

He's so strange. To be fair, he did say he was going to call me, and he actually did it."

Ricky laughs. "I had just expected more of a conversation, I guess."

"Expected or hoped?" Ricky asks, wiggling his eyebrows.

"Oh, come on. I don't know if I can see Paxton like that," I lie with a frown. Ricky and I both know that the truth is that I'm not ready to move on yet, despite my physical attraction to Paxton.

"*Aw*, querida," Ricky sighs.

"It's not a big deal. It's our last year, and then we're all leaving for college anyway. So it's not like I'm in a big hurry to get a boyfriend."

"That's true."

We both sit in silence lost in our own thoughts. I've told myself so many times in the last month that Dan and I would have broken up at the end of the year anyway. We would have gone off to separate colleges, and it wouldn't have worked. Eventually we would break up. He just did it a lot sooner, and a lot harsher than I expected. I don't know when it will stop hurting. "Well, maybe you can just fool around until college," Ricky suggests. I burst out a laugh because our thoughts couldn't be further apart.

"I don't think that's my style."

"Well there's only one way to find out..." Ricky says, poking my arm. I blush instinctively.

"No, I don't think so."

"Paxton could be a great person to–"

The Art of Moving On

I laugh and cut him off. "*Nnnooo*. No more talking. More Olivia Pope and Annalise Keating." He joins me laughing. He grabs the TV remote control from me and turns up the volume.

Chapter 11

I was a fool to actually think that Paxton and I were meeting before my photo

appointment with Dan at 3:30. I bounce around the halls and cafeteria until I finally give

up on Paxton. I see Dan is in the SC office setting up. I don't want to have to spend any

more time with Dan alone than I absolutely have to.

Once 3:30 hits, I walk up to the office. Before I reach the door handle, arms wrap

around my waist and drag me back a couple feet. I almost fall over, but the arms hold me

until I'm up on my own two feet. The arms release me, and I turn around to face

whomever just tried to snatch me.

"Jesus, Paxton, what are you doing? You scared the crap out of me." I place my

hand over my heart, feeling how quickly it's beating. He looks toward the office, and

The Art of Moving On

through the glass office walls I see Dan looking at us. Dan turns away quickly so his back is facing us. Paxton looks back at me with a relaxed face. I have no idea what his game is. I look right back at him expectantly.

"No need to bring Jesus into this, Emmy. I'll see you at seven." He pats my shoulder roughly and then walks away. I shake my head and sigh before I make my way into the SC office.

I can the feel the burst of thick hostile air as soon as I open the door, and it nearly knocks me backwards. I take a deep breath.

"Hey, Emmy," Dan greets me softly.

"Hi." I don't know what it is about his voice, or maybe if it's just that we're alone in a room together for the first time, but my throat clogs and my eyes feel prickly. I'm afraid if I attempt to speak again tears will come out instead. I knew this wouldn't be easy, but I wasn't expecting quite this sad of a reaction. Slightly violent maybe but not sad enough to barely be able to speak. I'm still standing right inside the door, and he's bent down clicking on a new lens on his camera. I don't know what to do or what to say, so I just stand by the door in silence.

"You can come stand right here. The lighting is best here, and the background isn't distracting."

Again with the fucking lighting.

He looks up at me and stops. "It's okay, Emmy. You know I won't bite," he says sincerely with a soft smile trickling his lips. I suck in my bottom lip to bite it. I will myself not to cry. His casualness is callous. I take in a deep breath through my nose and shake my head clear. I walk to the spot he points at against the inside wall. He looks

The Art of Moving On

through his camera and shuffles a few steps. "I think that'll work. Ready?" He asks quaintly as if I'm at Disneyland and asked him to take a family photo. I nod and paste on a pathetic, fake, closed mouth grin. "Great." He lifts the camera to his face. "One, two, three." He snaps a few photos from different angles and then lowers the camera. "Let me just see if we got it."

Awkward silence.

"Yeah, we're good. You've always been really photogenic," he compliments me, turning his camera off. He looks up at me. "Thanks, Emmy." He offers me his hand to shake. It breaks me.

Anger seeps out of my pores, my chin quivers, a tear tumbles down and all I can think to say is, "Fuck you." I don't wait to see his reaction to my words. Instead, I turn and run across the hall to the bathroom.

Ricky manages to coax me out before the meeting at which point I am feeling really embarrassed about breaking down. I was so sure that I could face him, but his indifference hurt more than the initial break up. I leave our meeting feeling foolish despite Ricky convincing me that I did the right thing, and my reactions were completely normal. It's not until Ricky and I walk out of the meeting and into the hallway that I cry again.

Someone stole the last Santa Spirit poster.

I forfeit. I thought senior year was supposed to be a breeze.

In a brave attempt to make me feel better, before we part ways in the parking lot, Ricky tells me, "At least you're going to Paxton's tonight."

More tears pour out.

The Art of Moving On

***

Right at seven I pull up to Paxton's house. He lives in the historic district of Cayden Springs. Although his house isn't technically a historical landmark, it's still an old classic colonial style house. It's smaller than most in width, but it's two stories tall. The outside of the house has dark gray horizontal paneling with dark green window trimming accents and shutters. It stands apart from the historical landmark homes in that the Wrights got to choose what color their house is. I like that the colors they chose allow the house to snuggle quaintly into the surrounding woods. The tiny lawn out front and all the bushes and flowers that line the house are uniformly manicured, and I wonder if Mr. Wright is one of those dads that loves his yard. I can see various soft yellow lights on through the windows and for some reason my heartbeat picks up.

The weird thing is that I don't know if I'm nervous about spending time with Paxton, or if I'm nervous to see Maria, his mom, again.

I'm scared.

I'm sitting in my car with the lights off in front of Paxton Wright's house, *scared*. I'm such a wimp. I shake it off and grab my bag. I get out, making sure to lock Betsy. My palms get sweaty as I step up on his porch. I lift my fist to knock exactly when the door opens, and I'm face to face with a bare-chested Paxton. I stop breathing. All of a sudden scared doesn't even begin to cover the emotion that stampedes over me.

He takes a bite out of the apple he's holding and just stares at me. I guess it's fair because I'm staring at him too. Except I'm not staring at his face and my outfit of jeans

The Art of Moving On

and an old white v-neck shirt leave far more to the imagination than his clothes…or lack thereof. A loud slurp from Paxton's juicy apple breaks my stare and I look up at him. "Stop drooling, Emerald, it isn't nice," he smugly corrects my manners, blocking the doorway. I look down and quickly wipe my mouth in case what he said is true and I really am drooling. I look up at his devilish grin. Cue my eye roll.

"Two things. A. Can I come in? and B. Can you put a shirt on?"

"No and yes. I mean, yes and no. Or no and no. Or…" he jabbers, slowly making way for me to enter. "Why don't you come in and we'll just see how it goes?"

I scoff and walk into a vaulted entryway with a narrow staircase leading upstairs. To the left is a dining room and I'm assuming the kitchen is beyond that. The next thing I notice is the giant black bear pathetically charging toward me. "Oh, Paxton, you never told me you have a girlfriend. My, what fur she has." I wait for the oversized dog to finally make it close enough for me to pet it. I squat down to greet the humongous jet-black ball of fur.

"This is Tiger and yes, she is the only woman I will ever love. She's a Newfoundland," he informs me, squatting down and petting her with me. Seeing Paxton with a dog opens this new element of Paxton that I never knew existed. Not that him having a dog explains any of his quirks…it's just a more personal, caring side of him than I'm not used to seeing. Although our picnic showcased the soft side of him, too. Maybe there's more to Paxton than a bunch of odd behaviors and random bouts of apathy.

"Tiger, huh?" I smile, shaking chunks of her fur around as she pants. "You have a dog that looks exactly like a bear, and you named her Tiger?" Paxton smiles brightly, and

The Art of Moving On

113

it goes straight to his eyes. It's quite exquisite. So beautiful, in fact, that I have to remind myself that the smile is for the dog and not me.

"Yeah. Why? What's your dog's name?" There's a hint of defensiveness in his voice. He stands up and I follow suit.

"Oh, I don't have a dog."

"Exactly."

I glare at him.

"Come on, my room is upstairs." A little butterfly in my belly flutters at the mention of his bedroom. We start taking the steps and I notice Tiger watching us.

"Tiger isn't allowed upstairs?" I wonder sadly.

He stops with his hand on the dark wooden banister and looks over his shoulder. "Nah, she can't. She's too old for the stairs."

"Oh," I reply even sadder.

I follow him through his bedroom door, and my eyes go wide. Never ever in my life would I have guessed that Paxton Wright's room is stunning.

That's right.

Stunning.

There's a large skylight in the middle of the room that is currently allowing the moonlight to filter through. He has a large (made!) bed with a green and black plaid comforter. It looks full and squishy, like there's a feather down comforter underneath the plaid. It looks outstandingly warm and inviting—dangerously so, in fact. I have to actually fight the urge to face plant on it.

The Art of Moving On

He has two small windows that face the back of the house and toward the dark dense woods. Above the two windows there's a small, round stained glass window. It's of no scene in particular but more of a non-objective piece of stained glass art. It makes me want to learn how to stain glass, an art form that I never took into much consideration before. I check out his messy desk that has homework, textbooks, and a bunch of filled composition books sprawled all over it as well as The Bible. I pick it up. "You actually use this?"

He looks at me like I'm crazy. "Yes, for Religion homework for the last three years. Don't you?"

I feel like an imbecile when I admit, "No, actually. I just make up some BS. But it's gotten me mostly A's so far, so…" I shrug my shoulders and go back to inventorying.

I make my way to the front of his tall, monster of a bookshelf. It's intricately sculpted from some kind of dark wood like mahogany, and it looks like it was done by hand. I reach out to feel the smooth wood, ignoring the dust that comes off with my finger. Next, I browse his books. I feel like a detective gathering intel on a person of interest. Paxton's letting me into this part of his world and I like what I'm learning about him. His books go from *The Hobbit*; *Me, Earl and the Dying Girl*; and *Harry Potter*; to *Fahrenheit 451*; *The Outsiders*; *The Great Gatsby*; all the way to *The Rules of Attraction*; *Looking for Alaska;* and *The Perks of Being a Wallflower*. "You've read all of these?" I ask in awe.

"Of course. You like what you see?"

Before I recognize the hint of innuendo in his voice I respond, "I love what I see." I look at him and his smug grin. I take a quick glance down at his naked torso. I put my

The Art of Moving On

hand on my hip. "I love what I see on your *bookshelf*." He moves his hands up and down his flexed chest and abs.

"My abs have never been called a bookshelf before but I'll take it as a compliment." I laugh and take in his insane body. Again. I take a mental picture for personal time later. Right now, I look away and try my hardest to ignore the needing sensation coursing through my body.

"Seriously, though, your books are great. You have excellent taste in literature."

"I think you'll find that I have excellent taste in a lot of things," he comments, tossing his apple in the trash. He grins at me and I roll my eyes but I can feel the corners of my mouth turn up, betraying me.

"You've read all those books, for real?"

"I have. Not everything is what you think it is. I read a lot. I also write a lot," he informs me, pointing to the composition books.

"You write?" I stroll back to his desk and lift up a composition notebook.

"Yes, and you're not reading any of it," he says, slapping the book from my hands causing it to flop hard on top of the heap of papers.

"Please?" I ask, purposely eyeing him up and down flirtatiously. He narrows his eyes.

"Are you *giving me eyes*? That's not going to work on me. Nice try," he says with his hands on his hips. I snort.

"Fine," I relent, looking around more. "We should start a book club." He chuckles.

The Art of Moving On

"Okay, what would our first book be?" We both think for a minute. "*Fifty Shades of Grey*," he says seriously. I burst out laughing. "Okay, okay, fine. How about *Twilight* then?" I double over giggling. "Fine, fine. I guess we can just re-read *The Great Gatsby*. It's my favorite." I stop laughing and straighten up.

"Your favorite book is *The Great Gatsby*?" I ask, doe-eyed. I feel a warmness spread either in my heart or in my undies. Any intellectual conversation about *The Great Gatsby* would make me feel things in both areas.

"Yes, and I can practically see your mating pheromones floating off of you, so we'll pause the discussion on *The Great Gatsby* for now." He waves his hand in the air in front of me like he's wafting away my pheromones. I blush fifty shades of red. "Do you want something to drink?"

"I'm okay right now, but maybe later. Thanks for asking." I fan my face trying to get the heat that built up inside of me to go down.

For the next hour we discuss (lightly argue) what exactly our project will be, and what our next steps are. I'm feeling really pumped about things when we decide to take a break. Tiger greets us once we get downstairs to the kitchen. "Hi, baby girl," I greet her, petting her head.

I follow Paxton to the kitchen, which is perfection and a million times fancier than mine. Marble countertops with stainless steel appliances. It's large and seems to contrast to the rest of the quaint house. As if reading my mind, Paxton says, "Mom added on to the kitchen. She loves cooking and baking, so this is her little sanctuary; the kitchen and the little greenhouse out back." I slide into one side of the breakfast nook and scoot over to the window that faces the backyard. I cup my hands over my eyebrows to try and

The Art of Moving On

see if I can see the greenhouse out of the window but no such luck. It's pitch black outside.

"My mom had a green thumb. She loved gardening. She was outside all the time, and that's why she looked so tan all the time. I actually get my skin tone from my dad."

"That's cool. So your dad has dark skin, too?" He asks, genuinely curious.

"Yeah but his is much darker. My grandma had really dark black skin, and my grandpa was white. Their relationship was pretty scandalous back in the day in the south. They grew up in Savannah. So, yeah, my dad has darker skin than me. I think I just look like I have a dark perma-tan," I joke. He grins. "I get my skin tone from him, but I have my mom's hair color which is why my hair is a lighter brown," I explain. He nods.

"I get my olive skin from my mom. She's Greek. Well, I guess you probably noticed that I look a lot like her. Anyway, how about some bubbly water and a chocolate chip muffin? My mom made them earlier." I want to ask about his dad, but if it's a sore subject I'd rather not bring it up right now. He's never said anything about his dad; there are no traces of any man in the house other than Paxton; and since Maria was at the game alone, I deduce his dad is out of the picture.

"That sounds wonderful," I respond, smiling up at him. He still hasn't put a shirt on, but as the night has progressed I'm thankfully getting used to it; so I've been able to keep my drool at bay. The sparkling water makes a *chug-a-lug* sound as he pours it out of the green bottle and into small square glasses. He grabs paper towels and puts two muffins in front of each of us. I gather my courage and ask him what I've been wanting to ask all night. "Thanks. Speaking of your mom…is she here? I'd really like to see her again. How about your dad?"

The Art of Moving On

"Gone," he says flatly.

"Uh…oh. Really?" I nervously pick at my muffin. His jaw clenches, and I see now that I've hit a sensitive spot.

"Yes." He throws a piece of muffin crumb in my face.

Okay, so he's deflecting.

"*Oof.* Thanks," I retort sarcastically and slightly annoyed. I want to get to know Paxton, but he doesn't seem so keen on letting me.

"You were supposed to catch it in your mouth but you missed," he tells me matter-of-factly.

"Ugh, *I* missed? There was no warning!" I reply, my eyes as big as saucers and my hands fly up in the air, then back down.

"What happened with Dan Cosgrove?"

I heave a massive sigh and groan. "That again?"

"Yes."

"Do you seriously want to know?"

"Yes."

This guy never quits.

"Why? You have to tell me why first," I demand. I don't know why he wants to know so badly; and I think whatever the reason is, he won't tell me.

"You're hurt. I don't like it, and I want to know why," he answers in a deep, serious voice.

"I am hurt, but there's nothing you can do now to fix that." He looks down in his muffin like a little kid that just got reprimanded.

The Art of Moving On

"Tell me what he did to you." For a moment our eyes meet and I get lost in the forest of dark green, bright green, and gold lines that make up the emerald color of his eyes. His eyes are so deep that it's nearly impossible not to get lost in them. Before I even realize what I'm doing, I start spilling the beans.

"He broke up with me after school at The Café while I was eating pie. He told me that he had feelings for someone else, and said our relationship wasn't working and hadn't been for a while. It was news to me. I was blindsided, I guess." He takes note of my droopy mouth and I fear when he looks into my eyes that he knows that's not all.

"What's the kicker?"

"The kicker?" I ask with furrowed brows.

"Yeah. The whammy. The surprise. The kicker. The thing that kicks you while you're down." He takes a sip of water and sets it down. I notice his hands for the first time. They're big, and his fingers almost meaty. His nails are short and well manicured, to my surprise considering he's outside playing soccer all the time. I contemplate on whether I should deny that there was a kicker, but because he sees it in my eyes he won't give me peace until he knows. Paxton Wright is relentless.

"He did it the day after we had sex," I admit with an embarrassed sigh, my cheeks growing warm. I leave out the part that it wasn't our first time. I don't think Paxton needs *that* much detail. "Less than twenty-four hours before, we slept together and held each other and told each other that we loved each other." No tears come out as I tell him, but my mood has taken a serious downward spiral.

"Emerald?"

"Yes?"

The Art of Moving On

"In my complete, unbiased but secretly biased opinion...Dan Cosgrove is a fucking idiot." I huff a small laugh.

"That was the first whammy. The second whammy is that he had been talking with Alexis before we broke up. But the kicker is that he acts completely casual and indifferent now, as if our relationship never happened. That's what really hurts me, even more than the timing and him talking to Alexis. I put in a devoted three years and I can't ever forget that, but he...he's dating Alexis now and it's as if the last three years never happened for him."

"Excellent example of the kicker." I push out the tiniest smile just for his sake. I look down at the muffin crumbs I'm playing with.

"After he took my yearbook photo earlier today he tried to shake my hand. *Shake my hand*, Paxton. His dick has been in my vagina, and he tried to shake my hand," I admit, getting worked up and angry. His eyes get big, astonished at my vulgar sentence. His cheeks flush and he squirms a little in his side of the breakfast nook.

"Well, no need for gross details, Em." I look at him with a deathly stare. He grins, playing off his astonishment. "So, what did you do?"

"I told him to eff off." My smile creeps back up because, *damn*, it felt so good to say that to Dan's face.

"Atta girl!" He lifts his palm for a high five, and I smack it. He gets up as if he just remembered something. He grabs an iPod dock on the counter and plugs in his phone. After a few seconds a song comes on. It's an instrumental piece I'm familiar with but couldn't tell you the composer.

The Art of Moving On

"This song is beautiful," I tell him. He stands in front of me offering me his hands. I look up at him.

"So are you. It's Canon in D Major by Johann Pachelbel. Dance with me." I allow his eyes to penetrate me. He knows his classical music. I wonder if I'll ever get to know everything about him to the point where he doesn't surprise me anymore. I doubt someone like Paxton Wright could ever stop being interesting or surprising. I'm in awe of his uniqueness and confidence.

I look at his hand and hesitate, but he doesn't give me an option to decline. He grabs me by the hands and gently forces me into his arms. He wraps one arm around me, keeping me tightly to his chest; which is shockingly warm even though it's bare. The other hand is holding mine up, like in a traditional dance. I awkwardly place my hand on his shoulder, trying to be cool.

His surprises keep me entranced, sometimes in a good way and sometimes annoyingly. He's so sweet but can just as quickly act casual and blasé. He's got tens across the board when it comes to looks: thick black hair, impossibly green eyes that radiate, olive skin tone, and to top it off, chest and abs that are perfect. I have imagined, more than once tonight, what it would be like to run my hands all over his body. I pray that he doesn't realize how sweaty my palm on his shoulder is. Gross.

It's taken the whole song for me to realize my head is nestled into his neck and my eyes are closed. The song ends, and I lift my head to find those vibrant forest eyes looking intently at me. He's still holding me against him firmly. He caresses my cheek with the back of his hand. I never thought I'd be in this position with Paxton Wright, the kid that's hassled me for the last three years.

The Art of Moving On

He cups my face and asks, "Do you want me to kiss you?" My eyes grow big at his forwardness. I open my mouth but no words escape me; all I can do is nod slightly. It's enough for him to lightly dust his lips against mine. He brings his lips back to mine with a full tender kiss. I feel the shattered pieces of my heart shift toward each other. His hand moves to the back of my head, and his fingers interlace my hair. The kiss deepens, but remains sweet, like the chocolate chip muffins we just ate. I start to feel a warmness and excitement down my entire body with such intensity that it frightens me. It's an innocent enough kiss but–

I pull away. "I'm sorry, Paxton, I can't. Seeing Dan today really messed me up plus–"

"Yeah. Sorry." His arms drop from me, and he takes a step back. He nods his head and looks down, embarrassed, scratching the back of his head.

"No, it's not you. I'm sorry. I'm still a little messed up and broken and angry and you know, we're project partners and Mr. Kirkland probably doesn't want project partners to sleep together–"

"Wow, who said anything about sleeping together?" His head bolts up, and his eyes go big. His hands fling up in innocence. His grin comes back. "Someone likes to dance in the gutter." I blush.

"Sorry. I didn't mean–Um–uh, Paxton–I have to go. It's getting late or something," I excuse myself and quickly gather my belongings. I ignore the heat in my face, surely knowing that my skin is beet red. I was absolutely in the gutter, like, *deep* in the gutter. It wasn't until he said it that I realized how much I wanted more than a kiss, and expected him to want more than a kiss.

The Art of Moving On

He follows me out to Betsy, and before he closes the door for me he squats so he's at my level. "I really need you to understand that not everything is what you think." I nod and assume he meant the kiss didn't mean anything. My heart slumps more than I care to admit.

"So, back in there…" I point to the house.

"Oh, no, that was exactly what you thought." He smiles and winks. He closes Betsy. I can't help but smile too, because it's actually a lie. I don't think Paxton was thinking about us sleeping together. I'm pretty sure that my mind was the only one that jumped from kissing to sex in about thirty seconds. It's safe to say that I'm insanely attracted to him physically. I don't know if it was just a carnal urge or if what I'm experiencing is founded in actual feelings for Paxton.

Chapter 12

"Agh!" I yell and jump a good foot in the air when I wake up late Saturday morning and find Todd Bartlett sitting at the kitchen table. He chuckles and flashes his heart-melting smile that makes his golden eyes shine. "What are you doing here, Todd?" I ask, testy that he's seeing me having just rolled out of bed with some serious bed head and zero make-up on. It's only Todd and he's sort of a friend, (a somewhat perverted one, but a friend nonetheless), still, I can't help but feel insecure. It doesn't help that even with scruff and messy hair he looks good, and his cologne makes my mouth water. Thankfully I put a bra on.

"Sorry, I came in for some coffee before I get started on the Camino. Want some?" I nod my head and stumble until I'm seated across from his chair at the kitchen table. He gets up and grabs a mug and fills it up. He sets it in front of me then goes to kitchen to pull the creamer out, grabs the sugar from the pantry and a stirring spoon. He places them all in front of me. I'm surprised that he knows where everything in the kitchen is. He's over every now and then, but I'm still impressed. I look at him with my eyebrows up. He shrugs. "I know you're not a morning person." I scowl.

"You don't know that," I snap. He smirks. "Whatever," I pout. I sigh deeply and slap my cheeks lightly to wake myself up in hopes that I stop acting like a jerk. I start spooning sugar in my coffee. "Thank you." He watches me for a few moments, and when I'm still spooning sugar into my cup, he calls me out.

"Enough sugar, sugar tits?" I roll my eyes so much it actually hurts. He chuckles. "What's been up? How's school?"

I stir my coffee and take a sip before responding. "It's pretty good. I have a project due soon for science. Hey, do you know Paxton Wright?" I'm not sure why I'm asking other than sheer curiosity.

"Paxton Wright…" he thinks for a minute. "Yeah…he's weird. And popular. Weirdly popular. Why?" He eyes me suspiciously. I keep my poker face, or at least I try to. He smirks. "You got a thing for Paxton Wright?"

"*No*," I respond like the accusation is absurd. He sees right through me and laughs. "What? I don't! I was just going to say that he's my science project partner!"

"Yeah, okay, Em, sure." He leans back in his chair with his arms behind his head. He stares at me amused. "Ah, young love. I remember the days…" I scoff.

"Todd, don't act like you've ever been in a relationship that's lasted more than a few hours. Also, you're only a year older than me."

The Art of Moving On

"Hey, the ladies all know what they're getting into. I don't mislead them. And I'm two and a half years older than you. I got held back in first grade," he confesses almost like he's proud. I nearly spit out my coffee laughing. "Oh thanks, Em. You really know how to make a guy feel secure. School just isn't my thing. It wasn't when I was five, and it isn't now." I recover from my laughing fit at his expense.

"I'm sorry. But you like doing what you're doing now, right? Going to trade school and working for my dad?" I ask seriously. Todd is one of the only students that graduated last year and decided not to go to college. Todd got into Mount St. Mary's on a lacrosse scholarship and was never much into academics. As far back as I can remember he's always had a greaser/grease monkey vibe. I think it's part of the reason he gets all the ladies. He's very good looking in a bad boy sort of way. He has golden skin, golden eyes, and golden scruff to match his short dark golden hair. He's a golden god.

"Stop staring at me, you're drooling," he accuses. I blush and wipe my mouth.

"It's just toothpaste you idiot." It's true, it is just toothpaste, but I was ogling. He's gorgeous but not at all my type.

"I love working for your dad. I love working on cars and bikes. It's what I want to do, you know? It's what I've always wanted to do."

"Good for you for doing what you want." We silently drink our coffee for a few moments.

"I'm sorry about you and Dan, Em," he tells me sincerely. "I'm not a relationship expert, but fuck that douche." I snort a laugh. My smile quickly fades. Does the entire town know about my breakup?

"Sorry," he tells me.

The Art of Moving On

"It's okay," I automatically reply, just as I've done for the last month since Dan ended our relationship.

"Lucky for you, I don't dip in the company ink. Otherwise you'd have a hot date tonight," he teases. I know he's kidding, even though he checks me out whenever he can get away with it and often even when he can't. Our friendship really is just a friendship. I think we both like it that way, like I said, not my type.

"I have date—with the entire basketball team. Be jealous," I retort. He tilts back in his chair and throws his arms up.

"I knew I should've played basketball instead of lacrosse!" He jokes. I chuckle and toss our empty coffee cups in the sink.

"Go be productive, Bartlett. I have stuff to do. I'll make sandwiches for lunch if you're still around," I offer.

"Hell yes, I'll be around." He gets up and starts to head for the front door as I head back to my bedroom to get ready for the day. Before he closes the front door behind him he loudly yells, "You're the best Emerald Evans-Green!" I smile and shake my head.

***

It's Saturday night, and I've found myself back at a basketball game. Ricky insists we sit with Paxton, Aileen, and Eli; and I insist that we don't. It seems like Aileen is always by Paxton's side and I don't want to be around them while they're together flirting or doing whatever it is they do. I win the argument, and we sit on the second row bleachers right

The Art of Moving On

behind the team. The two SC Sophomore representatives give the half-time announcement, and Ricky and I give them a loud awkward applause.

Ricky and I steal glances up at Paxton, and he seems very enthralled in his present company and in the game. I don't tell Ricky about Paxton and I kissing last night. Mostly because I think he'll freak out unnecessarily and make a bigger deal out of it then it actually is. He won't stop pestering me about how my night with Paxton went so I have to give him something. I tell him (okay, I ooze) about his book collection and how he pulled me up to dance with him in his kitchen while listening to classical music.

It's when Ricky and I are both stealing a glance that we hear a burst of yelling and a loud smack. The force of the ball hitting my left eye pushes me backward and onto the legs and feet of the people behind me.

The crowd lets out a resounding, "*Ooohhh.*"

I instinctually curse and cover my eye. A burning sensation spreads instantaneously around my eye, nose, and forehead. My neck and cheeks fill with heat, and I know I'm scarlet from sheer terror and embarrassment. Someone grabs the ball and the coach tells me to go to the locker room and get an ice pack from the ball boy. Ricky and I stand, and he helps me out of the gym. The ball boy—a squirrelly red head that I've never seen before—is right behind us.

"I'll go in and get you an ice pack, just stay here," the little Freshman ball boy tells me as if I was about to walk into the boy's locker room.

"Are you okay? Let me see," Ricky commands, carefully moving my hand away from my face. "Oh, chica…" He scrunches up his nose and sticks his tongue out.

"What?" I start to panic. "I already know it's swollen, I can feel it." My lid is weighing heavily on the rest of my eye. I can still see fine, but if I don't get ice on it quick it will swell even more.

"Do you want the good news or the bad news?"

The ball boy comes back out with a pack. He squeezes it until it activates, then shakes it up before he gives it to me. "Just hold that on your eye until it's not cold anymore. Sorry, about that. That's why most people don't sit in the second row. It happens sometimes. You'll be fine."

"Thanks," I mutter. He jogs back to the gym.

I turn to Ricky expectantly. "What's the news?"

"The bad news is you have a puffy eye that will most certainly turn into a black eye. The good news is that you'll have a puffy black eye that you can make up a cool story about how you got it." He does his best to look optimistic. I look at him with a pathetic frown.

"I *could* make up a story. Except everyone in the entire school just saw how I got it."

"Okay, you're grumpy. No biggie. I know exactly what we need. Advil, food, and ice cream. In that order. Stay here, I'm going to go ask if one of the Sophomore girls has Advil." He heads back into the gym before I can reply.

The coldness of the ice pack is slowly making my eye and forehead numb. The precipitation from the pack is starting to trickle down my hand like raindrops on a windshield. I have to switch hands because my left hand is going numb right along with my eye.

The Art of Moving On

"There's my pirate," a voice says from behind me. I groan and turn toward him, knowing there's no way I'm going to escape the inevitable mockery. "If you commandeer your own ship, can I be first mate?"

"No, you can't. You'll be swabbing the deck." He chuckles and flashes me a half-grin.

"Hey, I'll swab your deck any–" I interrupt him and slap him playfully on the arm.

"Paxton, nobody is swabbing anybody's deck."

"You sure about that?" He asks, inching closer to me. My nerves turn into a bundle.

"Yes," I respond unconvincingly, turning my head away from him embarrassed and slightly irritated that he can get to me to blush so easily and so often.

"Because last night…" He's trying to get on my nerves.

Or under my nerves.

Or, well, *in* my nerves is more like it.

I shake my head and let out a small growl. "Oh, quit it."

"Never." He lets a moment go by and then sincerely asks, "Seriously, are you okay?" His question softens me.

"Yeah," I inform him honestly. More precipitation from the pack leaks down my hand. Paxton puts his hand on the ice pack and lowers my hand off of it with his other hand. He takes my wet hand and not-so-gracefully wipes it off on the stomach of his shirt. Then he squeezes my hand a few times in attempt to get it warm. Finally he drops my hand. His sensitive gesture warms a lot more than just my hand.

The Art of Moving On

"Thanks, Paxton," I thank him coyly, purposely not looking in his eyes because I don't trust myself to not get sucked in by his charming good looks. "That was really sweet and a little bit weird and awkward of you. But mostly sweet." I finally glance up at him and he grins.

"No big deal. I did it for my own selfish gain. I don't want my date tomorrow to have a black eye *and* frostbite."

I smile and roll my one visible eye. "It's not a date. It's an 'outside-of-school-school field trip.' It's an Educational Research Outing."

"What happens if I hold your hand during this Educational Research Outing?" He dishes out his evil grin and wiggles his eyebrows suggestively. My eyebrows shoot up and I smile.

"Then we'll end up with matching black eyes." We're smiling together when Ricky rounds the corner to us.

"Well, *hellooo*," Ricky greets us, curiously shifting his eyes between Paxton and me. I can tell I'm going to have some explaining to do. "I don't mean to interrupt, *buuut* I got you medicine." He plops two pills in my hand, and I immediately turn around and walk to the drinking fountain to swallow them.

"Thanks, Ricky. Food?" I ask, turning back around. I throw the ice pack in the trash nearby.

"Oh, querida, you should have kept that on maybe a little bit longer," Ricky tells me candidly. I chuckle at his frankness and take a moment to appreciate that our friendship is strong enough to allow us to be so honest with each other.

The Art of Moving On

"Eh, it wasn't that cold anymore anyway. Food, please," I say politely and eagerly to Ricky.

"Paxton, do you and Eli want to come get food with us?" Ricky asks sickly sweet, batting his eyelashes. I make a confused face (or at least I think I do, my eye is pretty heavy) and look around us to see if Eli joined us and I just didn't notice. He didn't. Maybe Ricky's just trying to be nice and include him. Eli and Paxton have a big bromance after all. They're Captain and Co-Captain of the soccer team. Eli is pretty quiet and typically flies under the radar and Paxton is fairly loud and weird so naturally they make the perfect pair. Opposites attract, I suppose. As long as Ricky doesn't invite Aileen along I'll be fine.

"No, thanks. Gotta go. Can't keep the wife waiting," he says, nodding his head toward the gym then winks at Ricky. We start walking in our separate ways when he yells back, Can't wait for our date tomorrow!" I snort a laugh, and Ricky looks at me like I'm a nut.

Ricky escorts me to Betsy. "You have a date with Paxton tomorrow?!" Ricky exclaims, jumping up and down.

"I hate to kill your excitement, but no. We're working on our project tomorrow. It's not a date. It's an Educational Research Outing."

"*Suuure*, it's not a date—yet."

"No, really, it's not a date," I correct him firmly.

"I'll be the judge of that. Where are you going on this little non-date-educational-whatever-outing?" He asks with his arms crossed, nose in the air, and his lips pursed.

"The zoo."

The Art of Moving On

Chapter 13

I arrive in Betsy at Paxton's house at eight o'clock sharp Sunday morning. My left eye is droopy, a lá Forest Whitaker, and the color surrounding my eye is dark purple. I have no makeup on and my hair is in a sloppy braid. I'm sporting jeans, converse, and a giant green and gray Oregon Ducks sweatshirt.

"Well, aren't you a sight for sore eyes," Paxton comments before he even finishes getting in the car. His chipper attitude tells me he's a morning person. I wish I could say something sassy back to him, but he looks good even in jeans, a dark gray pull-over hoodie, and his hair looking like he just got out of tumbling around in his bed. I grunt at him, and he takes the hint. "Hey, I come in peace. My mother insisted I bring you a water in case the sun comes out, and it gets warm." He places a water bottle in my cup holder, and I can't help but grin. Maria's kind gesture warms my frosty, early-morning heart.

"Tell your mom thank you, please." It was so thoughtful of her to think of me. I'm eager to be able to see and talk with her again. I don't care if it leaves me in a puddle of tears. It's worth it.

"I will." Paxton ducks down to look up at the sky through his passenger window. "I don't think the sun will be coming out though." I hate to admit that he's right so early in the morning but...he's right. It's completely overcast. Not that that's unusual for the fall season in Oregon.

It's about a forty-five minute drive to the zoo, and Paxton insists on listening to death metal through XM Sirius radio. When I'm on the brink of killing him, he switches it to classical music. He never ceases to amaze me.

We pull up to the zoo parking attendant's window. Betsy has a lot of modern features but power windows are not one of them. The manual windows are a staple of an old car, and I'm happy to have them. I crank down the window and look at Paxton with my hand out flat.

He shakes his head in defiance. "I'm not paying. You said it wasn't a date." I scoff and roll my eyes. I fish out a ten and hand it to the parking attendant. We follow the flags and park in the appropriate, allocated spot. We walk to the ticket booths, and there are signs everywhere warning us that tickets are non-refundable, and the zoo is open rain or shine. I look up at the clouds, and they seem innocent enough. We each pay our twenty bucks, and find ourselves in front of the flamingos with Paxton looking at the map upside down.

The Art of Moving On

"All right, ma honey bee, what'd ya like to see first, huh?" Paxton asks me in a over-exaggerated Southern accent. I huff out a laugh but go along with it.

"Well, my honky-tonk man, I think I'd like to see them monkeys and apes."

"Ya know, honey bee, I'm gunna hafta disagree with ya. The elephants are a-callin' us."

"Well, all right, I suppose I can see the elephants first if that's what ma honky-tonk man wants, but then we gotta git to them apes."

"Anythin' for ma sugar dumplin'." Paxton crinkles the map under his arm and offers me his elbow. I accept it and we start walking.

We make it to the elephants just in time for a demo. They're doing a blood extraction to test the elephants for any possible changes in health. Five zookeepers guide the African elephant to these large metal cages reminiscent of the velociraptor cages in *Jurassic Park*. They use round, narrow whistles and hand signals to communicate with the elephant. I'm getting lost in the intricacies of the large creature from its dark curious eyes down to its toenails that have to be trimmed regularly. I'm so deeply enthralled that I jump alarmingly high when the elephant blows loudly through his trunk. When I startle, Paxton reaches out and grabs me. The elephant was none too pleased about the needle going into the vein in his giant floppy ear. Paxton's arm on my back feels so natural that I barely even realize it is there until he moves it and my back gets cold.

Almost three hours, two churros, a large tub of popcorn, and two slushies later (all of which Paxton paid for), and after he had convinced me to see the koalas, kangaroos, lions, pandas and aviary, we make it to the monkeys and apes.

The Art of Moving On

"Okay, so the goal here is to get a few minutes of the gibbon's singing," I confirm with Paxton.

"Do you have the recorder?"

"I have it on an app on my phone." I pull up the app. We patiently wait for the gibbons to sing. In the process we watch them swing, non-stop, all over their cages. After ten minutes we can't believe that they haven't stopped moving once. After twenty minutes we start to get bored.

"Let's go see the alligators and crocodiles," Paxton suggests.

"No. We can't leave. What if they start singing as soon as we leave?"

"Then we'll run back."

"You know I'm a terrible runner."

"No, I didn't know that. I'll run back. Or you stay here, and I'll go and then I'll run back."

"What! No, don't leave me," I plead. "I don't want to stand here alone."

"You're right. The males around here…" he huffs, "are nothing but a bunch of animals."

I snort a laugh. "Okay, okay, I get it but please don't leave–" I pause for a second and my eyes go distant. "Did you feel that?"

"Feel what?" The mere second that he finishes the question the clouds clash in a resounding boom. My shoulders close in on me, and I cower from the sound. Fat raindrops fall violently in a sudden downpour. Paxton and I look at each other, and in the seconds it takes for us to silently communicate and decide to run the distance into the

The Art of Moving On

Gorilla exhibit covering, we are already drenched. Luckily, I had the sense to jam my phone in my pocket. Paxton shakes out his head and water splashes everywhere.

"Ugh, Paxton!"

"Seriously, Emmy? You're drenched in water."

"Yeah, but you go it in my eyes," I whine.

"You mean eye. Your left eye is at half-mast so really you have one and a half eyes. And I know you want to roll that one capable eye at me, pirate, but don't you dare." He wiggles his pointer finger at me. My annoyance is quickly replaced with a taunting smile. It may or may not be because he's drenched with a few raindrops still falling down his face. He runs his hand through his shiny black hair causing it to stick up every which way. My mind immediately realizes that this is how Paxton must look getting out of the shower.

"Or what?" I ask, eyeing him up and down.

"I'll make it so you have to wear a patch over that bum eye of yours." He charges at me and flings me over his shoulder. I squeal and laugh. "Don't make me swab your deck, pirate!"

"Woah!" I yell with my head upside down, my face level with his belt. I shamelessly check out his butt from this angle. *Yup, still looks hot.* "Now whose head is in the gutter?" He doesn't get the chance to answer, because there is this insanely boisterous high-pitched screaming, hooting, and hollering.

"What the hell–"

"It's the gibbons!" I yell and he puts me down. I peak out of the Gorilla exhibit covering and learn where the term "ape shit" comes from. The gibbons are going bonkers

The Art of Moving On

and making every high-pitched sound you could ever imagine. "We have to record them! We have to go back out there!"

"It's *pouring*. Let's just do it from here. It's loud enough. You know they can be heard from a mile away."

"I know but we can't. The acoustics in here are weird and hollow. I promise it'll sound so much better if we go out there. Please? I need your help. Shelter my phone while I record it."

"How?" I eye his torso. He picks up the hint. "My sweatshirt's already wet. The water will seep through if we hold it over us. It's already almost soaked through." He tries to reason with me but I'm not having it. I shake my head and nod at his torso again. "You're kidding. My t-shirt?"

"It'll only take a minute or two," I plead.

"What about your shirt?"

"I can't take my shirt off in public. Also, I'm not wearing one." I can tell he's irritated by the way he tilts his head up like he's asking God for strength so I throw in a compliment. "Besides, you look way better without your shirt on than I do." This gets a nice smug grin out of him and his eyes shine like a piece of polished gold.

He leans in toward me as he pulls his arms in his sweatshirt to take it off. "I promise you, that can't be true. I'll go. You can stay here." He flings off his sweatshirt and tosses it on my face like a stripper. I try unsuccessfully to bite my smile. I pull the sweater off my head and sit back and enjoy the show. He looks drool-worthy without a shirt on.

Once Paxton's taken his shirt off and put his sweatshirt back, he darts out as quickly as possible toward the gibbon enclosures. I see him hit record, and our plan is working perfectly…for fifteen seconds. It was as if someone pushed the mute button. Every single one of the apes went dead silent. My jaw drops. The plan was to get a couple minutes worth of sound, not a few seconds. Paxton runs back to me under the manatee cover.

"Now what, pirate?" He wrings out his shirt.

"I don't know," I say, defeated. "How much longer do you think until they sing again?"

"Oh no, no, I know what you're thinking and no. We're not waiting for them to do it again. It could be hours." I nod my head. It was worth a try since I've invested thirty bucks and some gas to get here, but it's not worth Paxton catching a cold or pneumonia. Even his pants are nearly soaked through. I feel bad that I coaxed him into going back out in the rain. My guilt cloud descends.

"Okay, you're right. I don't want you to catch a cold or anything." We both stand in silence for a minute.

"Emerald?"

"Yeah?" I turn my head back at him and smile at the sound of my full name on his lips. It's like being completely wrapped in a fluffy new blanket that smells of fabric softener. It warms and comforts me to the core.

"Let's go back to your house and figure this out." He looks so sweet with wet hair and sopping wet clothes. I just want to take care of him, give him hot chocolate, and bundle him up in a soft towel. That's what I fully intend on doing.

The Art of Moving On

"Okay but can we go look at the alligators really quick first? I think they're on their way back toward the entrance." I grin coyly at him.

He nods like a shy little kid. We smile together. I turn and attempt to brace myself for walking back under the sheets of rain. He walks toward me, and I can't explain it but I just have the desire...I know that only one thing will make this moment perfect...so I hold out my hand for him to take it. He looks at my hand and then at me as if I'm offering more than just my hand. Maybe I will eventually. But for now, my hand is all I can offer him. He accepts with a grin. We nod together, and then make a run for the alligators making sure to stomp in every puddle on the way.

***

We pull up in my driveway and I notice Dad's car is gone. I say a silent prayer in relief that he's at the shop right now. He usually does paperwork on Sundays for a few hours. It's not that I don't want Dad and Paxton to meet each other; it's just...complicated. The only boy I've ever brought home was Dan. I'm not ready for them to meet, because I'm not sure what Paxton is to me yet. Sure, he's a classmate and project partner but...I think he might become more than that, more than a friend even; and if he does, then that's how I want to introduce him to Dad. It may sound silly, but I'm sensitive about it. Also, I honestly think part of me wants to be alone in private with Paxton. And that scares me.

"Emerald?"

"Yeah?"

"Are you okay? We've been sitting in Betsy for like two minutes. Are you sure you want to go in? Because your face looks worried." I shake my trance and look over at him. His eyes are filled with concern, but there's also hesitancy. I can't put my finger on why, but I can tell it's there. He's nervous or something.

"Yeah, sorry. Let's go get you warm," I say, trying to stop overthinking it. We make a run to my front door, and as I'm getting the door open he notices the car in the driveway for the first time.

"Is that your car too? It's awesome. It's like a mullet"

"Really?" I say, surprised that anyone would ever say that.

"Yeah, absolutely," he says, going full-on geek mode.

"How do you figure?"

"It's all business in the front and party in the back. It's the perfect combo of car and truck. It's completely practical." Seeing him gush brightens my eyes. I'm realizing there are so many things that make Paxton cute and likeable, more than his wicked good looks and stellar soccer playing. He's so well liked that I really shouldn't be surprised. I think he's friends with everyone at school. Well, maybe except Gavin now. I just never took much notice before, because he was always driving me bonkers. I never stopped and tried to understand him or get to know him until now.

"You do actually make it sound completely practical. I'm impressed. And kind of convinced." He smiles smugly. I shake my head at his cockiness. "I said kind of." I push the door open, and we walk in. I've always found it interesting having someone else walk into your house for the first time. I try to see it through his eyes.

The Art of Moving On

My house is nothing like Paxton's historical home. We have plush, cream colored carpet, for starters, and black and white tiled kitchen floors. We have a small living room with one big sofa and a small, brick-framed fireplace. From the living room is a hallway. Down the hallway is Dad's master suite, and to the left of the hallway is my bedroom and bathroom. My bedroom connects to the bathroom, but it's also the guest bathroom. Even though I'm not dirty, my stuff is still all over the place. I'm not dirty…just messy.

I pop off my wet shoes on the welcome mat, and Paxton follows suit. I take my soggy dark purple socks off and keep them in my hand as we walk further into my house. "Come on, I'll get you a towel." I show him to my room, and he takes it in slowly the same way that I took in his room. He zooms over my purple comforter, a few of my more colorful abstract paintings, my long, sheer white window curtains, and my messy closet that I always leave open. I curse myself for not being neater. I get nervous as he browses my bookshelf and looks at the wall of photos above my simple Ikea desk.

Nothing in my house is as nice or new (other than the house itself) as everything is in Paxton's house. I'm not ashamed or embarrassed of anything in my room, but I'm nervous all the same because whatever is going through his mind…I want it to be good. I care about what he thinks. Letting someone into your personal space is…well…personal. I don't let that many people in, literally and figuratively.

I take Paxton's socks from his hands and drop both of our socks in the middle of the room to start a pile of clothes for the dryer. Paxton's by my bed with his back to me. I pull out a dry sweatshirt from my closet. He's so taken with my wall of photos that I think I have enough time to do a quick swap without him seeing me shirtless. I commence the operation and of course right when the wet sweatshirt flops to the floor, Paxton picks off a photo and turns to me. His eyes bug out of his head.

"Hi," I say, awkwardly frozen, and confused if I should cover my stomach or my breasts. I'm wearing a bra so I'm covered there but my stomach isn't exactly that of a supermodel. My idea of exercise is typing a ten-page paper in one sitting. Ricky and I aren't exactly the outdoorsy, athletic types. I take co-ed weight training class with Ricky (instead of gym), but we mostly just tiptoe around everything and make up stats of how much we lift. I can confidently say that it's the only class that I worry about getting a "C" in.

"*Hhhey...*" He stares blatantly at me for a few seconds. I give up trying to hide myself. It's just like seeing me in a swimsuit really. Despite my less than perfect tummy, I do own a bikini...I never wear it, but it's still in my possession. "I was right." My brows furrow and I tilt my head to the left.

"Right about what?"

"You look better than me with a shirt off."

I blush and look away. I quickly change the subject. "Here, throw your clothes in the pile, and I'll put them in the dryer." I start to turn to grab my shirt when I see him start to shy away.

"Okay, well, turn away and don't look," he says, feigning shyness. He waves his hand, signaling for me to turn my back. I spit out a laugh.

"It's okay, buddy. I've already seen it."

He gasps dramatically. "Watch your manners, young lady," he says in his hoity-toity voice.

The Art of Moving On

"Take-it-off, take-it-off, take-it-off," I start chanting and throwing my fist in the air.

"Wow, just because you've seen it once you think you can have it anytime now, huh? Well, Emerald, I'm not that easy. But, lucky for you, I'll shed my clothes because you sacrificed them in the name of our Educational Research Outing, and it is your duty to save them."

I say nothing but cross my arms stare at him expectantly. He pulls both of his shirts off and tosses them into the pile of clothes. We stare at each other from opposite sides of the pile with our hands on our hips, shirtless, waiting for the other to do or say something. I'm beginning to feel the carnal urge bubble up from inside of me. I want to tackle him to the ground and have my way with him.

Wow, where did that come from?

I blush at my dirty thoughts.

"Put your sweater on," he says. "You're shaking, and it's still cold." I am shaking, but I don't think it's because of lack of clothes. I nod and do as he tells me despite my urge to jump on him. I realize he still has my photo in his hand.

"What photo is that?" I ask, nodding to his hand. He shows it to me. It's an old photo of my mom. She's sitting on a floor with green shag carpet, wearing a black Prince tank top with big, crimped 80s hair and red lipstick. Other than it being a photo of Mom, there's nothing particularly special about it. I just like how completely 80s it is and how badass she looks in it.

"It's my mom."

"She looks almost like my mom in a way. Not a ton, but there's for sure something familiar about her."

"Yeah." I look down shyly. I'm embarrassed to tell him that I like his mom so much for that reason. "I really like your mom." I start getting emotional. My voice gets shaky, and my eyes begin to pool. "It's the weirdest thing," I choke out with a lump in my throat. "She reminds me of my mom, and I've never really experienced that. I want to get to know Maria, and I know that's creepy and weird, but I can't help it. Just looking at your mom makes me feel better…like my mom is somehow nearby." A tear falls down unabashedly. He lets my admission sink in. Afraid of the silence I continue, "I'm sorry. God, that's so creepy. I shouldn't have said that. I'm sorry. I am fully aware that our mothers are not the same person. Oh no, that did sound right either–" I close my eyes and shake my head trying to organize my thoughts.

"Em, you can come over any time you want." I nod habitually because I've heard this speech so many times since I was twelve. "You don't even have to ask or tell me. You can just show up." He sounds sincere and serious. It takes me a minute to let it fully sink in that it's not just anyone telling me this; it's Paxton Wright, and for some reason it means so much more coming from him. It's like he's offering shared custody of his mother. The corners of my mouth curl up at the thought. I nod and more tears trickle down. My heart blossoms at his sincerity.

"There's only one condition," he says firmly. I look up at him waiting to hear it. I'm not used to him sounding so mature and definitely not this serious. "No shirts allowed. You can't wear your shirt. You have to come shirtless every time." I blow a laugh out through my tear stained mouth. I use the back of my hand to wipe my mouth. I

The Art of Moving On

love that he can make me smile no matter what mood I'm in. "Come here," he says waving his hands for me to come hug him. I step over the pile of wet clothes and embrace his naked chest.

He has this mind-blowing ability to open my heart. To make me feel better. *Happier.* I get wrapped up in the way he makes me feel mentally, emotionally and physically. His skin feels so good against my cheek and I want that goodness to spread all over me and consume me. Before my brain fully realizes what my body is doing, my mouth starts caressing his collarbone. I feel him tense, but he doesn't stop me. My hands slowly start to explore the different curves in his back and shoulders. His skin is warm on my lips as I make my way up to his neck. My brain shuts off completely and my body greedily takes complete control. I kiss up his neck, and his grip around me tightens.

When our lips finally meet it's with a neediness that I never knew existed. We rotate around and he pushes me against my desk. Every thought, concern and worry escape me, and all I can focus on is right here and now being wrapped up in Paxton's arms. I quickly rip my shirt off like it's on fire. His mouth moves lower leaving warm wet spots all the way down. He makes a move to unhook my bra and I've *never* felt such a rush of desire. I moan and whimper. If I was in my right mind I would be totally embarrassed that I just whimpered. I take it upon myself to unbutton my jeans so he'll get the hint that I want him—bad. His hand moves away from my bra to the hem of my jeans just as the sound of the front door opens. We jump apart so we're across the room from each other.

Oh my god, what just got into me? I've never been that bold in my life.

I grab my sweatshirt and throw it back on. "Put a shirt on," I hiss at him.

The Art of Moving On

"I don't have one," he whispers back. *Oh, that's right.* I pick up his wet shirt from the pile and fling it at him. "Seriously?" he asks incredulously, his annoyance blatantly showing. I nod firmly. He scoffs. "Fine, but if I get pneumonia it's on you."

"Fine. I'll nurse you back to health," I snap at him. "Just…get your stuff and follow my lead." I walk out of my room with Paxton in tow. Dad is in the kitchen sorting through some papers. "Hey, Dad." He looks up and does a double take. I know having another boy here is a surprise for him and a bigger surprise that Paxton is over without him knowing…while he was gone. "This is Paxton. Remember, I told you we're doing that gibbon rainforest project for my Environmental Science class?" Paxton stands straighter. Dad smiles curtly.

"That's right. You did tell me you were going to the zoo today. Hi, Paxton, I'm Roger." Dad walks closer to us and shakes Paxton's hand.

"Pleasure to meet you, sir." Despite looking like a wet beaver, this is the most mature I've ever seen Paxton. It's genuine too, not forced or uncomfortable. Then again, Paxton is a people-person. "We had an unfortunate downpour while we were at the zoo collecting footage. We got it downloaded safe and sound, so now Emmy's going to drive me home." I nod profusely even though it's a lie. I just want to get this moment over with quickly. This is not at all how I wanted Dad to meet Paxton. Right after his mouth was all over me. I try with everything in me not to blush.

"Let's go now so you can get home and into some dry clothes." I push on his arm to try and move us all along.

"Well, Paxton, it was nice meeting you. Maybe I'll see you over again soon," Dad says politely and casually.

The Art of Moving On

"Hopefully, sir. Also, that car in the driveway is awesome." Now he's trying to win Dad over. I roll my eyes at the car talk.

"Thank you. It's been a lot of fun to work on it."

"Good luck with the rest of it," Paxton says as I'm pushing him out the door.

"Thanks. Good to meet you, Paxton." Paxton waves from the driveway, and I have to practically force him to get into Betsy.

"Hey, where's the fire? I thought that went well. He seems like a cool dad."

"He is a great dad. A really great dad. I just would've preferred you two meeting under different circumstances is all." I waste no time on pulling Betsy out into the street.

"You mean, not right when my hand was about to swab your deck?" He grins crookedly. My eyes grow, and I blush so brightly that the car behind me probably thinks I'm a stoplight.

"Yes," I manage to say.

"Are we going to talk about that?" He asks seriously.

"No. We aren't. It's not happening. We can't do that." I don't know if I'm trying to convince myself of that or Paxton. I don't know what got into me. It was like a different person took over. It was so intense. *I* was intense.

"Whatever you say, pirate," he says apathetically, which tells me I said the wrong thing. I look over and he's looking out his window with a frown taking over his face. He's the cause of so many laughs for me. I hate seeing him frown. I hate that I'm the reason for the frown. It's a kick to the gut but I'm not sure what to say to make it better so I say nothing for the rest of the drive.

The Art of Moving On

149

***

I flop backward on my bed after I drop Paxton off. I stare at the dips and peaks of my white textured ceiling and try to find faces or animals as if the grooves are clouds floating by. Paxton got out of the car without a sound. He didn't even look at me. The guilt is weighing down on me and nobody is more shocked than I am at how badly I wanted his body. Well, that and nobody knows what just happened so they couldn't be shocked; but I'm sure if Ricky knew he'd be shocked, but I would still be more shocked than him.

What am I even thinking?

I turn and groan face-down in my feather pillow.

I can't believe how ready I was to let him have his way with me. Dan and I fooled around frequently enough, so maybe not having that intimacy for a while is making me loopy. I think I'm shocked because it's all happening so fast. Paxton is different. Things with him are different. Everything with Dan was so neat and calculated like our relationship was on a schedule. My relationship with Paxton is all over the place. One day he's packing me a picnic, one day he's throwing crumbs in my face, one day his mouth is all over me, and the next I act like a total jerk.

"Dinner's ready, sweet pea!" Dad calls from the dining room. I roll off the bed and join him at the table.

"Thanks for cooking, Dad." He places a section of a steaming casserole dish in front of me.

"Of course. It looked like you had been busy with Paxton and your project."

"Yeah." I purposely don't elaborate. If only he knew how "busy" we actually got.

The Art of Moving On

"He seems like a nice kid," he comments, shoveling food onto his fork.

"Yeah, he is." I blow on my food before putting it in my mouth. He's cooked some kind of hamburger, cheese and potato deliciousness. I glance at Dad and he's grinning.

"Emerald, come on. That boy is smitten with you and by the looks of it, I think you like him too."

"*Daaad*," I groan. My face betrays me and flushes pink. I wish I could sink into the white grout of the checkered tile floor and disappear.

"It's okay. In fact, I think it's good. You and Dan were together for a long time, and I think you should be going out and getting to know new people. It's okay to go on dates and things. You'll have plenty of time for serious relationships when you get older. That being said, I would also like to meet these guys before they take you out." I'm as red as a strawberry. "You don't have to be embarrassed, sweet pea, it's okay. I know you're practically an adult. Plus, believe it or not, I was young once, too."

"Nobody is taking me out. He's my project partner. We're friends. It wasn't a date," I ramble. He chuckles.

"You can deny it, but I can sense chemistry." I bust out laughing hysterically. Dad laughs with me but continues to talk through his laughs, trying to be serious. "Which is why—listen young lady—you are not allowed to be home alone with him again." My laughing subsides leaving me with a sore mouth. "Are we clear?"

I chuckle out one more laugh and then sigh. "Yeah. We're clear." He smiles.

"Good. You sound disappointed. That's how I know you like him." He points his fork at me then shoves it in his mouth.

The Art of Moving On

Chapter 14

Monday during our TA period, Ricky and I are in the library grading and whispering. I filled him in on all the details with Paxton.

"*See?!* I *knew* you guys had it bad for each other!"

"*Ssshh!* Library voice," I quietly remind him. He rolls his eyes at me. "I don't know what to do." The click and swoosh of the library door opening makes us look. Paxton comes in with his stack of papers to grade. We make eye contact; then he goes to the left, sitting at the table furthest away from us. His face doesn't show any expression whatsoever. That's how I know something is wrong. When Paxton isn't being loud, smiling brightly, making jokes or sarcastic comments, he's apathetic and somehow, that's even worse than sadness. It's really starting to get under my skin...under my heart...knowing that his apathy is because of me.

The Art of Moving On

"Querida, it seems like he's laid it on the line. I think he's made it very clear how he feels about you." I flick my red pen nervously. I nod.

"I mean, he hasn't actually said out loud how he feels about me," I try to reason then sigh. "But I think you may be right."

"No, Emmy, I am right." I grin at his assuredness.

"Okay, you're right. It makes me so nervous, Ricky…to know that he likes me. I don't know what to do. What if I mess things up because I'm stuck on Dan, like peanut butter on the roof of your mouth?"

"I know it's scary. Believe me, I know. And nice analogy, by the way. Peanut butter stuck on the roof of your mouth is the worst thing ever, and so is Dan."

"He is," I agree, slumping down in my chair. I steal a glance behind me to where Paxton is sitting. He's intently grading his papers. "What if I'm not good enough for him? What if I hurt him? What if he hurts me? I don't want to get hurt again like that. I really don't know what to do," I confess.

"Well, maybe that's okay for right now. You don't have to have all the answers right away. Give it space for a few days, and let what happened over the weekend settle in your brain. Process it. But don't overthink it, because that's your problem, you think too much."

"I never thought the valedictorian would tell me that I think too much," I tease.

"*Ay*, I'm not even close to being valedictorian." We're both quiet for a moment, lost in our thoughts.

"So, I should give it a couple days and let it be for right now?"

"Sure. Don't wait too long though. Also, you need to be open and honest with him. You have to talk to him eventually, but you can give it a day or two. There's nothing wrong with processing your feelings. Besides, waiting might help you muster up the courage." He begins to get a distant look in his eyes and then bites the inside of his cheek. I nod my head slowly, taking in everything he's saying.

"Okay. Yeah. I can do that." I nod, and then something dawns on me. My eyes go big for a millisecond before my shoulders collapse. I sigh and close my eyes. "No, I can't give it a day or two. We have our science project due the day after tomorrow." Ricky makes a pained face.

"Well, in that case, you better process fast or at least tell him you need space to process. You know you have feelings for him. You just need to figure out what those feelings are, and then if and how, you want Paxton to fit into your life." I can't help but notice a tinge of sadness on his face. I'll have to ask him about it later. Thank God for Ricky. I would be lost without him. I furrow my brows and think for a moment.

Paxton and I haven't communicated in any of our classes, not even in our freaking Environmental Science class, which means we have to hash out the rest of this project outside of class today or tomorrow. I start to stand up.

"Where are you going?" Ricky asks me.

"To go talk to Paxton."

"Right now?" He hisses at me.

"Yes. We have to figure out our project and I really don't want to have to call him on the phone. I would rather do it in person. I'm not good at phone conversations."

The Art of Moving On

"*Ay, ay, ay*," Ricky says, slumping down in his chair and using his hand as a visor to shield his face, like he's embarrassed to be seen with me. "Dios sea contigo," he mutters.

I snap my red pen closed and stand up. I adjust and smooth out my uniform to make sure I look okay. I take a deep breath and turn to walk toward Paxton. He doesn't look up until I'm standing in front of his table.

"Hi," I greet him shakily. He looks at me completely straight faced.

"You can sit down," Paxton allows, monotone.

"Thanks. I was thinking we could put the finishing touches on our project tomorrow so it's all activated and ready to go Wednesday morning. We can each do our parts, and then get together Wednesday morning before school and put it all together."

"Sounds good," he agrees, looking down grading papers. I can't deny that I have feelings for him because the cold shoulder he's giving me hurts like frostbite, and I don't know how to fix it quite yet.

"I'm going to be in the art studio with Mrs. Timlin today and tomorrow working on the posters for each restroom, if you need anything."

"I got it, Emmy. I trust you. I'll do my part, and I'll see you Wednesday morning," he says curtly. I nod, feeling like rejected.

"Okay. Really though, if you need help just call me or text me," I offer quietly.

"I'll be fine." He still doesn't look up at me. I want him to look at me. I want to be in his arms. I want him to make me laugh. I want to make *him* laugh. I want to feel him everywhere. I want to go places and talk in funny accents with him.

The Art of Moving On

Instead, I walk away. After a few steps he comments, "Your eye's looking better, pirate." The corners of my mouth turn upward.

It's better than nothing.

***

By Wednesday afternoon our art installation is complete. Paxton and I took our Environmental Science project and turned it into an art installation to raise awareness about the decimation of the rainforests and how it has made species endangered, particularly, gibbons.

In the main men's and women's restroom, we've rigged a music player and a small portable speaker. Every fifteen minutes the loud sound of the gibbons singing plays on a loop for one minute. We didn't get our minute of singing recorded so we just looped the fifteen seconds we did get to make it a full minute. On the wall of each of the restrooms is a poster stating the devastating facts of the destruction of the rainforests in Southeast Asia due to the growing desire for palm oil (used in foods and many skin and bathroom products, hence putting the installation in the bathroom). Underneath that we've listed the impact that deforestation has on gibbons, as well as facts about gibbons and what makes them such unique and valuable assets to the rainforest. Paxton used his tech savvy skills to organize all of the sound aspects, and I took my art skills to create stunning, educational visuals. We combined the two aspects for a guerilla-type (pun intended) art installation that will catch everyone with their pants down (pun also intended).

The Art of Moving On

The energy between Paxton and I has shifted this morning due to sheer excitement from both of us. Together we created something so uniquely us, we know the rest of the projects won't even compare. The air is charged as we walk the class to the restrooms and split so the girls and boys go in the respective restrooms. After the synchronized gibbon sounds went off we then explained to the class what gibbons are and how and why their habitat is being destroyed. Most importantly, we discussed with the class ways in which we can help. The class decided the easiest way to help is to spread awareness of the consequences of deforestation using thoughtful conversation and to boycott products containing palm oil.

After class lets out and the end bell rings, Mr. Kirkland pulls us aside and commends our excellent, unique, and engaging work. He informs us we will both be getting A's. We burst out of Mr. Kirkland's door reeling with pride. We jump and do a double high-five chest bump, laughing. The hall is already empty from students starting to leave to go home. The air is buzzing with a palpable electricity. I fling myself on him and wrap my arms tightly around him. He encircles my waist with his arms, bringing me in even tighter. I turn my head, without even thinking, to kiss him and he pulls back.

"Don't do it, Emmy."

"What?" He slowly loosens his arms around me.

"If you don't want to be with me, then you can't kiss me." I freeze for a moment, and then slowly nod as a pain seeps over my heart like tar—thick, heavy and dark. I reluctantly let him go.

"I'm sorry. I didn't mean to–Um, I need more time," I admit shyly. He nods his head as if he already knows that means I don't want to be with him. "There's something

The Art of Moving On

in me tugging at my heart still. I do have feelings for you, Paxton. But I'm scared, and I need to figure it out to make sure it's all real and genuine and not fleeting or…you know…" I shuffle our hands between us hoping he'll pick up on what I'm trying to say without actually having to say it. He furrows his eyebrows and then grins ever so slightly.

"Physical?" I can tell that crooked, smug grin of his is going to appear. I blush at my silliness. I've been constantly thinking about jumping his bones (and have actually tried to) yet, I'm shy about saying it out loud.

"Yeah," I reply softly. "I was hurt really bad and I need to make sure my head is on straight before I jump into–"

"Swabbing someone's deck?" He asks, fully grinning now. I smile and punch him in the arm. "*Ow.*"

After a moment of awkward silence we get back to seriousness. "I'll be here, pirate." He fist bumps my arm before we go our separate ways. I smile but it quickly fades, wishing I could figure out my feelings fast. I can't deny that I'm really into Paxton, but he deserves someone that's not caught in the sticky web of the past. I want to be able to be "all in" with Paxton. All or nothing. He deserves one hundred percent and nothing less. I *need* to be enough for him. Or he'll leave like Dan.

The Art of Moving On

Chapter 15

Paxton has given me my space, and I'm greatly appreciative. It's Thanksgiving break and after the food, football, and shopping, there's a party tonight. Ricky insists that we go, even though I would be content with us camping out on the sofa drinking hot chocolate and eating cookies on this Saturday night. *But* because it's Ricky, and he's been urging for us to go out more, I oblige. I pick him up in Betsy and have deemed myself designated driver since Ricky was the last time. That, and I have no interest in a repeat of the last party.

***

Rihanna is blasting throughout the house. It's been an hour since I've last seen Ricky. I can't seem to find him anywhere. I step out to the back patio from the large kitchen door and am mystically absorbed in a poof of smoke. I take a deep breath.

I've found the stoners.

I'm impressed with the cloud of smoke they've billowed. I walk around and contemplate sitting down. Alessia Cara's song "Here" begins playing out from the patio speakers. Ironic, considering I don't want to be here at this party and I'm under a cloud of marijuana just like the lyrics say.

"Hey, Emmy, do you want to hit this blunt?" Some girl that looks like Nancy Drew catches my attention. Her chair is parted just barely away then the rest of the group. The cloud of smoke still contains her. And me. Her auburn hair is a shoulder-length bob and curling out naturally on the sides. Actually, if it was a little longer and darker it would look like my hair. She's even wearing a yellow tank top. She is, without a doubt, Nancy Drew. I feel bad that she knows my name, but I have no idea who she is. I think she's a Sophomore…

"No, thank you. I'm actually looking for Ricky Rodriguez. Have you seen him?" It's a long shot but worth a try. She releases the smoke she had been holding inside. I don't plan to stay out here long, but I decide to pull up a patio chair and sit next to her.

"Yeah, actually. Last time I went inside he was with…what's that guy's name?" She stares into space for an awkwardly long time. She takes another puff of weed and blows it out, leaning toward me. Her face lights up, and she snaps her fingers. "Eli! He was with Eli, Paxton, and that girl he's always with…Aileen, getting beers."

The Art of Moving On

"Really? Are you sure?" I probably don't have to ask her. She is Nancy Drew after all. I can't believe that they were all hanging out together without me. It hurts even worse that Aileen is with them. A pang of jealousy punches me in the gut.

"Yeah. It was like thirty minutes ago though."

"You have an excellent memory for a stoner," I commend her, pushing the ugly jealousy away with a few deep breaths.

"Thank you!" She says with a big smile that makes her bloodshot eyes twinkle. She's very sweet and pretty, but I don't condone sixteen year olds smoking marijuana. I have the urge to smack the brown doobie out of her hand so it goes flying and into the nearby damp grass but, hey, not my kid. "Are you sure you don't want to hit this?"

"Yeah, I'm good on the reefer. Thanks though." Her eyes glisten. She looks so content that it's oddly comforting. Maybe I *should* smoke. It's really bizarre, but since I've found myself surrounded by smoke I think I like the smell of pot. Whatever she's smoking doesn't really smell skunky, like other weed I've smelled. I find myself gazing out at the lawn. I'm wondering what is going through her brain when she decides to speak again. I sink back into my chair and slouch.

"You're so cool, Emmy." I look at her surprised, and confused, but mostly flattered. "Cool" isn't a word that I'm usually associated with. Normally it's artistic, talented, or sometimes pretty.

"Um, Thanks." The words tumble out of my mouth slower than I intend. My eyes drift off to the grass again. "That's very kind of you to say." Part of me wants to ask why I'm cool, but I don't want to ruin the moment. We're silent for a few minutes, and I

The Art of Moving On

realize that it's not awkward at all. I am actually feeling pretty comfortable out here. It's not as cold as I thought it would be, and I'm finally starting to relax a little bit.

Wait, why am I out here again?

"Oh! That's right!" I don't mean for the words to come out loud, but they do anyway. "I'm going to go look for Ricky. Thanks, again." I'm starting to think I should hang out with the stoners more often. The ambience they create is something I think I can get behind. Too bad they feel like they need drugs in order to do so. I yawn, getting sleepy all of a sudden.

"No problem. I'll see you later," Nancy Drew replies, exhaling more smoke.

I walk back inside and spot Paxton laughing and drinking with Aileen across the room. I get paranoid that Paxton decided he doesn't want me after all. It seems like him and Aileen are together all the time outside of school. I don't know much about Aileen other than she's a year younger and very pretty. She's supermodel-thin with radiant, genuine red hair. Her face is covered in freckles that magically deem her as The Girl Next Door type. It's her flair in wardrobe that sexifies her and adds the Supermodel type to The Girl Next Door type. Together it's a deadly combo, and I might as well be green in the face with envy. I find my face frozen with a frown and eyebrows scrunched down in a V shape, staring intensely at both of them. Paxton must sense my eyes on him because when he looks up he finds my eyes immediately. His eyebrows come together in confusion. It takes a second for me to react and avert my eyes.

He walks straight up to me and asks, "What's wrong? You look constipated again."

The Art of Moving On

"Huh? I–I what?" I ask, confused and taken aback by his recycled comment…even though part of me wants to burst out laughing. Before I know it, I'm giggling like a little girl.

"What's wrong? Wait…" He leans in and sniffs me. "Are you high?" He asks in disbelief but a grin starts to grow on his lips.

"What? I–me? No–I was, uh–" I blabber, forgetting what I was going to say. His grin is now a full-blown smile. As if I wasn't flustered enough, his smile nearly knocks me back on my feet. His smile alone is enough to transport me into an alternate universe where only he and I exist.

Hm, I'm kind of hungry.

"Okay, if you say so. What's going on? I can tell it's something by your constipated face." I snort a laugh and then force myself to be serious, which is a lot harder than I expect.

"Stop calling my face constipated." I try to sound confident but my voice comes out shaky.

"I will when it stops looking constipated."

"You're so…" my voice fades out, unsure of what to call him. "My mouth is so dry. I need some water." I still can't remember what the point of this conversation is supposed to be. He hands me the bottle of water he's been carrying. I take a few small swigs and hand it back to him. "Frustrating!" I exclaim, remembering what I was going to say earlier. "You're frustrating."

"*I'm* frustrating? I'm just trying to figure out if there's something wrong or if you actually need to use the toilet. Come on, I can walk you there." He starts to walk away, but I grab his arm before he gets out of my reach.

"What? No, Paxton." I rub my dry eyes. "Why are you always with her?" I don't mean to say it out loud in an ugly whiny voice, but it comes out that way anyway. Between rubbing my eyes and whining, I'm certain I've regressed back to a five year old.

Paxton is looking at me with his eyebrows raised in disbelief. My face flares up, and I can already tell I've embarrassed myself beyond all belief. Jealousy is the most unattractive emotion a person can have. I feel as if I've just indicted myself. He's never going to want to be with a crazed, jealous person. I attempt to backpedal. "I mean, it's not my business, I guess–I just–I thought…you made it seem like we…" I sigh at my inability to communicate. I give in and just flat-out ask him, "How come you're always with Aileen?" It's impossible to ask in a way that doesn't make me sound jealous, but I have to know.

"Are you jealous?" He asks, his disbelief turning into amusement.

"No." I blatantly lie, and I can tell by his smirk that he knows it. "I just don't get why you would act like you want to be with me, but then you go and attach yourself at her hip. You guys are always together. It's just…" I struggle to find the right words, but I don't think there are any so I lamely settle with, "Rude to do that to me."

"*Rude?*" He says incredulously with big eyes. I can tell by his tone that I've used the wrong words. He's not happy, and I've never heard Paxton upset before. "What's *rude* is you leading me on." My face turns from pink to utterly pale because he's right.

The Art of Moving On

Ouch. "I've told you eight hundred times: not everything is what you think it is, Emerald."

He laces his hands together in the top of his head and heaves a groan. I look down, not even trying to stop the guilt and shame from consuming me. I deserve it. If Paxton likes other girls there's nothing I can do about it. *Plenty* of girls like him. Of course he's moved on. Any girl would be lucky to be with him. I knew I wasn't good enough. He lifts up my chin to look at him.

My eyes feel like they're going to betray me and let out tears despite how dry they feel. He looks sweetly into my eyes, which I know I don't deserve. His face softens. "Emmy, I told you I would give you space, and that I would be here. That hasn't changed. You have nothing to be jealous of because Aileen…is my *cousin.*"

I cover my face with my hands. I'm *horrified.* "Oh my god, I'm so sorry, Paxton. Oh my god. She doesn't look like you *at all*. I'm such an idiot."

"You are not an idiot." He gently pulls my hands away from my face unveiling my burning, red eyes. "I'm a jerk because I'm really glad you were jealous. I have to go back and hang out with her to stop that idiot Gavin from hitting on her. Speaking of douches, if he comes near you just kick him in the nuts. Don't hesitate. Just a swift knee," he orders me, lifting his knee, simulating kicking someone in the nuts. I nod and let out a small chuckle even though I'm still ashamed. "If he bothers you come tell me."

"Wait!" I exclaim loudly remembering the entire point of our conversation. He turns back to look at me. "Have you seen Ricky?"

"*Uuuhhh*, no, not really. I mean, I think I saw him wandering around. I wouldn't worry about it. *Uuum*…maybe go look in the dining room? There's a bunch of people in

The Art of Moving On

there." He's acting a little strange but I don't dare call him on it after making a complete fool of myself, so I let it go.

"Okay. Thanks."

"Later, pirate. Enjoy your high."

"I'm not high!" I yell after him. I sigh and watch him walk away, struggling with all the things I feel for him. I feel like a part of me is ripping the further away he gets. At the same time, I have a hormonal whiplash, and thoroughly appreciate the view of his butt. I snort a laugh and then immediately look around hoping nobody heard me laugh out loud while I'm standing alone.

I check the dining room but Ricky's not there, so I continue my search upstairs. I don't think it's probable that he's up here, but it's the only place I haven't looked. I start to open doors in case he's passed out drunk in a bed. I open the first door, and it's a closet. Not at all what I was expecting. I open the next door to the left of the stairs, and it's a laundry room. Again, not at all what I was expecting.

I open the next door down and get an eyeful of Ricky heavily kissing a very shirtless, Eli. I freeze like a deer in headlights. My mouth drops to the floor, and my eyebrows shoot to the ceiling. They rip apart lightning fast.

"Oh my god! I thought you locked the door!" Ricky snaps at Eli.

"I thought I did," he replies in a quiet voice.

"What the–"

"Get in here and close the door," Ricky hisses at me so violently that I obey immediately without even thinking about it. "Please don't say anything." They both scramble to put their shirts on. My mouth snaps shut. "I can explain everything."

The Art of Moving On

"You can't tell, Emmy," Eli begs in a deep, serious voice. "This can't get out. It will be bad for both of us."

"No, I–I wouldn't do that," I stammer.

"Seriously, querida. You and Paxton are the only ones that know and it needs to stay that way."

"Wait, *Paxton* knows and I don't?" I'm offended. I shake my head before they can say anything because I know I'm being self-involved. This isn't about me. "Sorry, I didn't mean that. You know I won't tell anyone." It all makes so much sense now. The awkwardness between them, the side-glances they share when they think nobody is watching, and when Paxton told me I wasn't Eli's type. That smart-ass. Silly me for thinking he was calling me ugly. It's all almost crystal clear.

"Uh…" *What was I saying again?* "It's getting late and…I–I got kind of hungry and want food. I'm–uh…sorry for interrupting. It's just…" I stammer out like a fool, avoiding eye contact.

"Getting late," Ricky finishes my sentence, squeezing out the rest of my brain fart. "I agree. Let's get going. Um…okay, here's the plan: I'll leave now and then wait like five minutes, or something, then you guys can come out together so people think you guys were alone in here hooking up. I'll meet you at the car."

"Wait, *what?*"

"*Okay-queridos-bye*," he says, rushing out the door leaving me alone with Eli.

I turn around and look at Eli who just shrugs his shoulders. I study him. He always seemed to me to be mister sportsman jock. He's big and beefy and…I don't think I've ever heard him speak more than like five sentences since I've known him. He looks

The Art of Moving On

more like a football player than a soccer player, and he's probably only an inch taller than me. He has a light brown buzz cut suited for the military. His complexion is less than clear, and he has eyes that are almost see through. If eyes are windows to the soul than I see how Ricky could fall for Eli. His eyes can almost compete with Paxton's. I never imagined anyone could even come close to having as beautiful eyes as Paxton.

My brain is spinning from everything that has happened in the last twenty minutes. I can't stop staring down at the ugly madras bedspread. It makes me want to vomit. I'm not great with decorating and fashion, but madras is the worst. Ralph Lauren, or whoever designs and uses this horrid pattern, should be taken out back. This is definitely a man's bedroom. Traci Dougan must have an older brother I don't know about. There's a dark blue painted wall with miniature sailboats adorning the walls. A crew oar hangs above the dark wood headboard. It looks like it belongs in Nantucket and not Oregon.

"Are you okay?" My head jolts up. I forgot Eli was even in the room. *That's* how quiet this guy is. *Or* how self-involved I'm being. Or both.

Wait, am *I actually stoned right now?*

"Yeah, I'm okay. Just…I don't know. How about you? Are you okay?"

He looks on edge…a little scared, but there's also a tinge of anger. His body is tense from head to toe. I wonder if he has a bad temper. He's a muscly guy that could do a lot of damage if he were to succumb to a fit of rage.

"Where's Paxton? I mean…is he your ride? Or do you need one?"

His body eases and his eyes melt from fear to shame like chocolate in the sun. Grim, dark and messy…and just plain sad. He has nothing to be ashamed of, and I wish I had words to reassure him of that.

"Yeah, he's here somewhere. I'm good. I'll just go find him. I'm sure he's running around doing something ridiculous." He lightly chuckles and I join him even though we're both forcing it out awkwardly. We make our way to the door.

"That sounds like Paxton, for sure." I miss him. I was just with him not even an hour ago and I miss him.

What's gotten into me?

There's a short pause. "Well, I'm going to go. I'll see you at school. Are you sure you're okay?" I ask one last time to be sure. He holds back to let me escape first.

"Yeah. Bye, Emmy. And thank you for not telling anyone," he thanks me desperately.

"Of course, Eli. I would never do anything to hurt you guys. Good night."

***

Longest. Car ride. Ever.

It's been nearly five minutes of complete silence since we got in the car. The elephant in the car couldn't possibly get any fatter. I can feel him look at me while I drive us back to his house. My mind is reeling. There are so many memories that run through my head, like a rapid slideshow of the last six years that I've known him. Moments where I knew he was gay and never said anything. Times that he seemed like he was in pain and

The Art of Moving On

169

needed to talk. So many memories where I should have been more forward and intuitive. Memories that I could have possibly made better for him if only I spoke up.

"Ricky, you know you're my–"

"Emmy, you know I'm gay," we both talk at the same time. My mouth makes an "O" shape, and I turn to look at him taking deep breaths. I focus back on the road and swerve us back into our proper lane, trying not to kill us.

"I–I mean, don't take this the wrong way, but…I kind of figured. I mean it's just that we don't ever talk about boys or girls, you know, when we talk about love interests. I'm sorry if I was wrong for assuming. I didn't want to push you to talk about it if you didn't want to," I spit out so quickly he probably barely understands me.

"I always did sort of assume that you knew. I regret not being honest and open with you about it. I'm not ashamed of being gay, I'm just…afraid. I just can't bring myself to tell anyone. You're my best friend. The Paxton to my Eli. I can tell you anything, and I know that. I do. I trust you with my life. I *know* this, and I still never said it because saying it out loud still feels like I'm pulling barbed wire out of my throat. I've kept a huge, major part of myself from you. I've never even been fully who I am when I'm with you, even though I feel the most myself when we're together. And now with Eli and even Paxton, too. Ugh, I'm not making any sense. You have every right to be angry and disappointed. I'm so sorry, Em. *Soy un idiota*," he looks down and shakes his head, angry with himself.

"You are not an idiot. Please don't feel bad for not telling me. I want you to know that you can tell me anything, seriously, *anything*. If you kill someone and need help burying the body then call me because I'll help you any way I can. I want to be that

The Art of Moving On

person you call. Well, I mean, don't ever kill anyone, but you know what I mean. I would never tell anyone. You can trust me, Ricky. I'm sorry if I haven't made myself more available or easy for you to talk to. I've been absorbed in Dan for months and now stupid Paxton." I can feel my eyes droop. I can also feel my face getting warm because I have no idea why I brought up Paxton in this situation. Ricky looks at me with big eyes and starts waving his hands in front of him.

"No, no, no, querida. You don't have to explain or apologize. I promise it has nothing to do about me not trusting you. I just couldn't say it, and…I don't know," he replies quickly. "Half the school probably assumes that I am gay but I still can't officially come out. My situation is…complicated to say the least. Honestly, I've never talked about it. *With anyone*. Not even you, and I tell you everything, so I'm sorry for keeping you in the dark." He rests his head on his hand with his arm leaning against the window. After a moment he looks over at me, and I'm still trying to find the right words to say because I don't think I've said them.

Instead, I lamely settle with, "Please know that I'm always here for you and willing to listen."

"Thanks. Te amo, querida." he sniffles and pauses for a moment. "Sometimes it *is* difficult to talk about, and other times I'm busting at the seams *dying* to talk about it," he softly admits. "You, Eli, and Paxton are the only ones that know. My parents don't know, and it needs to stay that way. You know how patriarchal and religious my parents are. I got a lecture about how tight my pants are a couple weeks ago. My dad kept telling me I look like a fag. They *will* disown me if they find out I'm gay. Coming out to them is not an option unless I have a death wish. They think you're my girlfriend even though I have

The Art of Moving On

denied it more than a million times. It's one thing to not fully be who I am at school but, Emmy, I can't even be truly myself when I'm at home." The suffering in his voice takes me by surprise. It's clear by his voice and his panicked yet hopeless eyes that the suffering has been intensifying lately.

"I can't even imagine, Ricky. I really can't. Is that why you don't like me coming over?"

"Yeah. Well, that and they *really* are loco, querida, no joke. My house is nothing but eccentric Cubanos running around yelling and eating all of the time. Its chaos." I chuckle and am grateful that he's lightened the mood at least a little.

"So…what's going on with Eli?" I glance at him while I pick at my cuticles nervously. I'm not sure if I should be asking about him about details with Eli but part of me is also squealing inside, dying to know. A gentle smile sneaks up on his face at the sound of Eli's name. It makes me grin.

"The Eli thing just sort of happened," he confesses. "When we were sitting so close together at the basketball game a few weeks ago we both felt this indescribable electricity. It was unlike anything I've ever felt. It was confusing and scary yet my heart unveiled in a way I didn't know possible."

I sigh and an "*aw*" comes out.

"I wasn't sure if he was gay though. I mean, I was pretty sure. I have a good gay-dar." I snort a very unattractive laugh. "He started playing with my hand while we were all squished tightly on the bleachers. I couldn't believe it, Emmy. This good-looking athlete was hitting on *me*.

The Art of Moving On

"After the game I was walking around for signatures and found Eli again. We got to talking and found out that we actually have things in common. Then we left together to this beautiful place in the woods, and…he kissed me. Like…he *kissed me*, kissed me. Like, I went dizzy and my body felt…sensitive and hyper aware. Every time he touched me I craved more. I still can't believe it happened." We look at each other, and we're both smiling. We share an understanding smile. He knows that what he and Eli shared is something that Dan and I shared. Something that I share with Paxton. The feeling is some place between love and lust. It's a beautiful gray area that's confusing, but you can get lost in it in a most decadent way. I shake my head and come back down to reality.

"Eli can't tell anyone because his parents would kill him which, I can relate to. He also said that it would ruin the soccer team dynamic if they all found out. It would gravely hurt his chances of joining a team in college and playing competitively after college. Apparently athletes don't want a homo on their team. And it *sucks* because he's *insanely* good, querida. You would think *he* was the Latino one, playing soccer that well. His talent is going to take him places and I won't get in the way of that."

I try to nod empathetically, even though the thought of Ricky getting in the way of Eli's life makes me sick. It shouldn't have to be that way.

"He told me that Paxton is his best friend, and that he's the only one that knows he's gay. Saturday after half-time at the football game Eli and I ended up sneaking off to kiss again. That's why you couldn't find me after the game. I slipped away when you were talking to Paxton's mom. You seemed like you were having a deep conversation with her so I dipped out to find Eli with Paxton again. After a little while, I left Eli to

The Art of Moving On

come find you. I'm so sorry I left you, Emmy. You shouldn't have had to deal with that experience with Paxton's mom on your own."

"It's okay, Ricky. You don't have to apologize. Neither of us knew that I would have a bizarre, visceral connection with Maria…Paxton's *mom*. I still can't get over it. Of all the people, Ricky…" I shake my head in disbelief.

"I know, querida. That was a whammy especially since you and Paxton have this *thing* now."

I groan. "I'm not even sure if there is a 'thing' or will be a 'thing.' Back to you and Eli in the room…" I trail off hoping my blatant attempt to change the subject works.

He sighs heavily and runs his hand through his thick dark brown hair.

I quickly backtrack taking his sigh as an over-step of his personal boundaries. "We don't have to talk about it. It really isn't my business."

"Paxton found us that room to hang out in and literally snuck us up there. He's been really supportive of Eli and I getting to know each other and exploring our relationship. I was sort of glad when you came in when you did, and I'm *sure as shit* glad it wasn't anybody else. Things were getting carried away. He makes me want to experience so many things, but it's unchartered territory and still makes me nervous. So, it was like divine intervention when you came in." He lets out a soft chuckle, and I smile.

"We've been sneaking around a little bit here and there. I was with him at the last party, too. I should've told you sooner, querida. I swear I was planning on telling you this week. The other day actually, but time just got away and I never did. This whole thing has been a whirlwind. It's all happening fast. Maybe too fast," he admits. My mind starts piecing more moments together from the last few weeks.

The Art of Moving On

"That one day at lunch…you were sad because Eli wouldn't even walk next to you, huh?"

"Yes. That was painful, but it put things in perspective. If our relationship is going to continue, then that's how difficult it's going to be when we're in public. We both feel like we still want to try being together though. We're *really* attracted to each other."

"That's good! Ricky, I've been complaining about a broken heart and being a huge downer while you've been exploring love for the first time. You probably want to punch me in the face, and I probably deserve it."

"No, you've been doing so well with your break-up. I know it hasn't been easy. I thought you guys were really going to make it, too. Your reaction to seeing Dan and Alexis at the pep rally was normal. Chica, if it was me I probably would have blown the whole school up like Christian Slater in the movie, *Heathers*." We laugh. The 80s movie, *Heathers,* is one of our favorite movies. The car ride has gone from uncomfortable to us joking around the same as usual. The elephant has officially left the car, even though something is nagging at me. The selfish part of me comes out.

"I don't mean to bring up Paxton again but–"

"Yes, you do," he cackles.

I can't help but grin and look down guiltily. "I'm curious as to why he knows. It's totally fine that you didn't want to tell me, I understand. I'm just wondering."

"That's an Eli thing. He trusts him. They're BFFs, Captain and Co-Captain of the soccer team, and all that bromance stuff. If Eli trusts him, then that says a lot about Paxton. I trust him too, Emmy. He's a kind of a 'wild card,' but he's a really good guy.

The Art of Moving On

175

And it's not that I didn't want to tell you…I just didn't know how. Like I said, I really was planning on telling you this week, but I just didn't make the time to...and if I'm being honest, I was scared. Saying the words, 'I'm gay' out loud feels like I'm standing on a cliff, and at any moment someone can push me over. It's a vulnerable feeling that's hard to explain."

I nod as I pull up to his two-story dark tan house. "Thanks for telling me and trusting me, Ricky." We have an awkward car hug.

"Thanks, querida. Te amo."

He's part way out the door before I call to him. "Ricky, don't be so surprised that a hot athlete wants to jump your bones. You're one of the most amazing people I've ever met."

He looks back down and sassily advises me, "I could say the same thing about you, querida." He winks at me and shuts the car door. I roll my eyes and grin. I watch him walk to his front door and it visibly looks as if a weight has been lifted off his shoulders.

***

I throw my keys and my purse down on the floor and collapse face down onto my bed. Tonight has been exhausting in the most confusing and random way possible. I roll over onto my back, put my hands under my head, and start to process everything that happened.

The Art of Moving On

As soon as Ricky told me he was gay, it was like his entire aura had changed; like he had this light radiating from him and his vibe was free. It was like he could breathe for the first time, and I didn't even know he was starving for air. I shiver and get goose bumps up my arms just thinking about it. He's been my best friend for years, and tonight he finally got to be one hundred percent him for the first time. It's nearly unthinkable as to how he survived—is surviving—without being completely who he is. I'm so incredibly happy for him and Eli but also deeply saddened that they feel like they can't even walk down the hallways at school together, much less hold hands anywhere in public. It hurts me to know that he can't have that.

At first, when Ricky told me that Paxton knows and has been helping him and Eli and supporting their relationship, I was jealous (okay, I still am a teeny tiny bit) that Paxton was trusted with their secret but I wasn't. The fact that Eli and Paxton had the kind of friendship where they did talk about their sexuality made me envious, too. I'm kicking myself for never bringing it up with Ricky or flat-out asking him about boys, especially since I can now see how much he's been suffering over the last few years. It makes me feel like a terrible friend. I know Ricky doesn't see it that way at all but a part of me still feels crappy.

After the jealousy hit, my heart thumped harder knowing that Paxton has been so sweet and helpful in fostering Ricky and Eli's relationship. I love knowing that he can keep a secret. If there's one thing Paxton is, it's loyal. It's one of the things I like most about him. I let out a tired sigh knowing that my internal struggle is about to strike me full force again. There are so many things about Paxton that I like.

No.

Love.

He's such a good person. I like him a lot, and I want to be with him. I do. I just don't know if I can. I don't know if my heart can handle it; if it's strong enough to be brave. I'm insecure, vulnerable, and scared; and I hate it. I'm a complete coward. My feelings for him can be so overpowering at times I find myself doing things that I never thought I would do…like practically stripping down naked because I'm so caught up in the heat of the moment. Our connection is undeniable, yet I still don't feel like I'm good enough.

I groan and force myself to sit up and put my PJ's on. I roll under the covers and try to get my wandering mind off of Paxton before I start to get hot and bothered. Or just bothered because I really don't know what I'm going to do with all of these intense physical and emotional feelings that are ready to explode.

I turn out my lights and shift my thoughts back to Ricky and how free his energy became on the drive home. Very little compares to the feeling you get when your best friend is genuinely the happiest you've ever seen them. I fall asleep with a smile on my face.

Chapter 16

On Wednesday morning, a miracle happens.

Ricky and I meet and walk down the main hallway planning the agenda for this week's SC meeting. Ricky stops us dead in our tracks. I'm finishing taking a note about getting those green Haribo frog gummy things back in the vending machines (don't ask) when Ricky shakes my arm.

"Hang on, I'm almost done."

"No, Emmy. Stop," he demands. I stop and look up to see that he's staring in awe at the walls. I turn my head and look. My mouth drops open and my eyes go wide.

It's a Christmas poster miracle.

All of my Santa Spirit posters are back on the walls. My breathing picks up because they're not just back on the walls. They've been turned into canvas prints. I cover my gaping mouth with my hand to keep from screaming. I don't know why, but whoever stole the posters had them printed onto canvas. Every. Single. One. They look *freaking beautiful.*

"Oh my god," I manage to muffle out through my hand.

"Uh, yeah," Ricky says, still in awe. "Ay dios mio, Emmy. They are *stunning.*"

A body comes up behind us and puts an arm around Ricky and I. I have flashbacks of the same arms around Ricky and I weeks ago. "I told you not everything is what you think, Emerald." I take a sharp inhale and look at Paxton.

"You?" I ask in a dream-like state. "You did this? Did you *plan* to do this?" He smiles.

"Mrs. Timlin and my mom helped me. She worked it out with the school so the prints, if you approve, can be auctioned off at the annual fundraiser in the spring. The school even agreed that all the profits would go to updating the art room and getting new supplies. I'm sorry for stealing them and not telling you, but I wanted it to be a surprise. Also, sorry for ripping that Picasso looking one. I ran out of time and someone was about to catch me so I ran and it accidentally got torn. I don't think you realize how amazing they are, Emmy. They're too awesome to just be thrown away after Christmas." He softly adds in my ear, "I hope you believe me. I'm here, Emmy. I'm all in. I'm not going to give up or leave you until you make me. I'll be here." He turns and walks away.

I'm in such shock I can't move. I'm swooning, doe-eyed in the direction that Paxton disappeared in. My mind is reeling a million miles an hour.

The Art of Moving On

"Dan," I mutter quietly.

"Um, *excuse me*?! Did you just say *Dan*?" Ricky looks at me like I've grown tentacles. I nod my head still incapacitated. "You have serious crazy eyes right now, and it's scaring me. Paxton did this, not Dan. *Why* are you talking about Dan? Please tell me you don't want to murder him. You would not do well in prison. Real prison is not like *Orange is the New Black*, Emmy," he spews out rapidly. He waves his hand in front of my eyes. "Are you even hearing anything I'm saying?"

"I have to talk to Dan," I state in a mind-racing trance.

"Ay Dios mio. I don't know what you're thinking, but can it *please* wait until after he takes photos at our meeting on Friday?"

"*Eeehhh yeee nnmm uuuhhh,*" I make noises as I think. "Yyyes," I conclude. I need that few days to think of everything I need to tell him. Everything I need to say to him to get it off my chest. Off my chest, off my shoulders, and out of my heart. Paxton just picked up the last remaining chunk of my broken heart and glued it right back into place. Before I hand it over to him, I need to make one hundred percent sure it's clean, clear and free.

***

"I thought long and hard after Dan broke up with me. I see now that our relationship was *too* easy," I admit. "It was boring. I was bored, and I didn't even know it. Even though I understand why our relationship didn't work it still hurts. The way he acts like it never happened hurts. Seeing him kiss Alexis hurts."

The Art of Moving On

"Those things are normal but they'll heal in time," Dad tells me Thursday night. "It's important that you've been able to take an honest look at the relationship. You learn something from every relationship you have, whether it's a good one or a bad one."

"Yeah, I guess that makes sense. This entire time I couldn't figure out what's been holding me back. I realize I have feelings for Paxton and I think I have for a while. Something about my relationship with Dan is still blocking me. The only thing I can think of to do is talk to Dan." I pull my legs up on the sofa and hug them. Dad has an auto-mechanics magazine on his knee that he was reading until I flopped down next to him and randomly started spilling my guts. Good thing he's used to it by now.

"You could do that. Might work."

"I don't know what to say though."

"Be honest. You guys were together for a long time, there is still a history and connection there that can't be brushed off with a handshake." I scowl at his mention of a handshake. He chuckles. "Sweet pea, if I could solve all your problems with Dan with a shotgun, I would. If you let me. If it was legal."

I smile. "I'll try not to kill him."

"I'll visit you in prison if you do," he kids. "And you know what? Sometimes things aren't always what we think." I groan. I've heard that line so many times now that I'm starting to think I don't know anything. It makes me want to bang my head against the wall. "For all you know, Dan could be having a hard time with your break up too just in a different kind of way."

"*Pfft*. Like what way?" I ask incredulously.

"I have no idea. That's why you have to find out. You'll get closure, and if you want to be with Paxton like you say you do, then you'll be able to do that without having any leftover strings that tie to Dan. You'll be string free." He wiggles his fingers around like "jazz hands." I smile.

"Yeah. Thanks, Dad." I'm starting to feel genuinely better about my decision to talk to Dan.

"You're welcome. And I mean it when I say there will absolutely be *no Paxton in this house when I'm not here.*"

An evil grin slowly spreads across my face like the Grinch. "But what if it's for, like, fifteen minutes? What if I just need to come in and grab something I forgot, and he happens to be with me?"

"Nope."

"Seriously? Not even fifteen minutes?"

"A lot can happen in fifteen minutes. You were conceived in fifteen minutes."

"*Ew!* Gross, Dad!" I smack him lightly with a sofa pillow.

"I'm teasing! I'm teasing. Thirty minutes max. No longer than an episode of *Sanford and Son.*"

"That's a really outdated reference, but I'll take it. I just have to actually tell him that I want to be with him...and talk to Dan." I sigh. It makes my stomach hurt just imagining the words I'll have to say.

"You're a beautiful young woman just like your mother was at your age. Dan's a freaking idiot. I never liked him that much anyway."

183

"Thanks, Dad." I grin and lean the side of my head against the sofa. "Hey, I saw the car out front, it looks great. Is it finished?" The El Camino had a fresh paint job by the time I got back from school yesterday. He always paints the cars last. The car is sporting a flawlessly shiny, dark green coat.

"It sure is. Looks good, huh?"

"It looks awesome! When are they coming to pick up?" I would love to see the look on the owner's face.

"She's coming by early afternoon on Saturday. Okay, I've gotta hit the hay. Have a good night. Don't stay up too late. Love you," Dad tells me, tapping my leg with his rolled up magazine.

"Love you too."

***

We spend the first half of our Student Council meeting taking care of business. Mostly, it was discussing the ins and outs of the Winter Formal Dance. I have very intention of taking Paxton as my date. And Ricky too. And Eli. None of them know it yet, and I haven't figured out how it will work out exactly, but I'll make it work. The second half of the meeting is spent wrapping gifts for Santa Spirit. It's our first round of gift-wrapping sessions, and it's mostly for Dan to take photos. He's kept silent and out of the way, demanding that we do business as usual and pretend like he's not there. It's not the easiest thing in the world for me, especially because I plan on talking to him when we're done.

The Art of Moving On

"Is everyone cool if I put on holiday music?" I ask the other members. I get quips of yes, so I begin to play the Pandora holiday station from my computer. "Sleigh Ride" starts playing and I hum to it.

I grab a fancy NBA certified basketball and set it in front of me. I murmur, "How on Earth am I going to wrap this thing?" I drape the paper over it and struggle to get enough paper to cover the ball completely. I have the ball in my arm with my other hand unraveling the roll of wrapping paper.

Once I move the roll up in the air it hits something and I hear an, *"Agh, oof."*

"Oh, shoot, sorry." I move the basketball and wrapping paper down so I can see whom I just hit. Dan is staring back at me completely aloof. I make a pained and contrite face. I hope he knows I didn't do it on purpose out of spite. "Are you okay? Sorry. This thing is kind of hard to wrap."

"No worries. Let me help you," he offers, taking the camera off from around his neck and setting it beside him. He scoots closer, and I can smell his old scent of vanilla. I don't know how or why but Dan always smells like vanilla and fabric softener. I would normally take a full inhale and relish in it. Today, it feels suffocating.

"Um. Okay. Thanks," I mumble, not wanting to be rude before I have this "clearing the air" conversation with him after the meeting. He takes the scissors and cuts the paper for me. "Hey, do you think we can talk when we're done?"

"Uh, sure, yeah, of course," he awkwardly replies. We're silent for a few minutes while we continue wrapping, cutting, and taping. "You know I always wanted us to stay friends," he comments sincerely. I give him a tight smile and nod. I don't want to be friends with Dan.

The Art of Moving On

This is why I need to talk to him, I remind myself. He helps me finish wrapping the ball and then goes back to taking photos. Ricky eyes me, silently asking me if I'm okay. I give him a small nod back from across the room.

Once everything is more or less cleaned up and organized, our meeting adjourns and everyone leaves except for Dan and me. Ricky gives me an especially tight hug and tells me to call him later. By later, he means right after I finish my conversation with Dan.

"So, how have you been, Em?" He sits down in one of the rolling chairs that surround our long executive table. I'm having trouble regulating my breath; so I take in one deep-deep breath, then blow it out through puckered lips and closed eyes. It's time to put on my big girl panties. I've been through so much with Dan in the last three years it would seem impossible that any conversation we have could be awkward or uncomfortable. My, how quickly things change.

"Um, I hate you, Dan." As soon as the words come shakily out of my mouth my eyes begin to sting and lump begins to grow in my throat. I try and take a deep breath. "Um, I didn't actually meant to say that. Sorry. You just–you...hurt me so freaking bad when you broke up with me. You were so casual about it. It was like I didn't even matter to you. I feel like you used me all the way up until that point." I pick at a piece of tape that got stuck to the table.

"I–" He starts.

"Stop. Let me finish." I throw my hand up.

He nods politely.

The Art of Moving On

"You told me the day before that you loved me. We slept together that night. Do you have any idea how badly it hurts to have been used in a physical way? It feels like you abused my body." He looks down, ashamed. I hear him take an uneven breath. He looks up at me with watery black eyes. I'm so glad that he's about to cry because it means that he has some remorse, that he has some feelings about it. It proves that he cares about what he did. I'm not proud of it, but it satisfies me to know that he feels crappy. He should.

"Emmy, I am so sorry. I think about it sometimes still and I am so disgusted with myself. It's the biggest regret I've ever had. Lying to you like that just to please myself. It was so wrong. It's been eating away at me, and I wanted to apologize. I swear I did, but every time you looked at me it was as if you were either being stabbed in the gut or as if you wanted to stab me in the gut. I didn't know how to say it. I've just been pretending that everything is fine." We both have silent subtle streams of tears flowing helplessly down.

"That's the other thing. You pretend like everything is fine. You started dating Alexis a week later, like I'm supposed to believe you guys hadn't fooled around—or God knows what else—while we were still dating. I'm not an idiot, Dan." I turn angrier but a hiccup comes out, compromising my seriousness.

"Emmy, I swear to you— nothing like that happened while we were together. Alexis and I had been talking, but it wasn't like that at all, I promise."

"I don't believe you, but it doesn't matter anyway. It doesn't make you any less of an asshole. You act as if the last few years never happened. Like you never loved me.

The Art of Moving On

Like I was nobody. Like our relationship was nothing to you. I was suffering, and you acted as if you had erased all the time we spent together."

He nods his head and then places his forehead in his hands. "I did. I hoped if I pretended long enough that things would be okay between us; then we could eventually be friends."

I intently look him in the eyes and ask, "Do you *really* want to be friends?" A sob slips out and I run the back of my hand across my mouth. "Because I don't want to be your friend, Dan. I'm sorry but I just don't. I think you're a massive jerk— and I'm pretty sure I will always think that. You really have no idea how bad you've hurt me." He shakes his head. More sleek tears tumble down his face.

"No. I don't want to be friends," he mumbles, his voice trembling. "I'll never forget the last three years—and I'll never forget how much I loved you. It's just not that way anymore, but don't think that I didn't love you—because I did."

I sniff and more tears leak out. His words hurt, but give me a release. I feel the burden, the hurt, and my tainted heart all being lifted. I meant what I said earlier about hating him. I want so badly to tell him that I hate him and actually mean it. But I just don't. I wish I could. It would make things so much easier but I just don't.

"I'm trying hard to get rid of this blame I have for you. I want to move on. There's someone else that I really like, and I want to be able to go out with him without carrying around animosity, heartache, and all the insecurity you left in your wake." He nods his head, and we sit in silence for a few moments.

"I want you to be able to do that. I hope you forgive me, Emmy, because I swear to you and to God that I am more sorry than you know."

The Art of Moving On

I roll my watery eyes because I'll never believe him. "I don't hate you, Dan. Lord knows I want to, but I just don't. I did try, and it was exhausting. I don't hate you, but I *really* don't like you. At all. I don't want to be anywhere near you, frankly. I don't want to look at you. I don't want to talk to you. I think it's best if we just stick to our own circles and be cordial when we have to."

"Okay." After a moment I decide the conversation is over and stand up. It's nauseating to be in the same room alone with him. Looking at his face and hearing his voice makes me want to vomit and rip my eyeballs out. Okay, maybe that's a little dramatic. He stands up also. "So, who is it? Who's the guy?"

I consider not telling him because it's none of his business, but he's going to find out soon anyway. "Paxton."

"Asshole," he mutters. My eyes dart up at him, confused and mad that he would ever even think Paxton is an asshole.

"What?" I ask defensively.

"I knew he always liked you the entire time we were going out, and it pissed me off. He didn't even try to hide it."

A single boisterous laugh falls out of me and a grin starts to grow. "Really? I never even noticed."

"Yeah, I know. Anyway…I am sorry, Emmy." I gather all my stuff and look at him before we both walk out the door. "Bye."

"Bye, Dan." I lower my head and walk out like I'm leaving a funeral. Once I push through the big glass doors of the school and get a fresh dose of air in my lungs I feel

The Art of Moving On

such relief. I stand next to Betsy and take deep breaths of air, each one more cleansing than the last.

CHAPTER 17

Saturday morning I wake up to Ricky drooling on the sofa pillow, an empty pizza box, a melted carton of ice cream, and a Netflix screen asking me if I'm still watching. I guess you can say things got a little out of hand. I sit up and immediately feel my bloated stomach gurgle. I groan and rub the sleep out of my eyes. My mouth feels sticky, and I realize that I have chocolate ice cream drool down the side of my chin. I need to be hosed down in the front yard; I'm such a mess. I shake Ricky's shoulder to wake him up, and when that doesn't work, I lightly smack his face a few times until he grunts. His crusty eyes open, and he shoots up to a sitting position.

"Oh my god. What time is it? *Jesus*, what happened last night?" He asks, noticing the disaster. "We morphed into a bunch of Neanderthals." He starts wiping his face.

The Art of Moving On

"It's ten. I just woke up. My head and stomach hurt. What were we *thinking*? I feel hungover, and I didn't even drink." I collapse back down on the sofa.

"*Ay ay ay. It's ten?* I have to go before my parents find out I've been gone all night, or before my sisters rat me out." He groans. "I feel gross. We have to find healthier ways to celebrate."

I smile. Last night Ricky and I celebrated my complete detachment from Dan. It's all onward and upward from here on out. I have Paxton in my sights, and I have to figure out a way to tell him how I feel. I also have to figure out how I'm going to ask him to Winter formal. And Ricky. And Eli. I have my work cut out for me.

Work has never looked so good.

I can't wait to see Paxton again, even as nervous as I am. Thinking about wrapping my arms around him and kissing him makes my heart skip a beat. I haven't felt this good in a very long time. Even when I was with Dan I hadn't felt like this in the months leading up to our break-up.

I stretch my legs and arms completely out, trying not to knock over the squishy ice cream container. Ricky stands up and gathers his belongings in a zombie-like state.

I feel like I have a food baby.

"You look like you have a food baby." He stares at me for a second. "Please tell me it's a food baby and not a real baby."

"*HA.* It's a food baby, you big jerk. Stop trying to give me nightmares. I have to clean and shower. Dad probably had a minor capillary waking up to this mess." The lady is coming to pick up the El Camino, and Dad will flip if the house looks anything less

The Art of Moving On

than pristine. I don't know if they'll have paperwork or business to discuss inside, so I have to get this mess cleaned sooner than later.

"*Ugh*, good luck with that. I would stay to help but these brown hands have come too far to start cleaning up a house that isn't mine," he jokes. I laugh loudly, and then immediately holding my stomach and groan. "I love you and you know I would help clean–"

"No, it's okay. Go before you get in trouble," I tell him as I lazily wave him off.

"Okay, thanks, querida. I'll text you later." He approaches the front door. "Now to begin my car ride of shame." I chuckle.

As Ricky walks out, Dad walks in. I hear Dad tell Ricky, "Drive home safe."

"I will, E.G., thanks!" Ricky shouts from out of the door.

"Hey, kiddo. Looks like you guys had fun last night," he comments, eyebrows high, in a clearly judgmental tone. I try to laugh, but only a puff of air comes out.

"*Too* much fun. I'll clean. How much longer until that lady comes?" I ask, my limbs still sprawled out on the sofa.

"About two hours. I just got back from the shop. Todd has things locked down pretty well so I'm going to stay here. I'll go in tomorrow for paperwork for an hour or so."

"Okay, cool. I'll figure out something for dinner."

"You need to shower first, smelly lady," he teases. "I'm real proud of you, sweet pea, for talking to Dan. I know it must not have been easy, but you did the right thing, and hopefully you're ready to move on." His words cover me like a warm blanket.

"Thanks, Dad. And I am ready to move on. I'm going to ask Paxton to Winter Formal…And Ricky. And Eli."

"All of them? And who's Eli? Do I even want to know?"

"Ricky's love interest and no, you don't want to know because I don't even know. I haven't figured out how to ask them all yet."

He chuckles. "Well, sounds like you've got a lot to do. Hop to it. I have to go make sure I have the paperwork all ready for the car."

"All righty. To the shower I go." I groan and grunt lifting myself off the sofa. Dad laughs at my pain.

"Oh," Dad stops me as I begin to saunter to my room. I stop and look back at him. "I don't have a problem with Ricky sleeping over but don't get any ideas about any other boys staying here overnight." He pauses for a second, and then points his finger at me. "And *don't forget the Paxton rule*." He smiles, feigning an evil grin. I grin and shake my head.

"I'll *try* not to," I tease him before closing my bedroom door.

***

Within two hours after Ricky leaving, I hear our screen door open, and then a knock at my bedroom door. "Sweet pea, the kid and his mom are just about here. She called and told me they're on their way."

"Okay, let me put my shoes on. I'll be right there," I holler through my closed bedroom door. I can hear him walk back out the front door. Once I lace up my Converse, I walk out of the screen door in a jiffy.

"Is it weird that we're just standing out here waiting for them?" I ask Dad.

"No. Not for me, anyway. For you? Probably." I laugh.

"Gee, thanks. Oh! That's them!" A sleek red car pulls up and parks on the side of the road.

Wait a second...

"Dad, that's not them, it's Paxton and his mom. What is she doing here? Paxton never told me he was coming over. I wonder if something's wrong." My heart starts to skip beats.

They're almost to us when Dad says, "*Uh*, sweet pea...that is them."

"*What?*" I exclaim at the bizarre coincidence. My jaw falls open. "Did you know?"

"Nope, but I do now," he admits.

I can hear Paxton say, "Mom what's going? Why are we at Emerald's house?"

"Emerald? The girl you–" she spots me standing next to Dad by our driveway. "*Ooohhh. Emerald is Emmy. Wow.* What a coincidence!"

"You didn't know that? Then why are we here?"

They finally reach us, and I stand awkwardly fidgeting because Paxton has no idea why he was dragged to my house, but I do. He looks completely baffled, but he comes up and hugs me anyway. I want to squeal at the simple gesture.

The Art of Moving On

"Do you have any idea what's going on?" He asks, and I just smile at him nervously. I look over to Dad and Maria who are both staring at us. Well, they're actually staring at Paxton. I turn to look back at him. "What's happening?"

"*Surprise!*" Maria yells. Dad and I follow suit. She runs to the El Camino and holds her arms up to it like she's one of those models on the Price is Right. Paxton tilts his head and furrows his brow. He's still confused, and it's adorable. "It's your new car!" His eyes grow as big as saucers.

"Are you serious?" He looks around at all of us and we nod. A smile slowly spreads across his face until he's beaming.

"Go look at it!" I push his arm.

"*Oh my god! Oh. My. God.*" He walks to it and Dad walks behind him. Paxton opens the car door and looks at Dad. Dad drops the keys in Paxton's hands. He squeezes them so tight that I can see his knuckles turn white from the bottom of my porch. He abandons the open car door and attacks Maria with a hug. He lifts her off the ground and sways her back and forth. She's through the roof excited, as much as Paxton. Their excitement is radiating all the way to Dad and me. I look at him, and we're both smiling to the point of giddiness. Four stunningly splendiferous people. That's right. *Splendiferous.*

"Happy eighteenth birthday, my beautiful son." My face turns into a look of horror and gets frozen there.

Oh shit. It's his birthday.

"My birthday's not until the end of the week!"

Phew.

The Art of Moving On

All my tension eases. *Thank God.* I have a few days to figure out what to get him. It's interesting how badly I want to get into Paxton's pants, yet I don't even know when his birthday is. Our relationship couldn't be more opposite than Dan and mine's, but I'm grateful for that.

Paxton is now sitting inside the car checking out all its glorious interior features. I know they're glorious, because when it comes to cars, Dad either goes big or goes home. "I have no words at how amazing this is and how much I love it. Thank you, Mr. Evans-Green!"

"You can call me Roger, son." They shake hands.

"Thank you, Roger. I promise to take good care of it."

"I only care that you take good care of my daughter," Dad replies sternly with a firm nod.

Aaand it gets awkward.

I haven't had the chance to tell Paxton that I'm all in too. Paxton only stumbles for a second.

"I absolutely will." He shoots a look at me that can only be described as vulnerable. I bite my bottom lip and smile. I wink at him and he grins. Dad notices.

"Oh shoot. She hasn't told you yet. I forgot. Just pretend like–"

"*Dad*, stop!" I beg him, shaking my head but also grinning. He takes the hint.

"Maria, would like to come in for a minute to fill out the rest of this paperwork? Can I offer you a drink? Tea, lemonade, water?" Dad asks. The twinkle in his eye when he looks at her doesn't escape me. I'm going to have to talk to him about that later. If he's been talking to her all this time then he knows that she's not married...which reminds

The Art of Moving On

me that there's so much about Paxton and his family that's still a mystery to me. I intend on learning every single detail that he's willing to share.

I mosey on over to Paxton who is leaning against the car with his hands in his pockets. He's wearing jeans and a blue flannel shirt that darkens his green eyes. He gives me a smoldering look, and it's enough to make me go weak in the knees. I grin shyly at him. "So…"

"So…" he counters, nudging his shoe against mine. My cheeks hurt from smiling so much. "Did you know about the car this whole time?"

"No! I had no idea. Crazy, huh?" He nods with a smile. A moment of silent passes while I figure out how to say what I want to say to him. I was planning on having more time to gather all my thoughts into one coherent and romantic speech to sweep him off his feet. "Paxton…"

"Yeah?"

I decide to stall on words because he looks too damn cute for me not to kiss right now. I wrap my arms around his neck and pull him down to me. I plant my lips against his with as much sultry and seductive flare as I possibly can. By the way he breathes into me I can tell it's working. Before either of us gets carried away, I tear myself away. "I meant that," I tell him about our kiss. "Can we be together? Like *together* together?"

His eyebrows raise and a devilish, suggestive grin paints his face. "Like *together* together?" I laugh and sense the heat rising to my face.

I laugh at his stupid, dirty question. "Get your head out of the gutter!" I whack his arm playfully and he laughs. "I mean, can we date exclusively? Will you be my boyfriend?"

The Art of Moving On

"I think I would like that. Very very much. Even more than I like this car."

I bite the corner of my mouth. He takes me in from head to toe and meets my eyes brazenly. My entire body screams for him to touch me. "And also maybe *together together.*" I smile as bright as the sun.

"You want to swab my deck, pirate?" He teases.

"Ha-Ha. Real cute. So…pick me up at six tonight in your sexy new car?" The sexual tension floating between us could be cut with a knife.

"Make it five. *Aaand* my mom works the night shift at the hospital tonight. Wink, wink, nudge, nudge."

I fall into a fit of giggles.

"Yeah, I got it. Loud and clear. Take it easy with those hormones, huh? How about we just see how the night goes. Is your mom a nurse or something?"

"Fair enough and yes." He sneaks me a sweet kiss on the mouth and then one on the nose before our parents come back out.

"Let me know if you ever need anything else," Dad kindly tells Maria as they walk out the door…both smiling.

"Thanks again, Roger. It's been a real pleasure. I hope to hear from you again." They shake hands and turn toward us. Before it gets awkward I speak.

"All right, I'll see you in a few hours, Paxton. Good to see you again, Maria."

"You too, Emmy." She comes and gives me a hug. I find it bitter-sweet that she doesn't smell like Mom. Her scent smells more like citrus and amber; whereas Mom always smelled of lavender. My heart flops and doesn't know what to feel.

The Art of Moving On

We exchange final goodbyes, and Dad and I walk into the house. We just stare at each other like...*wow, that just happened.*

"That was her," I inform him. "Maria. She's the one that reminded me so much of Mom that I cried."

"*That was her?*" He asks, surprised. "She's the one that *I* told *you* about that reminded me of Mom."

"This entire thing is really strange," I admit, bluntly.

"Yes, it is. So, are you officially dating Paxton?"

"Yes," I announce proudly. "I am."

"I'm happy for you, sweet pea. He seems like a good kid. His mom did a great job raising him."

"Just like you did a great job raising me."

He slings his arm around me and pulls me in. "Thanks. I had the best help anybody could ever ask for for most of it." His comment makes both of our eyes water. I know him and Mom both raised me, but I have to give him buckets of credit. Dad raising a twelve year old all by himself had to be the hardest curve ball that life threw at him. He knocked that ball way out of the park. I couldn't ask for a more amazing dad.

"Don't forget the Paxton rule."

***

I waste zero time as Paxton and I arrive at his house after he took me out to dinner and a movie. As soon as he unlocks the door and we walk in, I kick the door closed with my foot and pounce on him. He's shocked for a second but is quick to wrap his arms around

The Art of Moving On

me, bringing me close to him. His hand moves to the back of my neck and into my hair. I start at the bottom to unbutton his blue flannel shirt. As soon as I get his shirt part way undone I slip my hands over to his sides. He grabs my hands and pulls apart from our kiss.

"Sorry. Are my hands cold?" I ask breathily.

"No, it's not that," He quips. "Bedroom," is all he says. I nod my head in agreement. He grabs my hand and leads me to his charming bedroom, running up the stairs like a couple of—well, like a couple of horny teenagers.

"I love your room." I don't get the chance to say anything else because now it's his turn to pounce on me. He backs me up against the closed door and starts kissing me. His fingertips grab the bottom hem of my simple black dress. He lifts it a little and then looks into my eyes. He finds the answer in my playful eyes and lifts the dress over my head in one swoop. He takes a deep breath and places his forehead gently against mine.

"I really hope you believe me when I tell you that you're beautiful." His words make every nerve in my body scream.

I don't know the exact time, place, or moment when I first trusted Paxton, but I think I *always* have trusted him to some degree. In the last three years, he's always been there. For many different, weird, random moments, he was just always there. I don't remember a time in high school when I *didn't* know him, when he wasn't a part of my life in some bizarre way.

"What are you thinking?" He whispers, his face still inches from mine.

"Do you trust me?" I look up into his glowing eyes.

The Art of Moving On

"Probably more than I should, pirate." That look of deviance is back in his eyes, and now mine are filling as well. He walks me backwards until I hit the edge of his bed, our eyes daring the other to make the next move. I decide to and in a split second I finish unbuttoning his shirt and am eagerly yanking it down his shoulders. I like undressing him, something Dan would never let me do. Everything was always concise and repetitive with Dan. It had to be the same way every time. He is neurotic like that.

"I like taking your clothes off." I reach for his jeans and begin with the button and the zipper. His eyes grow wide. I can hear him swallow hard.

"I like it, too. *A lot.*" I start to kneel to try to yank down his jeans not so gracefully. I feel Paxton's warm hands on my shoulders immediately and he pulls me back up on my feet. "You don't have to do that, Emmy."

"I want to." I don't leave any more time for discussion because I don't want to waste time with him. He stops me again before I can get his pants down.

"Em, let's just...kiss for a while." His hesitation is obvious, like he doesn't want to pressure me into doing anything. If he's rejecting me right now I will die of embarrassment and probably lose my self-confidence forever.

"Um, okay, if that's what you want. Things are really different with you, Paxton, and I like it. I don't feel like pressured or anything if that's what you're worried about it." He nods and looks into my eyes as if he sees the world in them. He pulls me up so I'm standing in front of him again.

He kisses my fingers before letting them go. He starts kissing me intently and after a few moments he swiftly unclips my bra.

Okay, he's clearly *had practice doing that.*

The Art of Moving On

I'm shocked for a second at how quickly he did it. He notices me tense up slightly. "Oh god, I'm sorry, Emmy. I should've asked if that was okay," he quickly spews out his words. He immediately reaches back to re-hook my bra, and I let him.

"No, no, it's okay, I promise. It just surprised me at how quickly you undid it," I explain. "I'll never do anything I don't want to do, okay? Trust me."

He nods and kisses my forehead, cheek, and then the corner of my mouth. His hands venture to my lower back, and then he squeezes my butt. I squeal. "I've dreamed about doing that every single night since the first time I met you."

I laugh loudly at the thought, because the first time Paxton and I saw each other was while we were taking our placement exams before freshman year. Now that I think about it…after our bathroom break, I came back and there was a grape Jolly Rancher on my desk. I can't believe I forgot about that. My eyes would stare at the crinkles in the wrapper every time I needed to think of an answer.

"Yes, I left the candy on your desk and yes, I had a hard-on the entire time. I was fourteen, and you were the most beautiful human I had ever seen," he admits, reading my mind. I laugh and blush. "I did horrible on the test because I couldn't stop staring at you. I had to switch into Honors and AP classes half way through freshman year because the regular classes were too easy. Everyone was really confused as to why my exam scores were so low." I laugh and lean my forehead on his chest.

Once we both stop laughing he says, "Hey, come here." He leads me to lie on his bed and puts a pillow under my head. He wraps around me like a warm blanket.

"I've wanted you since the first time I laid eyes on you, Emerald Evans-Green." He kisses my shoulder. His words…they mend every crack, every split, every hole of my

The Art of Moving On

heart and fill every open spot, every nook and cranny, and every area of my heart that was once void or unknown. I wiggle around so I can face him.

"Everything with you, Paxton—absolutely everything—is different and new in a way I never knew existed. It's unimaginable. I didn't know what I was missing." We intertwine our fingers together between us. Paxton puts our hands to his mouth and begins nibbling at the twisted rope we've created. It makes me smile.

"Emerald…I've never had sex," he mumbles, looking down at our hands. My eyebrows rise slightly.

"Oh…um…" I stammer, taken aback by his blunt confession.

"Yeah, I've never had sex." He's wearing a sheepish grin.

"Why?" I ask him sincerely. "I mean you've been with other girls…"

"Yeah but after it got to a certain point I would have to stop. It didn't feel right with any of them. Maybe it's because they weren't you. I really was waiting for you. That's no bullshit." I look down and feel heat rising on my cheeks. He lifts my chin forcing me to look up at him, and I can't help but swoon.

"Maybe I am the right person," I say shyly, unable to wipe the smile from my face.

"I think so but there's really only one way to find out…"

I smile brightly and he chuckles.

"And what would you have done if I Dan and I never broke up?"

"I'd probably die a virgin."

I laugh loudly until tears come out of my eyes. I beam at him, and move my hand to his neck to play with the shorter hairs. I look into his green eyes. "Well, I'll be here whenever you're ready so you don't have to die a virgin."

"Good because it's probably going to be soon. Like right now," he jokes, rolling on top of me. I giggle and toss my head back.

"*Nooo*. It can't be now. It should be special." I playfully push him off.

"It *will* be special," he insists, kissing my nose. I nuzzle into his chest and his arms wrap around me. All my thoughts drift away, and his comforting smell relaxes me. There's no place else in the world that I would rather be right now.

After dozing off for a while, I force myself to get up.

"I have to go," I tell him. "I'm tired."

He groans. "*Boooo*."

"I know, I know but…I'd really like to take one last spin in your sexy new car."

"Now you're talkin'!" He jumps up and pats my butt playfully. "Up and at 'em, pirate," he shouts, already pulling his shirt on. I start to get up. "I have another date *wiiiith* …"

Just when my heart stops, thinking he's telling me he has a date with another girl, I realize he's struggling with what to name his car. My heart starts to beat again.

"What about Shonda? Oh, what about Ross? That way I'll be driving Betsy–"

"And I'll be driving Ross," he finishes my sentence before blowing out a laugh. He tackles me back to the bed and kisses me. I giggle. "That was so geeky. And Sexy. And I know that broad could sew damn well," he adds. "But it has to be a girls name.

The Art of Moving On

Ross sounds like a boy's name." I roll my eyes dramatically. "What about Selena? Since she's kind of a Latino car. It'll be like a tribute to Selena."

I laugh. "What do you know about Selena?" I ask, giving him the side eye.

"I know plenty," he states confidently, crossing his arms in front of his chest.

"Oh, yeah? Like what?" I ask with a smile plastered across my face. I haven't been able to stop smiling all night.

"I know *thaaat*…she was a singer that got killed by the president of her fan club."

I laugh knowing that's probably the extent of his knowledge. "Okay, okay. Fair enough."

He smiles smugly. I flatten down my dress and comb my hands through my hair so it doesn't look like I just went through a romp in the woods. Or a romp in a bed.

"All right, pirate, let's motor."

"Motor?"

"Yeah, I'm bringing it back."

"What? No. You can't do that. I'm bringing it back," I say territorially.

"Not if I bring it back first." We leave his room as he shuts the lights off.

"You wouldn't," I argue, walking down the stairs behind him.

"Last person to the car is a rotten egg." He takes off before me. I yell and run out after him. He makes it to the driver's side door and proclaims, "Beat you, Em!"

"*Maybe*…but you left your front door open." A slow evil grin grows on my lips.

"You play dirty." He shakes his head at me and starts to walk back to lock his front door.

"You know you like it," I call out to him. He looks over his shoulder and winks.

The Art of Moving On

When we get to my house, Paxton walks me to my door. He tells my goodnight and a gives me a respectably sweet kiss. He shoves something in my hand then walks back to Selena. Once I watch him pull away I open my hand. It's a grape Jolly Rancher.

Chapter 18

"No."

"Please?" he whines.

"No," I respond firmly.

"Please, querida."

"No," I reply for the tenth time. "You have to do this on your own. I want to be there, but I just don't think it's a good idea if I'm there. It's a family thing, and I don't think it will go very well if you tell them while I'm there. They'll probably ask me to leave, and it will be even more awkward."

Ricky's decided to come out to his family, and is determined to have me there when he does it.

The Art of Moving On

"I had such a freeing feeling after I told you. My spirit was uplifted or something — it probably sounds stupid but it's true. I haven't thought about when or how to tell them I just feel like I have a rock in my gut that gets heavier and drags me down whenever I'm home. My dad is going to kick me out of the house. It's going to get ugly."

"You can always stay here," I offer.

He's spent weeks trying to sneak around in order to spend time with Eli. They begged Paxton and I for the four of us to all go out on Friday night so that they can spend time together under the guise that we're all just hanging out in a group. Of course we are going to agree to the shindig, but we, too, hate that they can't be themselves out in the open. We can't fix all of their problems, but we will both help them when we can. We've been trying to be as supportive and helpful as possible. But this request crosses my line. It reeks of bad idea. No, *horrible* idea.

"Thanks, querida." He looks sadly down at his hands on his lap. We're at my house sitting on the sofa taking a break from watching *Ted Talks* on Netflix. "If he doesn't kick me out of the house, then he'll probably kill me."

"He's not going to kill you, Ricky."

I don't think.

"I don't know a lot about your dad, but I highly doubt he or any of your family members are murderous," I attempt to reason with him. He stares ahead lost in a haze of doubt. He sighs in sorrow. And then I sigh in guilt—for what I refuse to do and for what I'm about to say.

"Maybe don't tell them yet? I mean, if you really think they'll kick you out of the house…or kill you. Wait until you go off to school. You'll be leaving so they can't really

The Art of Moving On

kick you out of the house. It'll be a fresh start for you. You can be an out gay man at college. It will be like a whole new life for you if you want it to be. I'm *not* saying that to deter you from telling them; I'm just throwing out another option. I *fully* support whatever decision you decide. " He gives me a small nod, thinking it over. "You also don't have to decide right this second."

He sighs heavily again. His brows are furrowed, and I know he's really taking in what I said. "I'll think about it some more. You may be right. It's just so heavy, you know? I feel like I'm really opening up and finally becoming the person that I truly am. Going home and having to stifle that has been destroying me, Emmy. Now that I've had this taste and experience of being free it hurts even more to go home than it ever has in the past." He glances at me and sees the pools in my eyes. I can't help it. My heart breaks for him. When he hurts, I hurt. I nod and sigh. Again.

"I'll be here for you either way, but I don't think it's a good idea that I'm there when you tell them. I'm sorry, Ricky. I really really am. It's not because I don't want to be there for you. It's because it really is a family thing and your parents will probably ask me to leave. I know if you absolutely want to do this that you are strong enough and capable of handling this situation. I know you, Ricky. You've tackled every obstacle and busted your ass for the last handful of years to get into Mount St. Mary's and to get a scholarship for college. You are a badass, Ricky Rodriguez. And hey, if you really want, I can wait in my car outside of your house while you tell them and if you need to make a quick getaway I'll be ready. I'll be your getaway driver." I flash him what I hope is a smile, but the tears trickle down subtly.

The Art of Moving On

"Thanks, Em." I scoot over on the sofa and wrap my arms around him. He rests his head on my shoulder and attempts to hold back his own tears. We break apart, and because this conversation has turned into a sigh fest we both sigh at the same time.

"Just be careful if you keep sneaking around with Eli alone. If someone finds out it could really blow up in your face and Eli's. Have you talked to Eli about coming out to your parents?"

"Yeah, I have. He said he'll support the decision if it's what I really want. He really doesn't want me to come out at school though. That part is okay with me. We're almost out of here, and I've made it this long without officially coming out of the closet at school. I wouldn't want to jeopardize anything on Eli's end either. I'm pretty sure everyone at school already knows I'm gay which is why we have to be even more careful about us being seen together. *Ay!* Why does life have to be so complicated, Emmy?" He groans and plants his face down in the cushion that separates us.

"We need ice cream and more intellectual, inspirational speeches." He drags himself back up and leans his head on the back sofa cushion like a sad puppy.

"I couldn't agree more. I couldn't be more thankful to have a best friend on the same wavelength as me." I smile brightly at him. I slide down the sofa and we give each other another big swaying hug.

I get up and make my way to the kitchen leaving him with his thoughts for a few minutes. He certainly has a lot to consider.

Ricky's hands are over his face like he's saying a silent prayer for guidance and strength. When he opens his eyes there's a bowl of ice cream with whipped cream right in front of his face. He looks up at me and we both grin. Ice cream helps everything.

The Art of Moving On

"You're the best, querida. If Paxton ever hurts you, I'll kill him."

***

School seems like a whole new place now that Paxton and I are officially together. Aside from people sneaking glances, anyway. Since I've talked to Dan, there is no more sauntering to classes, no more dodging him and Alexis, no more moping in the hallway, no more panic attacks, no more angry feelings toward Dan, no more animosity, and no more Ricky having to deal with a mess of a best friend.

It's Friday and Paxton's birthday. He picked me up for school this morning and I surprised him in the car with a cream filled donut with a candle in it. I surprised him even more once we got to school and he opened his present. His eyes illuminate.

"Selena's greatest hits?!" He yells, even though I'm right next to him in the car. I laugh. He rips open the CD like it's Christmas morning and pops it in the CD player. The beat begins and he starts dancing. I laugh, ecstatic that he's ecstatic. I wish I could've gotten him more, but time was limited, and I had my work cut out for me trying to figure out this Winter Formal situation. He unbuckles my seatbelt, grabs me and pulls me to him. I've decided that it is really nice not having bucket seats. He kisses me playfully. For once, I don't care at all if I'm late to class.

There's hooting, and howling, and slapping of the car's hood. We pull apart to find Paxton's soccer buddies, including Eli, in front of the car ogling and cheering at us. My cheeks burn like fire. They all continue to walk and give us a hard time. "Ingrates," he tells me. "The whole lot of them." I smile and give him a small kiss.

The Art of Moving On

"Happy birthday."

"Thank you. I love my CD."

"Good."

He climbs out of the car and walks around to my side to help me with my stuff. I have a big bag of supplies. I told Paxton that it's stuff for an art project for Mrs. Timlin's class, but it's really supplies for me to ask him, Ricky and Eli to the dance. I've got it all planned out and am asking all three of them together after school today.

***

As soon as the bell rings at the end of the day, I head to the art room to pick up my supplies. I've already told Ricky, Eli and Paxton to meet my outside the SC office at 4:30. I told Ricky that I need the office because I wanted to use it to ask Paxton to the dance. He offered to help, but I planned to set it up when I knew he would have his mentor meeting with the school counselor to discuss applications for colleges. In lieu of helping me, I told him he could come watch while I ask Paxton. Ricky begged me to tell him how I was going to ask him, but I refused to give anything away.

I told Paxton that I was decorating the office for Christmas to really get everyone into the holiday spirit now that we're getting down to the due date for all Santa Spirit donations. It's halfway true because I plan on leaving up some of the decorations I use today. He asked if he could help but I lied and told him the other members were helping me. I asked him to meet me outside the office so we can drive home together.

The Art of Moving On

I slipped a note in Eli's locker to meet me outside the office to talk to him about something. I left it vague and knew that he would think it had something to do with Ricky or Paxton. I hope he didn't mention anything to either of them.

I sneak my way from the art room down to the office and immediately get to work. I have fishing line tied to numerous white, sparkling plastic snowflakes and white string holiday lights that hang down like icicles. I begin hanging them from the ceiling using tape and a stepladder that I schlepped down from the art room.

After I hang all of the lights and snowflakes, I reposition the room. The large rectangle table remains in the center of the room with all the rolling chairs tightly tucked in. I've wheeled the white board in between the table and the back of the room. I've stacked Santa Spirit presents behind the white board and stacked a particular stack that I could hide behind. I tape a sign on the outside of the door telling the boys to come in.

At four-thirty I have everything in place and am hiding behind the stack of presents. The room is shimmering with lights and snowflakes. A few moments later I can hear the boys hesitantly open the door.

"I'm really confused about what's happening right now," Ricky says while walking in.

"Check out the board," I hear Eli instruct them.

"'No one snowflake is the same. Look at the snowflakes to discover a hidden message,'" Paxton reads the board.

"*Ay dios mio.* What is she doing?" I can tell by the tone of his voice that Ricky already has an idea of what's going on. He knows me too well.

The Art of Moving On

"This is perfect," Paxton says with excitement in his voice. I have to keep myself from squealing. My heart is hammering, and I have so much adrenaline.

"What on earth is going on, you guys?" Eli asks.

"We have to look at the snowflakes," Ricky can barely say before Paxton starts reading. I knew he would love figuring something out like this even though it's not hard.

"'Will.' The first one says 'will.'"

"This one is blank."

"You," Eli reads, jumping on Ricky's words.

"'Yes.' 'Will you yes?'" Ricky questions. "That makes no sense. We have the order wrong. What's that one say?"

"This one's blank too," Paxton replies. "Oh! This one says, 'All three of you.'"

"Okay… 'Will you, yes, all three of you,'" Eli says. "This one says 'go with.'"

"Ay, ay, ay, chica está loca! This one says, 'Me to.'" It takes everything in me not to bust out laughing.

"This one's blank," Eli says. "Quit grinning like a fool, Pax, and read what it says." I can tell Eli is smiling from the sound of his voice, and I know Ricky well enough to know that he's smiling, despite himself.

"It says, 'Winter formal.'" I pop out from behind the gifts and the white board.

"Will you guys be my date to Winter formal?" I shyly ask. I know they'll all say yes but my cheeks are pink anyway. Before I know what's happening, Paxton picks me up and swings me around.

"Yes." He starts kissing me little kisses all over my face, making me giggle.

"Even."

The Art of Moving On

Kiss.

"If."

Kiss.

"I have to."

Kiss.

"Share you."

Kiss.

"With these guys."

He kisses me full on the lips. My heart starts hammering again, my knees go weak, and my body starts craving him. I grab him around the shoulders, and he pulls me into a tight hug. Ricky and Eli cough loudly. We pull apart and my face flushes even more.

"Um, excuse me. We haven't given our answers yet," Ricky reminds me.

"Sorry," I say meekly. I bite my bottom lip and raise my eyebrows in anticipation of their answers. Ricky and Eli look at each other, smile lovingly, and nod. The short moment between them seemed small, but it interestingly intimate at the same time. It pulls my heart strings to know that Ricky has found someone special.

"Yes," Eli answers, smiling. "Thank you, Emmy."

"Of course we'll go with you, querida." He holds his arms out for a hug.

"Group hug," Eli announces, grinning. They come to us and wrap their arms around me.

"Thanks, guys. I promise we're going to have fun."

The Art of Moving On

"Now I have to figure out what to wear," Ricky says, already stressing out. Eli laughs.

"Now if you'll excuse us, gentlemen. Emerald and I need to go so she can give me her *other* birthday present," he says suggestively.

"*HA!* You wish! Get your head out of the gutter," I say playfully.

"You guys are gross. I have to go anyway." Ricky turns to Eli. "I'll text you later?"

"Sounds good." We all walk out the door and say goodbye. Paxton grabs my arms and then twists in front of me. He uses my arms to pull me up on his back. I wrap my legs around him like I did that night when I drank too much. He gives me a piggy-back ride out to the El Camino so he can drive me home.

"So, about that birthday present," I say in his ear. "You'll get it....eventually." I kiss below his ear. He lets out a groan.

"Everything about you drives me crazy in the best possible way. You know, we don't have to do it on a set schedule if you don't want to. I mean, I want to do it. Like right now. But you're in charge. I want you to be comfortable, and we can do it when you want to," he tells me.

"You melt my heart. Everything feels so much better when we're together."

"I couldn't agree more which is why we're going to listen to Selena all the way to my house. *Aaand* I hope you don't have plans Sunday night because you and your dad are coming over for my birthday dinner with me and my mom."

"What? Really?" I squeeze my arms and legs tighter around him.

The Art of Moving On

"Yup." He sets me down on the passenger side of Selena and opens the door for me.

"I can't believe you planned that. I should've done that," I say, starting to feel bad that I didn't think of it. I wanted to take him out to dinner but I'm saving money so I can pay for all four of us to have dinner before the dance. Dad told me he'd pay me to help him with paperwork.

"Nonsense. My mom actually worked it all out. She told me this morning."

"Oh...that was nice of her." He nods, in response. I start to think as I'm getting settled in the car. Paxton starts the car and after a few moments of silence, my brain becomes alert to this sickening feeling in the bottom of my stomach. I don't like it. I don't like it one single bit. "So, if Maria worked it all out, then that means she's been talking to my dad…"

"Yeah…"

"Do you think they've been talking? Do you think they like…" My heart pangs and my stomach drops.

"I don't know if there's anything like what you're suggesting going on. Let's not think about it right now, okay?"

I nod, but my mind is still freaking out and reeling with questions. I saw the way they looked each other at the house, and I got an uneasy feeling then too. Dad wouldn't do that. My heartbeat picks up as I feel panic wanting to settle in.

"Emmy," Paxton says firmly. "Emerald, look at me," he demands louder. He snaps me out of my impending panic, and I look at him. "Don't worry about that. Please?"

The Art of Moving On

"Uh, okay. Y–Yeah. Sorry. It's just–"

"*Ssshhh*, no more of those thoughts right now. Instead, think about how much you like kissing me. Oh! Hey! Look what I taught myself during TA period." He changes the track on the Selena CD and he starts to dance. I can't help but laugh. I was wondering why he wasn't in the library during TA period. He's such a goofball. I wouldn't have it any other way. When Selena starts singing so does Paxton.

Every.

Single.

Word.

In Spanish, right along with her voice. My mouth drops and my eyes grow.

"Oh my gosh, you did *not* learn all the words to this song!"

"I did!" he exclaims and continues singing. I laugh hysterically all the way to his house.

"Paxton, it's your birthday and somehow, you've managed to make the day extra special for me. I should be doing all this for you." He kisses my hand and looks me in the eyes.

"Don't say things like that. I love surprising you. It makes me happy and it's exactly how I want to spend my birthday. Plus, you surprised me by asking me to the dance. That was hot."

"I'm falling in love with you," I blurt out. It's seems so soon but it's true. He makes me feel so happy and so full of love. I'm letting go of timeframes, and the idea of "normal" and everything that people say about relationships, and just going with how I feel right now. And right now, I'm pretty much enamored with him. He holds the sides of

The Art of Moving On

my face. He swallows hard, my heart is about jump out of my chest in anticipation. The butterflies in my stomach are flittering around as if my tummy was their garden.

"Those words are the best gift I could ever ask for. I'm pretty sure it was love at first sight for me." He kisses me softly and slowly. I'm so glad I'm sitting down because I'm certain my legs would give out on me from swooning.

"Paxton Wright," I say when we pull apart. "You make me feel like the luckiest girl in the world."

"Good. You are," he jokes.

***

"It's pretty crazy that we both have single parents—you and your mom and my dad and me, and we're both the only child," I casually bring up as Paxton and I eat birthday cupcakes in the breakfast nook at his house.

Paxton looks at me with a raised eyebrow—a warning look. He's getting better at reading me, and it's a little unnerving.

"I'm not saying anything about our parents…liking each other." I cringe, and he smirks. "I'm just saying it's interesting that we're the only child to single parents," I state harmlessly. Well, not that harmlessly. I've been trying to think about other things for the last hour or so, but my mind is being weighed down. His smirk fades, and he looks down as he swallows a bite of his strawberry birthday cake.

"What's wrong?" My heartbeat picks up wondering if he saw our parents doing anything other than talking. I'll die if that's the case. Dad can't date, and he especially

The Art of Moving On

can't date my boyfriend's mom. He just *can't*. Paxton's head stays down and bites the corner of his mouth. *Oh god.* "Paxton, you better tell me what's going on right now or I'm going to flip out." He looks up at me alarmed that I might leave. And if he doesn't spill the beans I just might have to storm out of here dramatically. The idea of our parents—of *Dad*—dating is really no laughing matter to me, and if he knows something that I don't then we're about to have a really big first fight as a couple. I cross my arms and give him an icy glare. He sets his fork down on his plate.

"You know when you asked if my dad was around?" He looks out the window with a frown.

"Yeah…" I respond suspiciously.

"Well, it's true he's not around. He lives in Seattle." He pauses, and I realize that I really don't know that much about Paxton. I did wonder about his dad, but he shut down when I asked so I never pushed it. I know Paxton didn't grow up around here, but I never even thought to ask him where he used to live. I'm a rotten girlfriend. *Rotten, rotten, rotten.* My insecurity begins to grow as does my frown. "Hey." He grabs my hand. "What's wrong?" I look up at him and shake my head.

"Um, nothing. Sorry. What were you saying about your dad?" His expression darkens again and he sighs.

"He lives in Seattle with his wife and three kids," he finally spits out. I hate to admit it, but I'm relieved that what he is saying has nothing to do with Dad and Maria. I instantly feel like a jerk when I notice that his arms are crossed and shooting a deathly glare at some pine tree out the window. He's obviously very unhappy about this, but I don't know how to respond. I decide to use the same tactic he used on me, and I grab his

The Art of Moving On

hand. He looks down at our hands and continues to talk. "He cheated on my mom so they got divorced, and my mom and I moved from Seattle to Portland which is where I went to middle school before we moved here the summer before high school. My dad has two stepdaughters and a son with his new wife. Amber is twelve, Annie is ten, and AJ, is seven." I quickly do the math in my head. "I know what you're doing and yes, she got pregnant while he was still married to my mom."

I frown and look down at my half eaten cake. "Do you ever see them?" I ask even though I'm afraid to.

"I used to have to go back and spend summers with them but when I got to high school I told him I didn't want to go anymore, and he didn't even care. I haven't seen him since I moved here four years ago."

Ouch.

"My mom got a position at the hospital in Portland right away, and then when I was about to finish middle school a position opened up at the hospital here and she got the job. She grew up here," he explains, his expression softening making it clear how much he loves Maria. I nod.

"I remember her telling me that when I first met her at the football game."

"So, there it is. I'm not an only child." He looks down as if he feels guilty for not telling me sooner.

"Thanks for trusting me enough to tell me that." I stand up and move to his side of the nook. I put my knee on the seat and then try to scoot myself on top of his lap squeezing myself between his chest…except I don't fit and let out an, "*oof*" and end up with my back to him in a strange twisted position between the back of the seat and the

The Art of Moving On

table. My leg is scrunched up and Paxton's arm is awkwardly draped around me. He chuckles and my cheeks turn pink. I try to maneuver back to my feet but Paxton doesn't let go. I sigh. "I gained a few pounds after Dan broke up with me," I sheepishly admit. He kisses my head and starts to help me to my feet.

"Well, don't lose it because you are absolutely perfect."

Yup. Best. Boyfriend. Ever.

I squirm and finally get back on my feet, and he slides out of the booth seat. "Come on, let's go upstairs." He swats my butt, and my eyes go wide as I squeal.

"Where did *that* come from?" I ask smiling. He grins and lifts his shoulders up feigning a guilty look.

"What can I say? I like your butt." I turn away and bite the massive smile that's about to show. "Now let's go," he tells me as he grabs my hand and pulls me into a faster walk to the stairs. "We have some kissing and some heavy petting to do before my mom gets home." I burst out laughing and he joins in.

Chapter 19

It's late Sunday afternoon, and I'm setting lunch on the table for Dad and myself. I've been nervous all day after telling myself that I *will* ask him before tonight's birthday dinner for Paxton about him and Maria. He's never dated anyone since Mom died and honestly, I might have an anxiety attack right now if he tells me he likes Maria. The thought makes me nauseous every time I think about it. Dad turns off the TV and joins me at the table.

"Thanks for cooking lunch. You would not believe the amount of paperwork I have for us to do. Todd is great at working on the cars, but he stinks at paperwork. I have a lot to catch up on," he shares, as he puts some salad on his plate. I nod silently and stare down at my chicken sandwich. We both start eating silently until he looks up at me suspicious. "Sweet pea, what's wrong?" He asks like he's not sure he wants to know the answer. I gulp down a bite of food.

"Um," I start and then take a drink of water. Anything to prolong my questions for him. "Um. So. I noticed that maybe, you know, that um, maybe you and Maria m-maybe, uh, like—"

"Okay, sweet pea, I know what you're going to ask me." He sets down his sandwich and wipes his mouth.

Oh god. Time for serious talk.

"It's okay, Emerald, I knew we were going to have to talk about this eventually so it's okay. You can look at me." I reluctantly look at him. He takes a deep breath. "I have been thinking about asking Maria out. Possibly tonight, actually." My body completely deflates, and I sink down in my chair. "I said I've been thinking about it, but I haven't done it. I know there's a lot to consider in this situation. I'm not just Roger Evans-Green, a person. I'm Roger Evans-Green, Emerald's father. I take that role seriously, and I take you into consideration with every choice I have ever made for the last seventeen years, okay?"

I nod my head and feel my eyes start to pool. My mind is racing in a million different directions. My stomach is doing flips sloshing around acid causing me physical pain. My heart that was mended feels like it's breaking all over again but in an entirely different way...a way I didn't know hearts could break. "What about Mom?" I ask, my chin quivering and my throat swelling. I blink and the tears begin to cascade quickly down my cheeks.

The Art of Moving On

"Emerald, I think about your mom every. Single. Day. And I have since the moment I laid eyes on her years ago, and I will still think about her every single day for the rest of my life. I will never stop loving her." I look up at him and his eyes are watery now too. "Not a day goes by that I don't feel her presence. When Maria came to me at the shop about Paxton's car, I had a very strong feeling about her, and I think it went beyond her having a couple of features in common with your mom. I felt a strong pull to her."

I'm full on sobbing loudly now and somehow an "*oh god*" manages to escape my mouth. He ignores my ugly crying and continues to talk. "I want to ask her out. It's been six years since your mom passed away. Don't you think I deserve to continue to live my life trying to find happiness?"

I let out a wail and attempt to use the back of my hands to wipe my eyes. My chest is tightening and my lungs starting to burn. I can't believe he's making me feel guilty right now. He sighs in frustration.

"Emmy, I know this is weird for you. I get that. But you're verging on the edge of ridiculous right now. You need to calm down, or you're going to hyperventilate. You're not twelve anymore. You should not be acting this way. I haven't even told you what Maria and I discussed about how a possible relationship would affect your and Paxton's relationship."

I instantly stop sobbing and inhale a massive breath of air. I glare at him.

"What do you mean what you and Maria discussed? I thought you said you hadn't asked her out yet." My hands bunch up into fists.

"I haven't asked her out, but I have told her how I feel. I told her I had to take you into consideration, and that she and I need to take into consideration your and Paxton's

The Art of Moving On

relationship. Honestly, I thought you would be more level headed about this. I can't

believe you haven't even thought about my happiness."

Again *with the guilt!*

"*Aaaggghhh!*" I growl. I jump up quickly, sending my chair backwards to slam on

the floor. I grab my car keys on the key hook by the front door and bolt out of the house

not caring about my wallet or my cell phone.

"Emerald! Get back here! Where are you doing?! We have dinner with them

tonight!" He yells after me.

I ignore him. I've never moved so fast in my entire life. I'm backing out of the

driveway and am on the street before Dad can even catch up to me. I take off down the

street without looking back.

Now what?

***

"Emmy!" Ricky's mom, Eliana, screams my name and roughly pulls me through the

front door into her arms. I sob into her shoulder, and she holds me so tight I can barely

breathe but it feels so perfect. She sways me, and I see Ricky out of the corner of my eyes

coming out of his room upstairs. He sees my splotchy, runny-nosed face and takes the

stairs down two at a time.

"What's wrong?" He shouts at me, sounding just like Eliana. He wraps his arms

around both of us. I start hiccuping. "Take deep breaths. It's going to be okay," He

instructs me even though he doesn't know what's happened yet. I start taking deep

The Art of Moving On

breaths as much as I can between hiccups. Each hiccup hurts worse than the one before. "Mamá we're going to go upstairs." Ricky has to physically remove Eliana's hands from the grasp she has on me. She nods and lets go of me completely. I instantly get cold and shiver.

"Emmy, come down later, and I can heat up some food for you." She kisses my head and gives me one last squeeze before she trots back to the kitchen.

He looks at me and we both take a deep breath at the same time. He nods his head toward the stairs and I follow him up. Once we're behind the security of his bedroom door I plop face down on his firm bed. It's harder than I expect and I groan from the sting from my chest and stomach.

"Querida, tell me what's going on." He sits in his desk chair and reaches over to shake my foot. "Please don't suffocate yourself in my pillow." He tries to lighten the mood, but I turn over and keep my limbs dangling off the side of the bed like a dead person's would. I catch him making a sour face, noticing my morbidity without me having to say it.

"Dad wants t-to ask out M-Maria." He stares blankly at me for a few seconds to figure out the significance of what I just said before I answer his question. "P-Paxton's mom." His eyebrows shoot upwards. My chest starts to tighten again after hearing the words out loud. It fucking *hurts*.

"Oh god," he groans, leaning over and putting his head in his hands. "Emmy, I'm so sorry. What else happened?" He asks curiously. I sit up and prop myself up and on my hands. I sniff, and my chin quivers.

The Art of Moving On

"I could tell that there might be something between them when she picked up Paxton's car, and then she organized a dinner for all of us with my dad without me knowing. They've been talking. I finally got the nerve to ask him about it today. We are supposed to go to their house for dinner tonight." I stop in fear of sobbing again. I take a deep breath, and a few tears trickle out. I can't go to dinner. I *won't*. I look at Ricky who is literally on the edge of his seat waiting for me to continue.

"And?"

I continue reluctantly. "He told me he wants to ask her out, and I flipped. He and Maria already talked about it, and he told her how he feels about her but said that he was going to talk to me before asking her out," I hastily explain. He nods his head but still looks confused.

"So, he wants to date Maria but wanted to check with you first?"

"*Ugh*, when you say it like that, Ricky, it doesn't sound so bad but it was! *Is!*" I snap at him. "He completely guilt tripped me saying, 'don't I deserve to be happy? Aren't I allowed to continue with my life? It's been six years since Mom died,'" I tell him in a voice mocking Dad's.

He raises his hands in defense.

Here it goes.

He's going to play devil's advocate. I can tell by the calm look taking over his face. I'm not sure that I'm ready to hear the voice of reason just yet. I shoot him a nasty warning glare.

"Don't. Don't you dare," I warn him with my finger pointing at him.

"Emmy."

The Art of Moving On

"No." I look away from him.

"Emerald Evans-Green, *mírame*," he demands in a deep, serious voice.

I growl and reluctantly find his eyes. He reaches over to grab my hands. I meet him half way and scoot so my feet are on the ground.

"First of all, is this about your mom, or is this about a potential relationship between your boyfriend's mom and your dad?"

My eyes immediately move down to the carpet in guilt, but even in my guilt the anger still rises. "Both. How could he do that to my mom? How could he do that to Paxton and me? We just started our relationship and now what? Our parents are going to start dating? What if they get married, Ricky? Paxton's going to my boyfriend and my stepbrother?" I shudder, even though that's not what has completely caused my meltdown. It's part of it, but only a small part. It really is about Mom.

"*Yyyeah*, that is kind of weird but Emmy, seriously, one date does not mean they're going to get married. Or even begin a romantic relationship for that matter. You should not be too concerned right now about Paxton becoming your stepbrother, and you know what? Who cares? It's not like it's incest or anything." My eyes go wide, and I lean over the bed making dramatic puking noises. Okay, maybe it is bothering me more than a little. He rolls his eyes even though he very well knows that was not the best thing to say to me right now. "I'm sorry, but I think you should just table that thought and worry about crossing that bridge *if, not when,* it ever comes. Besides, I know you, Emmy and you're easy to read, and you're level headed, and somewhere deep inside you know that you're being irrational–"

The Art of Moving On

"You're supposed to be on my side, Ricky!" I whine and complain like a child who is moments away from kicking and screaming on the floor. I'm regressing. I feel like I'm twelve years old all over again, and all I want to do is stomp my way to my bedroom, and give Dad the silent treatment for days like I used to after Mom died. I'm *furious,* and I want to stay that way.

"I am on your side. We have to talk about your mom. Why is this bothering you so much? He talked to you about it first, didn't he? He hasn't actually asked her out yet, right?"

"No, *I* brought it up. *I'm* the one that asked. God, he made me feel so guilty, Ricky. It's so unfair."

"You know what that means, right? Feeling guilty? I know you do. You're just being stubborn and refusing to admit it."

I give him a murderous glare for calling me out. He throws his hands up in surrender even though we both know he's right and I'm wrong.

Wrong, wrong, wrong.

I refuse to admit anything right now, which is why I know he's going to say what I already know out loud for me to hear.

"You only feel guilty when you know you've done something wrong. You're feeling guilty as hell because he's right, and you know it. You *do* want him to be happy. His happiness *does* matter to you. He's your dad; you love him."

I take a deep breath and prop my head on my hands. The burning in my eyes comes back, and my stomach churns as I hesitantly start to come to terms with what I've said and how I've reacted.

The Art of Moving On

"When I was younger the thought of him dating made me so sick, but after years passed that fear dissipated because he never seemed interested in seeing anyone. I quit thinking about it. The entire situation has all added up, and it's just overwhelming. He wants to date a lady that reminds me a little of my mom, and not just that, but it happens to be Paxton's mom. You know, my *boyfriend's* mom. Of all the women in all the world..." I shake my head.

"I get where you're coming from, and you're not wrong. It is overwhelming and intense." I look at him confused. "*But* you're being irrational when it comes to your dad dating, and you know it."

I slump my shoulders and pout. "What about Paxton and me?"

"It's something that needs to be figured out, for sure. You told me though that he and Maria had talked about it. Be glad that they're taking you and Paxton into consideration. Does Paxton know about any of this?" I shake my head.

"I don't know. I haven't talked to him. I don't even know what to say to him at this point. I stormed out before my dad could finish talking. I was so upset. I didn't grab my wallet or my phone."

He winces. "Emmy, you're dad is probably freaking out right now. You have to go home. I think you're making it worse by running away." I frown angrily and flick his kneecap hard. "*Ow!* Jeez. You can stay here for a while if you want but you have to call him. And you have to stop hitting me."

"I can't do it, Ricky. I can't go back, and I really can't go to dinner. I need more time. I'm still too angry."

The Art of Moving On

"Lie down and take a nap. When you wake up you can either go home or eat dinner with my family. If you stay then I'm going to come out of the closet in the middle of dinner. Ultimatum, bitch."

My jaw drops to the floor.

***

"Wake up!" Ricky yells in my ear. "Hora de la cena!"

I lift my head and attempt to rub the grogginess out of my eyes. "How long was I out?"

"Like two hours. We're about to have dinner, and my mom made enough food for you. Well, technically she always makes enough food for the entire neighborhood. So, what's it going to be? Dinner here or go home? I'm sure that your dad has had a minor heart attack by now. If you stay, I think you should call him." He's standing next to his desk in front of his door with his hands on his hips.

I sigh and rub my face with my hands. I think for a moment as he looks at me expectantly and nervously. "I don't want to go home, but I can't stay here. I promise I'll come back over if you're willing to come out anytime after today. I *promise*. But if you come out tonight—right now, I can't be here for you the way I need to be and should be. I've been gone for a few hours no with no contact with anybody so I would have to leave right after dinner. But if you're ready to come out tonight then you should."

The Art of Moving On

He nods his head and we're both silent for a few minutes while he contemplates and plays with his bottom lip, I try and get my wits together about what's going to happen when I get home. Finally, I break the silence.

"You know what? Fuck it. Let's have dinner," I announce standing up from his bed.

His head turns up from looking at the carpet and his eyebrows raise to his hairline. His lip snaps out of his fingers to make a "*blop*" sound. He takes a deep breath.

"*Ay, Dios mio.*" His breathing picks up. "*Ay, Dios mio,*" he repeats, shaking out his hands and bouncing up and down like he's trying to pump himself up. I'm getting butterflies in my own stomach just watching him. "Are you serious about this, querida?"

"Yeah, I need to get out of my head, and you've been wanting to do this for weeks now. I'm here, and I need to not think about myself. It's a win-win for both of us. If you're ready, then let's do it. You're brave, Ricky Rodriguez. You can do this. You deserve to be you wherever you are. *Especially* when you're at home." I give him a nod of encouragement and the best smile I can muster up.

"Ricky! Dinner!" A girl's voice calls from downstairs.

"*Mierda,*" he mumbles. He looks me dead in the eyes, terrified, and says, "If they kill me, you can have everything I own. Don't give shit to María though. What am I saying? She will have already stolen everything of mine, probably," he babbles.

"Ricky! Snap out of it. You can do this. Nobody is going to die," I announce confidently.

He opens the door before I can respond, and we're attacked with voices. He was definitely right about his family being loud.

The Art of Moving On

"Delfina, I told you to go call Ricardo and Emmy for dinner!"

"I did!" Delfina, Ricky's nine-year old (and youngest) sister, insists. "Míra, there they are." She tells her mom, Eliana, as we round the corner into the kitchen. Delfina points her little finger at us.

"Emmy, you and Ricardo go sit down. María will bring you a drink," Eliana tells us.

"I will?" María replies with an attitude.

"Si, tú debe," she sternly answers.

A door off the kitchen hallway shuts loudly. "Why didn't anyone call me for dinner?" Liliana, Ricky's oldest sister, asks. She appears out of the basement looking like she was sleeping. Liliana is two years older than us and is generally moody. She's strikingly beautiful with long dyed caramel colored hair that differs from the rest of the family's dark brown and black hair.

"Ugh, I did, Liliana. You just don't ever listen to anything," María whines. María is four years younger than us and is the one that gets under Ricky's skin the most.

"Whatever." Liliana rolls her eyes, and then sees Ricky and me sitting. "Hey, Emmy." Just as she sits down with us Eliana calls for her.

"Liliana, get in here and carry this bowl to the table!"

She hastily gets up and mumbles, "Do I have to do everything here?" Ricky snorts. She shoots him an icy glare. "Shut up."

As everyone brings the dishes and food plates to the table, Ricky's dad, Efraín, walks in from the other room and sits down at the head of the table. He works construction and is an intimidating man with large shoulders. I glance at Ricky who is

The Art of Moving On

looking pale. I can feel his knee under the table bouncing up and down. Now that his dad is at the table a sense of quiet has come over the room. I swallow loudly, starting to regret my decision to stay. If *I'm* nervous I can't even imagine how Ricky is feeling.

"Hola, Emmy. It's good to see you. I'm glad mi hijo has brought you for dinner," Efraín greets me. I give him an awkward half smile.

"Thank you, Mr. Rodriguez."

"Now, let's pray," he commands, holding his hands out to myself and Delfina.

We hold hands and say the Lord's Prayer. Well, they say it and I lamely sit there listening to it in Spanish. We all dig in, passing the steaming bowls and plates around. I get enough rice, beans, and chicken to feed an army.

Once we start eating I find that I slowly start to lose my appetite. I have no idea when Ricky plans on sharing his "news". I eat slowly and steal glances at Ricky who, like me, is just shoveling around food on his plate. I give him a questioning look, and he nods. He sets his fork down on his plate and takes a deep breath. I follow suit. It's game time, and I'm sick to my stomach not knowing how this is all going to turn out.

"So, I've been wanting to tell you all something for a while now..." Ricky starts. His hand finds mine underneath the table, and he starts squeezing it hard. I give it a squeeze back to encourage him to keep going. "Um, I'm–I'm..." He pauses to take a deep breath and then comes right out with it. With a surprising amount of conviction he states, "I'm gay."

Everyone's silverware drops to their plates with a chorus of "*tink*". I look down at my food. I turn my head up slightly after nobody says anything right away. Liliana is stifling a laugh and has her mouth covered. Obviously she knew. I look to the left of her

The Art of Moving On

at María who is looking at Ricky wearing a concerned expression, scared almost. She definitely already knew. Next to her is little Delfina who has no idea what's going on, because her eyes are bouncing around looking for answers. Ricky's hand releases mine just when his mom sniffs and his dad slams down a fist on the table. All five of us kids nearly jump out of our chairs.

"Tú eres un maricón, eh?" Ricky's dad menacingly accuses. Ricky looks up to the ceiling trying to not let his tears spill out. "Mírame!" Ricky turns his head down to look at his dad.

"Sí," he meekly lets out.

"Lo sabía," he says in a deep, low voice. "Mi hijo menor es un pinche maricón!" He barks out to the room then slams his palm down on the table, scaring us yet again.

"Efra, No digas esas palabrotas!" Eliana lets out as best as she can with her napkin to her nose and tears streaming steadily down her cheeks.

"Cállete, Eliana. Estás escuchando esto? Tú hijo es un jodido maricón," Efra spews out quickly and harshly at his wife. She squeezes her eyes closed and covers her mouth. His neck is so tense I can see his bulging vein from across the table. I have no idea what he's saying, but judging by his expression and the hissing, raging sound of his voice I'm guessing it's bad. Real bad. I look at Ricky, and he has just as many tears as his mom. Delfina looks terrified, María's chin is quivering and her eyes pooling, and Liliana looks bored.

"Dinner is over," Ricky's mom declares, staring at the table in front of her catatonically. "Emmy, go home querida."

The Art of Moving On

"Um–yeah, yeah, of course–um, thanks–uh, bye, everyone," I stutter out as my chair skids across the linoleum floor. As soon as I stand the girls stand up to disperse silently. "Ricardo, walk Emmy to her car."

Ricky nods his head and responds, "Sí, Mamá." She doesn't look at us as we walk past her.

As soon as we make it out the front door we both take a huge gasp of air. The tension inside was suffocating. I link elbows with him as we walk to Betsy.

"Talk to me. What's going through your head?"

"I–I don't know if I even have words," he admits, sniffing. "My dad hates me. He said some pretty messed up stuff. I shouldn't have done it in front of María and Delfina. They should not have heard what he said," he sobs loudly. I immediately wrap him in a hug. "I think I broke my mom's heart. I thought she'd be hysterical, but her heart was too shattered. I broke my mom, Emmy. I *broke* her," he confides. I squeeze him as he shakes and cries into my sweatshirt.

"Your mom loves you. You didn't break her. You could never break her. I don't think anyone could break that woman. Not even your dad. I saw the way she looked at your dad after he said all that stuff. She could have killed him just with one look. You didn't break her heart." My eyes well over as thoughts about my own mother creep back into my thoughts. I rub his back before we break apart. "Do you feel better?"

"Honestly?" He wipes under his eyes and blows out a breath. "No. I don't feel very good right now. I'm second-guessing everything, but...I think I will...feel better, I mean."

The Art of Moving On

"Good. I think you will too." After a moment we both look toward his dark tan stucco house. The front porch lights bleed out into the front yard to allow light to flood into the perfectly trimmed lawn. He looks back at me.

"I don't want to go back in there," he admits.

"I don't want to go back home either," I agree somberly. I groan. "Living life is *haaard*, Ricky," I whine. "I'll see you tomorrow at school if my dad doesn't kill me before then." I turn to open Betsy's door.

"Ha, yeah, likewise, querida. It's scary...not knowing what's going to happen."

I sigh. "You can say that again." I climb in. "I'm still angry," I randomly admit.

"I know you are, querida, I know you are."

"I'm so scared."

"So am I."

I sniff trying to keep the tears from forming again. "I love you, Ricardo Rodriguez."

"And I love you, Emerald Evans-Green."

***

My fear consumes me, and I'm pretty sure I'm going to die from it. I'm shaking as I get out of Betsy, having sat in her for a good fifteen minutes just staring at the street in front of me before I left Ricky's. Dad is going to be so mad at me.

So so so mad.

The Art of Moving On

I'll never be able to leave the house again. I'm terrified as to what is going to happen the second I walk in the house. I sulk to the front door not in any particular hurry. I'm just not ready for this to be real. Any of it. I don't want to see the look on Dad's face right now. My heart drops to my stomach for the umpteenth time today.

I cautiously open the screen door and push open the front door, my eyes glued to the ground. I look up but Dad has already jumped off the sofa and is staring at me with his mouth over his hand like he's going to be sick. His eyes are red and watery. He's been crying. I'm the worst daughter on the face of the planet. He stays and stares at me, trying to breathe through his hands that are clamping over his mouth. I look back down at the ground in utter and complete guilt. Neither of us moves for several moments. He stares at me while I stare at the carpet. Finally, he removes his hands and gasps for air.

"Emerald," comes choking out of his mouth, and before I know what's what his arms are around me so tightly that it's hard to breathe. My knees want to give out on me. "Are you okay? You can't do that to me, Emmy. We're a family. I can't lose you; do you understand? It's just me and you, so I can't lose you. Don't ever do anything like that ever again. Anything I have ever done has been done with you and your mom in mind. Please, please, please don't ever drive away like that again." I remain in his arms, waiting for the words, "disappointment," and "ashamed," to fall from his lips. He is silent and keeps me so close that my face is pressed firmly against his itchy sweater. I have to will myself to speak without him pushing me to.

"I'm sorry, Dad," I croak. My chin starts quivering. I know I'm about to lose it even though my cheeks are raw, and I'm physically and emotionally exhausted. He grabs

The Art of Moving On

my shoulders and pushes me away with his hands firmly grasping my shoulders. He bends down to look me in the eyes.

"I love you. Are you looking at me?" I move my eyes back to his intense ones. He moves his grasp from my shoulders to either side of my face so he's tightly holding my head in place. "I love you. You're allowed to have thoughts, feelings, and opinions; and you have every right to express them. But do not *ever* run out on me ever again. I. Can't. Lose. You. So go to your room and go to sleep. You're not going to school in the morning until we've had a long discussion about what you did, and what's going to happen now. I'm extremely upset, but I think it's best if we sleep on it. Now go to your room, please."

I nod my head and turn to go to my room. He rests his hands on his head, then looks at the ceiling. Before I get to my room I look back at him and say, "Dad, I love you too." He takes a deep breath and blows it out along with a sigh.

"Go to bed, Emerald."

I give him a small nod and continue my sulking.

I face-plant on my bed pathetically.

What the hell I have I done? Why am I still angry?

I slip into a dark, torturous slumber.

Chapter 20

"Hey, what's going on? I've been trying to get ahold of you since yesterday. Your dad called and said you guys weren't coming, but he didn't say why." Paxton wastes no time talking to me once I go through the school doors during lunchtime.

Dad and I stayed home and talked until I needed to come finish out the rest of the school day. I would've really liked to just stay in bed all day sulking and wallowing in self-pity, but he wasn't having it. I'm basically grounded for life. Oh, and the Winter Formal that I invited three people to? Yeah, I can't go anymore. Once Dad got over the initial scare of having me storm out, he became very angry. Even after I told him he was right, and told him that it's fine if he wants to ask her out. After all, she's better than some strange woman. I didn't tell him that last part. I'm not at all happy about them going on a date, but he deserves to be happy. I'm nothing but a selfish little brat.

Selfish, selfish, selfish.

I walk past Paxton, looking like a zombie. I ended up tossing and turning all night beating myself to bits with all this frustration, confusion, and resentment. I just want it all to go away. I don't want to see or talk to anyone. I don't want to have to tell Paxton, Eli, and Ricky that I can't take them all to the dance anymore. I don't want to hurt them. They'll all have to get other dates, and it will crush me when Paxton agrees to go to the dance with one of the other eighty girls that have probably already asked him. Maybe that's just as well. He deserves someone better than a crappy, boring girlfriend who is also a crappy daughter.

Crappy, crappy, crappy.

Is this what it feels like when you need to break-up with someone?

I'm flat-out depressed. I want to hide in my bed and never leave the house ever again.

Paxton follows me to my locker. He looks at me expectantly, not happy that I just breezed past him ignoring him. "What happened?"

"My dad is probably going to ask out your mom." My face remains expressionless as I swap notebooks. He fidgets and looks down. My entire body is tense, and I really don't want to listen or talk to anybody right now.

"Yeah, she told me she was interested in him." He shrugs his shoulders. "She's dated before. When I was younger I didn't like it too much, but I don't really mind her dating. It's really weird that it's your dad. No offense to your dad, but it kind of freaks me out that they want to date considering we're dating." He sighs. "But it's her life, you know? I can't stop her, and I'm not angry at her for wanting to be with someone who makes her happy. She's a good person and an even better mom. She deserves it. Even if it weirds me out." He shudders.

"Shut up, Paxton!" I lose it. He freezes, and his eyes darken. "Yeah, I get it. She's a good person, he's a good person, you're a good person, and everyone's a good fucking person. I'm the stupid, selfish, childish, little brat. I get it, okay? So just shut. Up." I snap at him and then slam my locker closed. It's so loud that it echoes through the hallway.

"*What?*" Paxton's jaw drops to the floor and he immediately steps in my way. "You're not any of those things. Why would you say that?" I sidestep him, but he's too quick. I throw my head back and groan. "Talk to me. What happened?" My tears come back. I've lost all control of them. Even when I try to stop them, they still pour out of my red, burning eyes.

"I'll talk to you later." I push past him and bolt to the ladies room.

The truth is, I want nothing more than to collapse in his arms. He makes me feel safe and needed. That's all I want right now, but I'm so furious with myself. I'm angry that I'm angry. I'm sad that I'm angry, and I'm angry that I'm sad. It's confusing, but I know that I don't deserve him. I kick the concrete wall and throw my bag down. The late bell rings, but I ignore it and continue to cover my face with my hands and lean against the bathroom wall trying to ignore the acid in my stomach begging to come out. I hear footsteps entering the bathroom, and I try not to groan out loud.

I just want to be alone. No. I just want to be with my mom. Why can't she just be here?

The Art of Moving On

244

Before I can lock myself in a stall someone calls my name.

"Emerald," a deep voice says.

I jump and let out a squeak. "Paxton, what are you doing in here?!" I whisper-yell at him.

"I'm coming to console my girlfriend," he whispers back from across the bathroom. "I'm here to help her, and be here for her. Even if she elbows me, or punches me in the nose, or slaps me, or even runs away from me. I'll just keep following her trying to make her feel better because I love her. Now, why are we whispering?" I stare at him wide-eyed as soon as the word "love" escapes his mouth. A shiver runs through me, and I swallow down the bile in my throat. He walks a few feet toward me, and I try to back up but remember that I'm already against the wall. He crosses his arms and takes another two big steps toward me. "I love you, Emerald Evans-Green, and you're not going to be able to get rid of me that easily."

His confession makes me dizzy, and I squeeze my eyes shut. This is all too much to handle. My chin starts to quiver, and I look down at the small gray tiles that line the floor. I shiver again. "You can't love me. I'm not good enough for you, Paxton," I admit quietly.

"That's bullshit, and you know it." His loud voice makes me look up at him in panic. "I don't know exactly what happened, but I'm guessing it has to do with your dad and my mom. It doesn't matter what they do, Emerald. Seriously, look at me. I mean this: it. Does. Not. Matter. What. They. Do. Because they are not us. We can't let other people affect our relationship because our relationship is yours and mine—it's *ours* and nobody else's. Don't let your mind get carried away. If you and your dad got in a fight, I'm sorry.

The Art of Moving On

It doesn't seem like you're angry with him though. You're mad at yourself. Don't be. Your dad loves you more than anything, and *nothing* will ever change that.

"I love you, and you really aren't going to get rid of me. So stop thinking this, 'I don't deserve you' crap, because it's not true. My heart is mine to give, and I've already given it to you. I'm not going anywhere." He's somehow managed to cross the entire bathroom and is now inches away from my face. I release a shaky breath. He smirks, and it makes my knees wobbly. Even his smug smirk makes me weak in the knees. "You're stuck with me, pirate." I don't have the chance to respond because he grabs the side of my head and crashes his lips to mine in a heated kiss that causes my entire body to blush. He moves one hand to cradle the back of my head, and moves the other to my waist, and pulls me closer. He moans into my mouth, and through all fogginess of my mind I fully realize that my gorgeous and perfect boyfriend is kissing me like a maniac in the school's women's bathroom. I'm so going to get detention. I gently push him back.

"That was the best kiss in the entire world," I whisper.

He smiles. "You're welcome. Are you feeling better?" I roll my eyes at his cockiness but shyly nod my head. He makes everything better. He grabs my hand and starts leading me out of the bathroom. "Let's go to class. If they see me in here, they might suspend me from going to the dance or something stupid. We're still going to talk about this more…just not in the girl's bathroom."

And just like that my stomach drops and I stop in my tracks. He turns and gives me a questioning look. I attempt to swallow down the lump in my throat so I can tell him.

"What's wrong? Do you need me to kiss you again?" He starts to hold me again, but I take a step back and let go of his hand.

The Art of Moving On

"I can't go." I look down and mess with the button on my shirt. "I can't take you guys. I'm basically grounded for the rest of my life." I sigh and my eyebrows pinch together in frustration. He doesn't even hesitant.

"Eh, that's okay. We don't have to go." He kisses my forehead.

I look down and mumble, "You don't want to go with someone else?"

"Nah, Eli and Ricky can figure their situation out themselves. They'll be fine without me," he says casually, playing with my brown hair as if I didn't yell at him ten minutes ago.

"I meant a girl. You're not going to go with another girl? Don't you want to?" I'm terrified of the answer. I feel sick to my stomach. His eyes grow huge.

"*No*. Emerald, I literally just told you that I love you, and I mean it. You're my girlfriend, so get it through your head. Clearly I do need to kiss you again." He grabs me and kisses me fiercely. Somehow this kiss is even better. I allow myself to sigh and fall into him. When he stops I'm completely out of breath and I don't want to open my eyes. He holds my shoulders until I regain my composure.

"Now just what do you think you're doing in here, Paxton Wright?! This is inappropriate!" Our religion teacher, Mrs. Novoa, exclaims utterly horrified. Paxton and I instantly break apart. I push back my shoulders, stand tall, and nervously straighten out my uniform. "You should not be in the ladies room, Paxton. Emmy, do you have a bathroom pass?" I shake my head and nervously bite the corner of my mouth. "This kind of behavior will not be tolerated! What has gotten into you two? You will both have detention. Get to class right now before I take you both to the Principal's office to call your parents. I will not stand for this and, frankly, neither does God. What is with kids

The Art of Moving On

these days? Ramona and Brett last year, and you guys this year? Control your hormones!" We both stand in front of her fidgeting, listening to her tirade. "Don't just stand there! Get out!" She shoos us out of the bathroom.

We wait until we're around the corner to start laughing.

***

"*Gasp.* Is that you, Emmy? Or your ghost?" Ricky asks me cautiously as he greets me at my locker after school.

"Oh my god, Ricky!" I hug him desperately. "I'm so glad to see you and so glad you're alive!"

"You and me both," he chuckles. He sways me in his arms. "My dad won't look at me, and my mom tries to speak to me but stops every time like she doesn't know what to say. This morning she was mumbling something about me not giving her grandkids. She already has two grandkids, and even if I decide not to have kids, she still has three other daughters. Doesn't make any sense. I am starting to feel better though. Despite the mess, my soul does feel better." I can't help but give him a small grin and soft eyes. "What happened when you got home? When you didn't show up this morning I thought you actually did die. Thanks for answering all of my texts and calls this morning, by the way," he adds sarcastically.

"I'm sorry about not answering, and I'm sorry, but I can't go to the dance with you guys. I'm grounded. For life, actually. And my dad is going to ask Maria out." His

The Art of Moving On

eyes widen as he slowly absorbs the super abridged *CliffsNotes* version of what happened when I got home last night.

"You can't go to the dance? That was one of E.G.'s punishments?" I nod my head, trying not to allow the fury to come out. He brings his fist to his mouth and thinks for a moment. "Okay, well…I think we have enough bodies to cover setting up the décor before the dance, but do you think there's any way that he'll let you come help clean up on Sunday?" My eyes dart back and forth, and I nod my head wondering how he could miss the point of the news.

"I can ask." I lean in closer to him while I zip my backpack. "What about you and Eli though?" He sighs finally allowing his disappointment to show. He shrugs his shoulder.

"It's not like we'd be able to dance with each other anyway. Besides, he and I have been sneaking around for almost six weeks. The dance won't change any of that. No matter what, I still have to go show my face. I'll just go casual and stay for a couple hours, then leave. I don't have to be there the whole time. I don't even want to go now that you're not going. It all just sounds like a big Student Council chore now. Maybe when I'm done, we can all go out and do our thing?"

"I'm grounded, Ricky. Like, forever. I'm forever grounded. You can look up grounded in the dictionary and there will be a picture of me. I'm so grounded—"

"*Ay ay ay*, yo sé," He cuts me off before I get morbid. He purses his lips. He's not going to allow me to wallow in my pity. I did that enough after Dan broke up with me. "I'm sorry that you're grounded. It could be nice though. Just take some time, and work your thoughts out. Focus on your art." I grunt and roll my eyes. "You need an after-

The Art of Moving On

school snack. You're hangry. I'll pick up a slice of pie for you from the café and drop it off at your house in like thirty minutes."

"Oh, I don't know if that's a good idea. *I'm grounded* and...I've gained a few pounds over the last couple of months." He looks me seriously in the eyes.

"Querida, pie is always a good idea and you know it. You're grounded, meaning you can't leave the house, but that doesn't mean that I can't come over. Is E.G. even there right now?" I shake my head. "So it's settled. I'm bringing cherry pie because despite your few extra pounds I think you need a few more. No arguing, querida." I grunt again like it's my second language, and he takes it as acceptance. He gracefully closes his locker. We walk to our cars together. He throws his arm around me, and I lean my head on his shoulder.

"I don't know what I did to deserve you," I softly comment. Soaking in the indescribable feeling of the sun shinning on my face, radiating through me and changing my attitude.

"Easy. You're a good person, querida. I don't know what I would do without you. Seriously. I never would have made it through last night if it weren't for you. Stop being hard on yourself. You're beating yourself up. Don't let the anger eat you alive. *Stop* getting in your own way. Forgive yourself. Everyone's allowed to fly off the handle occasionally. You're still seventeen not thirty-five. It's okay to act your age sometimes. *Our* age." He sighs tilting his head to the sun.

The Art of Moving On

Chapter 21

It's Friday evening and even though much of my anger has dissipated throughout the week, I still don't *feel* right. Mine and Dad's relationship is off and our family doesn't feel right. It's more than just the Maria thing, but I can't put a pinpoint on it exactly. It's gnawing at me and I don't know what to do.

I walk out of the house carrying a heavy bag of trash to throw away. Dad is supposed to be at work for another hour or so, but someone's working on a car that I've never seen before in our garage. Todd rolls out from underneath the junker and hits his head. I can't keep myself from laughing. His eyes immediately go to me. He shakes his head at me and jogs over.

"Here, I'll take care of it," Todd offers, taking the trash from me.

The Art of Moving On

"Thanks." I walk with him to the far side of the house where the big trash can is kept. "What are you doing here? The Camino is done."

"I could say the same for you," he retorts. I smirk and look around.

"I live here, remember?"

"Likely story," he mutters jokingly. He glances down at my bare legs. I have on my short pajama bottoms and loose light pink tank top with a sports bra underneath. His cheeks turn pink. I silently laugh to myself.

I'm making the man-slut, Todd Bartlett, blush.

"What's with the car?" I ask as he tosses the bag in the big black bin.

"I just bought her. It's a 1971 Boss 351 Mustang," he proudly touts. I cross my arms, and my eyebrows go up trying to convey that I have no idea what he just said. He quickly looks down at my chest thinking I don't notice, but I do so I uncross my arms. He smirks, and I shake my head.

"It's a piece of shit," I confidently respond. He guffaws. My smug grin grows. "Just calling it like I see it, Bartlett."

"She might be rough around the edges *now*, but when I'm done with her, you'll be *begging* me for a ride." He shoots me his panty-dropping smile that shows his dimples. I roll my eyes at his cockiness and try not to blush. Todd looks like he should be modeling shirtless on a biker magazine. But he knows he's hot and uses his wicked good looks to get laid any time he wants. I start to walk back to the house without saying anything. I can feel his eyes on me, and I know he's checking out my butt. I swing my hips more than usual just to mess with him.

The Art of Moving On

I get to the door and before I go in I yell over my shoulder. "Todd, put a shirt on! You're ugly!" I turn around and can hear him laughing loudly as I close the front door. I chuckle and shake my head. He really is a good guy though. One day he'll meet a lady, and she'll sweep him off his feet. Yes, *she'll* sweep *him* off his feet. Mark my words.

I start my homework on the kitchen table. I'm taking a drink of lemonade when Paxton walks in unannounced with an annoyed look on his face. "Why's that asshole, Todd Bartlett, in your driveway without a shirt on?" I nearly spit out my lemonade. I cover my mouth, forcing myself to swallow the juice before I burst out laughing. "Seriously." He stares at me with his hands on his hips. He's so cute when he's jealous. I jump up and wrap my arms around his neck, giving him a flirtatious kiss that leaves him wanting more. "Why'd you stop kissing me? I didn't even get to cop a feel," he whines. "Can we hang out?"

"No, you're only allowed to be here for fifteen minutes, per the 'Paxton Rule.' I'm also on strict lock down, so I really don't think you should be here right now. I don't want to get into more trouble. My dad is *really* mad at me. I don't think he's ever been this mad at me."

"Wait. There's a *Paxton Rule*? I have a rule named after me?" He asks proudly. I smile up at him.

"Yes. You're not allowed to be here for more than fifteen minutes if my dad's not here."

"I hate that rule!" He pouts. "I get fifteen minutes, but Bartlett can strut around the house without a shirt on? Hardly seems fair."

The Art of Moving On

"You're kind of cute when you're jealous." He crosses his arms and grunts. "My dad should be home shortly, and I have to start fixing dinner. Thanks for coming by." I walk him to the front door. He grunts again when I open the door for him to leave.

"I hate this. And I hate Todd Bartlett." He looks at Todd over his shoulder and his eyes narrow. I have to try really hard to stifle my laugh. The relationship between Todd and me is completely harmless. We mess with each other, but we both know we're not the other one's type. We just don't have those feelings for each other.

"I hate it, too." I get on my tiptoes to give him a quick kiss.

"Uh-uh." He objects to my chaste kiss. He shakes his head. He grabs my waist and lowers me into a dip, kissing me until I feel the electricity all the way down to my bones and my legs nearly give out. When I'm back on both of my feet, I'm in a drunken stupor. His kisses make me feel high and forget about all of my problems. "Don't look at Todd Bartlett. If he looks at you, tell me and I'll kill him." All I can do is nod.

Todd who?

That kiss was freaking amazing.

The Art of Moving On

Chapter 22

Tonight is the night. It's the night of the dance, and just happens to be the night Dad and

Maria are going to dinner and a movie. I do my best not to gag every time I think about it.

He left to pick her up about thirty minutes ago.

I'm sitting on the living room floor with my legs spread out surrounded by a

bunch of art and magazine clippings for a decoupage project I decided to start. Turns out,

being grounded is boring as all hell.

I'm in the middle of cutting when I hear a shuffling near the front door. I freeze,

and my heart immediately beats in over-drive. I stay completely still to make sure I really

did hear something. After a moment of silence, I convince myself that being grounded

has made me go crazy, and I go back to cutting. Another sound makes my head bolt up, and I stop breathing. With scissors and magazine clipping in hand, my heartbeat picks up again as more rustling comes from the front door.

Holy crap. Someone's trying to open my front door.

I tiptoe to the door hoping that the trespasser can't hear my intense breathing or my erratic heart. I keep my scissors in my fist ready to attack.

Wait.

It's probably just Paxton trying to sneak over. Coming to my senses, I lower my attack hand and exhale, releasing all my tension. I unlock the deadbolt now that I can hear the screen door opening. I pull the door open ready to jump out and scare Paxton.

"Agghh!" I let out a high-pitched scream so loud that the dogs start barking next door. I raise my attack hand again. I jump back just as Todd yells, equally loud, and blocks himself with his hands.

"What the hell, Emmy? You scared the hell out of me!"

"I scared *you*? No, *you* scared *me*!" I shout back and take a few steps back so he can come in. I rest my hand on my chest trying to calm myself down and lower my heart rate. "What are you doing here?" I close the door behind him.

"Calm down. Your dad wanted me to come check on you to make sure that you're here, not at the dance, and definitely not with Paxton; because you're supposedly grounded," he informs me as if his presence in my house is obvious. He stands in front of me in all his leather jacket, facial stubble, golden-eyed glory. "Are those scissors in your hand?" I look down and my knuckles are turning white from squeezing my scissors so hard. "Were you about to stab me?" He asks, offended. I loosen my grip.

The Art of Moving On

"Uh, yeah. Sorry," I mumbled embarrassed. We both face each other and look around awkwardly. "Well…"

"So…" he looks at me expectantly after a moment. The awkwardness is thick from having almost attacked each other. Okay, from me almost attacking him. "Well?"

"Well, what?" I quip.

"Can you please put the scissors down? You're making me nervous." I grin, setting them down on the coffee table. He walks around the sofa and flops down on it.

"Getting comfortable?" I look at him, not at all amused that Dad sent someone— no, not just someone, he sent *Todd*—to come check on me. He reeks so much of bad boy you can smell him from down the street before you can even hear his stupid motorcycle. He starts looking at all the clippings and craft supplies that cover part of the floor and the entire coffee table. "I don't need a babysitter."

"It looks like Martha Stewart threw up in here." He smirks at me, and I gasp dramatically.

"It does not," I argue, putting my hands on my hips. "It looks like a young, obviously talented, thoughtful, intelligent artist threw up in here," I state confidently. When he doesn't respond, I sit back down to my spot on the floor and start cutting again, pretending it isn't weird that Todd is sitting on my sofa babysitting me.

"Is that a cigar box?" He points to the box a couple feet away from me, on the outskirts of my mess.

"Yeah, I take one that's not in the best shape—not the expensive ones—and give them a new life. I decoupage it. Pretty cool, huh?" I glance up at him, and he's inspecting one of the older ones I've created. It's covered in the sheet music of my favorite song,

The Art of Moving On

Dark Eyes by Bob Dylan. I then laced a gold strip on every edge and pasted few large sheer, jagged, light pink hearts on top of the music sheets. It's pretty girly, so I find it adorable that he's so amazed by it.

"Will you make me one?" He asks looking at me with child-like eyes. I look up at him with my eyebrows raised.

"Mister Leather Jacket, Manly-Man, Todd Bartlett, wants a decoupage cigar box?"

He looks at me seriously with pleading, hopeful eyes. "Yeah. You're really good at this. Make me a box, and I'll come by next week and change Betsy's oil, air filter, wipers, and check the alignment."

"Really? Okay." I agree even though I can pretty much do all of those things to Besty myself. "What do you want on it?" I concentrate on my cutting while I wait for his response. I glance at him after a brief pause, and he has the biggest smirk on his face. "What? Why are you looking at me like that? Do I have something on my face?" He's full on smiling at me now, dimples showing and eyes sparkling.

"What? No. Your face is perfect," he says quickly as if I was insane. His hands rub the stubble on his jaw and he looks away from me. I clear my throat to cover the awkward pause that lingers after his compliment. The front door swings open, and Todd and I both jump a foot in the air. Paxton walks in like he owns the place, the same way that Todd did.

"Yeah, your face is perfect. Why are you here, Todd?" He asks defensively. Todd starts to get up off the sofa.

The Art of Moving On

"I'm actually here to make sure *you're* not here." He stares Paxton in the eyes for a moment, and there's some kind of male testosterone communication thing happening. I sit on the floor doing my best to translate what's going on between them. Paxton's eyes are dark and practically scream that he is majorly displeased that Todd is here. "I'm not here to cause problems." He brushes past Paxton on his way to the door, just barely bumping his shoulder. Paxton jaw tightens. "Don't worry, mums the word." Before he walks out the door, he looks over his shoulder at me. "Naked chicks." He winks at me and closes the door behind him. My eyebrows pinch together confused.

"Why was he here, and why was he talking about naked chicks?" Paxton demands to know before he moves any further into my house.

Naked chicks…Naked chicks…What was he talking about?

"*Ooohhh*. His box." I chuckle. "He wants naked chicks on his box." I hold up a cigar box. "I told him I would make him one. Why?" He has one eyebrow raised. Jealous Paxton is pretty hot. "Do you want one too?"

"Yes," he pouts, then straightens and points at me accusingly. "Don't distract me with your cute art and sexy legs in those tiny shorts. Why was he here?"

"My dad sent him to check on me," I tell him, casually looking back down at my clippings.

"Swear to God?" He asks in a deep voice. I can hear the vulnerability in his question, and I look up at him with soft eyes.

"Yes, Paxton. I would never just be hanging out with Todd Bartlett. We literally have nothing in common. I didn't even know he was coming over. I promise." He relaxes, and nods his head. He looks down at his shoes and rubs the back of his head.

The Art of Moving On

I take the time to look at him and take in what he's wearing tonight. He's wearing his typical plain white t-shirt and brown bomber jacket with dark blue suede shoes. His hair has grown out a little so it flops to the side, but it's still messy. He looks like a really sexy hipster/greaser combo. I bite my grin and ignore the fact that just looking at him makes me blush.

"I'll tell you what, I'll make you a box, but you're going to have to pay." I raise an eyebrow and bite my lip. He catches my drift and walks closer to me, grinning.

"Pay, huh? What kind of payment are we talking about exactly?" I see a light flash in his eyes and I smirk.

"Take your shirt off."

He smiles at me and does as I ask. He tosses his jacket over a chair and then flings his shirt in my face. I giggle. I bury my head in his shirt and sniff it. "You smell so good."

"That's because I showered for you. See how lucky you are to have me?"

I roll my eyes but can't wipe the goofy grin off my face. We just stare at each other taking the other one in—him in his sexy style, and me in pink pajama shorts and tank top. I blatantly sigh, admiring his muscles and dreamy hair. Yeah, dreamy.

"Take your pants off," I demand quickly without thinking. His eyes go round, surprised at my command.

This is not at all what I had planned for tonight considering I'm grounded, but part of me was really hoping he would at least try and sneak over. I look from his pants back up to his face. He's silently asking me for the go ahead, so I nod at him. He bites his growing smile and reaches down to unbutton his pants.

The Art of Moving On

"I like it when you're bossy. Can I grab your butt now?" He asks politely, and I crack up giggling.

I walk over to him, wrap my arms around him, and kiss him deeply. He grabs my hips and pulls me close to him. We fall back on the sofa, and I giggle again.

"Wait. What time is it?" He looks up at the clock on the wall. "We have twenty minutes until I need to go. I dressed up in my suit and told my mom I was going stag with Eli since you couldn't go. I dressed up and drove away and everything. Went to Eli's house for a little bit. Once I knew it was safe, I went back home and changed and then came here." He leans forward and kisses me. "We only have twenty minutes, pirate. We have to make them count." We both chuckle and go back to kissing. When I feel his warm hand grab my boob I moan and then push him away a little, trying to sit up. "What's wrong? I'm sorry if I pushed that–"

I stop him with a kiss. I lick his lips and nibble on the bottom one. I get him to shift with me on the sofa so now I'm on top of him. "Nothing is wrong. I enjoyed that." I kiss his neck and start to work my way down to his chest. "I love it when you touch me." I continue my kisses all the way down to his belly button, and start to undo his jeans. I pick up my kisses, and he groans. Not exactly the reaction I was going for... He tugs on my arm and leans up on his elbows.

"No, Em. Seriously, come on, you don't have to do that. We can just talk, or kiss, or stare at each other, or decoupage, or something." He looks at me so sincerely and sweetly that I swoon. Hard.

I give him a devilish grin. I push his chest back down on the sofa, and he lets out a definite moan this time.

The Art of Moving On

***

Paxton is throwing his shirt back on right when Ricky bursts through the door like he owns the place, too. My house might as well be a revolving door tonight. He is holding a pie and dressed in black fitted suit and thin purple tie. His hair is perfectly styled to the side, and his face is shining bright. His eyes go up at the sight of Paxton putting his shirt on, but he recovers and shoots me a knowing grin. I blush, doing my best not to jump up and down and giggle from happiness.

"I didn't mean to interrupt." He stifles a laugh, also noticing Paxton's silly smile. "I brought apple pie!" He announces walking all the way into the house.

"Ricky! Apple was my mom's favorite! I'm so glad you're here. I can't wait to hear all about the dance. Tell me everything. How did all the decorations look? Did you see Eli? You look so handsome! Did you get photos? I want to see them," I shoot out questions eagerly, bobbing up and down on the sofa unable to control my excitement after all.

"Hold on, querida. Let me get slices of pie first. Then we gossip."

"That's my cue to go. I'll see you tomorrow morning. Clean up right?"

"Yes!" Ricky answers for me. "Nine. I'll have donuts for everyone."

"Awesome. I'll see you guys in the morning. Don't forget your dad will probably be home soon."

"Thanks. I'll see you in the morning." I smile sweetly at him from my spot on the sofa. We look at each other for a moment, biting our grins. My heart beams at him, and I

The Art of Moving On

hope with everything in me that he knows how much I love him. He looks at me with an adoration that I've never seen on anyone before. It's such an intimate moment that I ignore Ricky out of the corner of my eyes fidgeting with a box of apple pie. He coughs, breaking our trance.

"Ahem. I'll just go to the kitchen and get these slices ready," Ricky offers and awkwardly makes his way to the kitchen. Paxton walks back over and kisses my head. I want to grab him and kiss him all over again.

"I'll see you in the morning. Don't get in trouble, okay?" I nod, and he kisses my cheek before walking out the door.

After the front door closes Ricky walks back into the living room and hands me my slice of apple pie. "Querida, spill the beans now, because *vato* just had the goofiest grin on his face. One that I'm now familiar with. *Sooo…* Did you guys have plans to see each other behind your dad's back? And Maria's back," He mumbles the last part awkwardly. I fidget, and the smile wipes clean off my face. "Sorry. That was weird. I shouldn't have said that."

"I mean, they had to have known, right?" I shrug my shoulders.

He takes a bite of pie and moans. I swear he goes cross-eyed. I take a bite but refrain from moaning despite the pie being freaking delicious. "Oh my god, querida…this pie…" I ignore his pie moans.

"They decided to go on a date the night of the dance, and I happen to be grounded. Like, they had to know Paxton would sneak over, right? Dad's not dumb, Ricky. He had to have known that." I've already convinced myself, so it doesn't really matter what he says at this point. He shrugs his shoulders.

The Art of Moving On

"Probably. Maybe. It is weird that he would ask her out tonight, of all nights. Maybe this is him extending an olive branch in some weird parent-y way." My jaw falls open, and my eyes go wide. "What?" He asks innocently.

"An olive branch? Like to hang myself from? Like Judas did?"

He snorts so loud it hurts my ears as much as it probably hurts his throat. He spits out the mushy bite of pie that's in his mouth so he can laugh. I stare at him wide-eyed, expectant and worried. "Querida, no. The opposite. But, whatever, forget the olive branch. Maybe this was his way of throwing you a bone."

"Oh. I don't know about that. Things are still not back to normal here. He sent Todd to come check on me and to make sure Paxton wasn't here."

"He sent Todd to babysit?" He asks for confirmation before he fan girls. Like I said, Todd is the epitome of rugged and sexy. The face that he looks much older just adds to it. Ricky loves running into him whenever Todd's here running an errand or doing something for Dad. I nod and roll my eyes. He squeals and then swoons, completely abandoning his pie on the coffee table. "How did he look? What was he wearing? Did you get a good look at his butt? Oh my god, tell me everything he said!"

"Oh, I don't know, Ricky. Hey, how was your date with your *boyfriend* tonight?" I look at him accusingly.

"Don't look at me like that. Todd doesn't count. He's not even a human. He's a god. An idea. Unattainable." He lies back on the sofa and sighs. "So much has happened in the last couple months, huh?" He looks over at me. I put my pie down too and collapse into the sofa cushions.

The Art of Moving On

"So much. We go through three years of high school, and in two months everything is flipped upside down."

"Yeah and the dust will start to settle. It's going to get better, and when it does everything will feel *right*. You know? It'll feel like this is how it's meant to be. We're getting there, querida. I can feel it. Even though home sucks and my parents still won't look at me, I still feel better and better every day."

"Yeah," I respond hesitantly. I feel that way about Paxton and me, but certainly not about *everything*.

"You're not feeling any better about your dad and Maria?"

I frown, and my eyes droop. Ricky can always see right through me. My name just officially changed to Debbie Downer.

"No. I mean, yes. I don't feel like I did before, when I was at your house. I don't know if it will ever feel right. It's so confusing. I *like* Maria like as a person. My boyfriend's mom is dating my dad. It's weird, and I don't think that aspect will ever not be weird. I'm worried about the future. Their future. Mine and Paxton's future. All of our futures. There's still something else though..."

"Did your dad ever talk about that with you like he said he would?"

I nod, maintaining my droopiness. "He just said he and Maria won't interfere with our relationship. He said that Paxton and I should go about our business." I stare at my pie for a few moments. My throat tightens and my chest starts burning. I haven't talked about this with anyone since last week when I flipped out. I've been trying all week to shake the feeling...to move on from my fear of change...my fear of leaving Mom behind.

The Art of Moving On

"D-Do you...do you think it's weird that my dad dating someone that's not my mom, really bothers me more than anything?"

"Querida, this entire thing is weird." He reaches over and takes my hand. He holds it for a few moments before tilting his head to this side like he just got an idea. "Do you ever talk to your mom?" My head bolts up, and I stare at him like he just grew three heads. "I mean, have you ever like written letters to her or…you know…gone to visit her?"

I look down and feel my eyes start to tingle. A flood of emotions washes over me with a forceful impact causing my heart to physically hurt. A softball forms in my throat, and I can't swallow. I solemnly shake my head. He squeezes my hand.

"She's gone but her spirit isn't. If you talk to her or write her letters, Emmy, she *will* get them. Not in the literal sense, obviously, but I know she watches over you."

Tears trickle down my cheeks quickly but silently. I scoot over and hug him. We break apart, and he winces when he sees the darkest face he's ever seen on me. I'm in a black hole, and I need her to get me out. I *need* my mom. I've needed her this entire time. I've needed her since the second God introduced us, and the second He took her away from me.

"Querida, I really don't want to leave you like this, but your dad is probably going to be back soon. If you ask me to stay though, I will. You know I will."

"Thanks, Ricky. You should go. I can't take any more punishments. This is hard enough as it is." I sniff as he nods his head in understanding. I stand up and walk him to the door. "I love you so much." He pulls me in and holds me tightly.

The Art of Moving On

"You know what you have to do right?" He asks me softly. I meekly nod with my head against his shoulder. We hug for another moment before letting go. "It's going to be all right. I know it, and you know it deep in your heart. Everything is happening the exact way it's supposed to. Have faith, querida. Te amo." He kisses my cheek. "I'll see you in the morning for clean up. It's okay if you want to come late, or if you need to skip out just text me."

"Thank you, Ricky. And thanks for the pie." I let out a small laugh that sounds more like a sob. He starts walking to his car, and I shout out to him. "Mom would've loved it. It's funny that you brought over her favorite on tonight of all nights."

"Te amo. I'll see you at nine."

I give him a small, knowing smile. He smiles and waves back before ducking in his car.

I close the door—and lock it this time. I plant face down into the sofa trying to gather all my thoughts and emotions. There are some things you can't explain. Some things you just simply *feel* and there are no words to match them. I know Mom is watching over me. I could *feel* her with Ricky and I just now. The sensation was overpowering. I know she was with us because Ricky went through all the trouble to bring over an apple pie, then found out apple pie was Mom's favorite. He ate the apple pie that was so freaking good he had a foodgasm. Yes, *foodgasm*.

There's only one thing that stands out in my mind…he bought and ate that pie without question, thought or hesitation, like it was the most normal and best thing he's ever done, and…

Ricky *hates* apple pie. He always has.

The Art of Moving On

You can't always see faith, but sometimes it shows itself in small, weird enough ways to keep us believing. Call it just an apple pie, or call it whatever you want to. I call it a sign. Because the one thing that I needed tonight was that apple pie. It made me realize what I need to do. What I've been needing to do to actually move on. There's another conversation that I need to have.

The Art of Moving On

Chapter 23

I wrap my coat around me and tighten my scarf. There isn't a breeze, but the chill reaches

my bones. It only took a minute for my nose to turn pink and the sniffles to start. The

sniffles get worse as I walk up the grassy knoll to Mom's headstone. Her headstone is

black and shiny granite engraved with gold vines. It reads:

Anastasia Evans-Green

The Best Daughter, Mom and Wife

For Thirty-Five Perfect Years

I got to pick out the headstone, as morbid as that may sound. I wanted to be a part

of it—saying goodbye to her in this way. At first Dad objected, telling me kids shouldn't

have to deal with these adult matters, but I wanted to. It was helping me say goodbye to

her. I wanted to make sure she had the very best of everything—the best flowers, the

The Art of Moving On

most beautiful headstone, a burial spot with a pretty view, and everything. It was important to me, which is why Dad let me pick out any headstone I wanted. I picked this gorgeous one, and I remember seeing him wince when he looked at the price. I told him nevermind and that I could pick something different, trying the hardest I've ever tried in my life not to cry. Then he pulled me under his arm and told me, "This is the last thing I'll ever be able to buy your mom, and I want it to be the most beautiful thing in the world, no matter the cost. She would love this, not just because it is the most beautiful option, but because you picked it out. I love it, too."

Tears are now streaming down my cheeks in full force. The chill in the air mixed with my wet cheeks instantly has me shivering all over. I place a bouquet of white roses on the frosty grass. I step back and hug myself. I take a breath not knowing where to begin.

"Mom," I manage to croak out. I take a deep breath and try again. "Mom. Um, I–I miss you." I pause and squeeze my hands together, nervous to admit how awful I've been. Before I even speak again, sobs start spilling out.

"I've been s-so selfish l-lately." I squeeze my eyes hard, trying to get all the tears out, but it's no use. My eyes just keep pooling. "I m-made Dad so m-mad at me. I couldn't h-help it. It h-hurt so b-bad, Mom. He went on a date. And I hate it." My chest caves in at the admission, the guilt all consuming and crushing. I bring my hands, which are now in hard fists, up to my temples. "And I h-hate myself for it. The guilt, Mom, it's destroying me. P-please help me, M-Mom. I n-need you so bad r-right now." I sob and wipe my face. "I just want you to be here. Every day I get up knowing that a p-piece of me is gone and isn't coming back." I sniff loudly and wipe my nose with the back of my

The Art of Moving On

hand. "It's gotten easier but…I just…m-miss you so m-much that it hurts me so freaking bad sometimes. But D-Dad has found this l-lady…and he likes her." I sob a few times before I continue. Between the tears and the snot, my entire face feels frozen over. "I-I like her too. It's Paxton's mom. Paxton is my b–boyfriend, and I think I'm in love with him." I pause and breathe deeply. "The only thing is that she's n-not you. But he likes her, and she m-makes him ha-happy. B-but I want you to know that she'll never be you." Another sob escapes. "And D-Dad knows b-but I had to tell you because even though it's hard—like, really hard, Mom—she m-makes him happy and I n-need him to be happy. No matter what. He's all I have now that you're g-gone. He's the b-best Dad, Mom. You'd be s-so proud. He deserves hap-happiness. So even though M-Maria—that's her name—will be in our lives, you're irreplaceable and w-we think about you every d-day. And m-miss you every day. And love you every day. Nothing and n-nobody will ever change that. Ever. I'll never leave you behind."

At some point, I collapsed to the ground. My head pressed against her headstone, and my arms are wrapped around it, desperately wishing it's Mom. I remain collapsed against the cold granite with my eyes closed. I can feel the frosty grass melt beneath me and seep through my jeans, but I can't move. I need to stay here just a little bit longer. I need to hold on to her just a few minutes longer. I need to wait until I know she heard me. I know she can. I feel her sometimes just like Ricky was saying last night. I *know* she watches over me. Slowly my breathing settles, and my tears stop. I feel the weight lifted off my shoulders. I let go of the guilt that clouds my heart. An incredible force of peace rushes through me. My face is numb, and so are my fingers, but I swear I could fall asleep right here and now. I feel *calm*. I feel her light. It feels *right*. *I* feel right. For the first time in months. I hear a sniffle.

I slowly open my eyes and give Dad a small smile. He's crying and has a bundle of red roses. He walks on the crunchy grass and places them near the white roses I brought. They look perfect there sitting on top the frosted green grass in front of the black and gold granite. I let my arms fall down to my sides and lift my head up so it's not resting on the cold headstone. Dad wipes his tears. He leans down to me, and I wrap my arms around him as he pulls me to my feet. He holds me close and rubs my back. His warmth is slowly melting my bones. He kisses my head, and then rests his head on mine.

"I love you, sweet pea. You're not selfish. You are kind, loving, and beautiful just like your mom." I sigh into his long wool coat.

"It's okay if you want to date Maria, Dad. If she makes you happy then that's all that matters. I'm so sorry for everything." I hiccup.

"I understand, sweet pea. We make each other laugh. It's nice being around her." He kisses my head again. "Come on, let's go get breakfast before you have to go clean the dance mess. I'll walk you to Betsy and you can follow me." I nod my head.

"Dad? How did you know where I was?"

"You left at 6:30 in the morning. When I realized you were gone, I knew that this is where you would be. I don't know how I knew. I just did. Maybe your mom told me." I nod, understanding completely.

"Hang on. There's something I forgot to tell her." I jog back up the knoll to her headstone. "Mom, thank you for making Ricky bring over that apple pie." I release a part-laugh and part-sob. "I know that was you. I love you, Momma." I jog back down to Dad and get in my car, following his truck to the café for breakfast.

***

"*Yeeeesssss!* My beautiful, amazing, talented…" Paxton pauses as I come closer to him. I let the school's doors swoosh close behind and immediately walk to Paxton. "…and red-eyed, puffy pink cheeks, crying girlfriend is here. Babe, what happened?" My heart flutters when he calls me babe. It's geeky, but I love it. "Are you okay?" He wraps his arm around me. He's wearing a long sleeved, hooded black Henley, dark jeans and those blue suede shoes. AKA he looks delicious. I don't know how I got so lucky. He pushes me away just enough so he can see my face. "Beautiful, what are you thinking? Talk to me." His hand cups my cheek and I lean into it and sigh, a faint smile appearing.

"I was just thinking how hot you are and how lucky I am to have you." I step up and kiss him softly. He smiles.

"I'm the lucky one, and I can't wait to see you naked because you're the hottest person I've ever laid eyes on," he admits seriously.

I giggle and whack him in the arm. "Quit it."

"Tell me what's really going on. Please?" He moves his hand to my hip and plays with the hair that falls on my shoulders. I look around for the first time and see Ricky. He senses me and looks right at me. We stare at each other and without words, he knows I did what I had to do this morning. Mom sent Ricky to me. I love him. He gives me a small smile and a wink. After Ricky and I have our moment, I look back up at Paxton,

The Art of Moving On

and he appears totally lost and looks between Ricky and I. "Tell me now. Did something bad happen?"

"No, no." I lead him by his hand, and we sit on two chairs that are still lining the wall from the dance. I take both his hands and look at his sparkling green eyes. "I went and visited my mom this morning." His eyes grow wide for a second before he nods. "I mentioned you." He grins. "But I really talked to her about Maria and my dad. I had a lot of things weighing on me. I told her about how I was feeling and I let it all out. It was really hard, and it took a lot of me. She understands everything. She always has."

"And then what?"

"And then it was gone. It was like her light, her essence, hugged me. My guilt was lifted. Her spirit gave me peace and clarity. That probably sounds so dumb, huh?" I look up at him. He shakes his head.

"No, Emmy. It's not dumb at all. I believe she looks after you. She's your angel. I get it." He squeezes my hands. A tear escapes my eye. Before I can swipe it away with a finger, Paxton leans over and kisses it. "How are you feeling now? I'm sure we can leave if–"

"No, you can't!" Ricky yells with a trash bag in hand and light blue crepe paper stuck to his shoe. "Look around. Eli and I cannot do this alone. All those sophomores ditched us." He grunts and goes back to picking up cups with a stank look on his face. I grin.

I look behind Ricky, and sure enough Eli is standing there taking down taped snowflake cutouts and other wall decorations. I look around the rest of the cafeteria and it looks like Sleeping Beauty vomited all over. Everything is a different shade of blue and

The Art of Moving On

covered in sparkles. There are black streaks on the floor from kids dancing and black marks from spilled punch that got walked over. It's nasty. We're going to be here for a while. I turn back to Paxton, still holding my hands.

"Tired. I feel very tired." My eyes are puffy and heavy. My face feels sore from all the cold and wiping of tears. Ricky walks to us, bends over and places his hands on his knees so we're eye level.

"Querida. I'm so proud of you. Now get these mop heads attached to your feet because we're dancing." He gets the crazy look in his eyes as he flops down four white cotton mop heads. "Here's some duct tape. Tape it up, dip your feet in purple Fabuloso, and show me your moves." He smiles and joins Eli across the cafeteria who is already almost done taping his shoes.

"I knew I shouldn't have worn these shoes." Paxton winces. I smile and slap my legs.

"Let's get to it!" We all strap up and dip our feet.

"Wait, wait, wait. We can't dance without music!" Paxton pulls up his music on the phone while Ricky awkwardly wobbles to the SC office to get the speaker. I try not to giggle, but I fail and end up laughing hysterically.

"Oh, *HA HA HA*, querida. You're the one that's going to have to nurse me back to health if I break my ass!" We all laugh.

Paxton puts on one of his favorite compositions. "Moonlight" by Beethoven. Ricky looks up at me once it begins to play. "Really?" he asks disgusted. "No Beyoncé? Classical? This is really happening?" We smile at him and nod

Paxton grabs my hand and pulls me to him just like he did weeks ago when we were in his kitchen. Being in his arms, fully enveloped by him, is starting to feel like home. Instead of slow movements, he's leading me in big steps so we can actually get the floor clean. He pushes from me, holding my hands, and we both start moving across the floor like we're ice skating. I look over and Ricky and Eli are skating just like we are. They're laughing and holding hands, openly and freely showing their affection for each other. Ricky slips, but Eli catches him. Before he brings Ricky to his feet, Eli uses this advantage and kisses him passionately. I look up at Paxton expectantly.

He holds my face and kisses me so softly that I can barely feel his lips brush against mine. I mumble against his mouth. "Tonight's the night, Paxton. It feels right." His eyebrows rise like he's asking if I'm positive. I nod. "I want you." I use our closeness to sneak a grape Jolly Rancher in his pocket so he can find it later and think of me. He kisses me sweetly and holds me close.

I take a moment to be grateful. The cafeteria is still a mess, but it doesn't matter because I'm surrounded by people I love. Eli and Ricky are being who they truly are. They're laughing, touching, kissing, and looking at each other like they see the world in each other's eyes. We are beautiful. Right here and right now, we are who we are, unashamed, flawed, and beautiful.

I wouldn't have it any other way.

The End.

The Art of Moving On

Acknowledgements

Thank you for reading and supporting me as an author! If you enjoyed this book, please consider writing a review! They are crucial to us indie authors! I always write my acknowledges unedited so bare with me!

Thank you to all my beta-readers that read this as my 2015 NaNoWriMo project, then welcomed Ricky Rodriguez's voice into their hearts by reading the full-length manuscript, and then read the 25,000 new words I added in after that. Your time and graciousness is appreciated!

Thank you, God, for giving me this story. Thank you for putting artists in my life that were able to help me through my confusion and doubt. (I'm looking at you Amy Sue Burt.)

Thank you to Katie for being accessible for all my questions regarding content and art. Your opinion matters so much to me.

Thank you to the graphic designer, Tiffany Lee. Thank you for working on this even while you were out of the country. Your patience is immense and so appreciated.

Thank you to the editor, Julie Henderson. I'm sorry my grammar sucks. You're a saint. Thanks for being there from the very beginning of this story and understanding me. This is obviously unedited and it might be killing you to see. Sorry!

Last but not least, thank you to my mom and dad who (for whatever reason) have supported me. Like The Beatles song says, "Of all these friends and lovers, there is no one compares with you. In my life, I love you more."

The Art of Moving On

Made in the USA
San Bernardino, CA
03 June 2020

72643963R00155